Untamed Highlanders

The temptation of the wild...

Meet these wild Regency Highlanders, who have
grown from unlikely friends and mischief makers
at boarding school to some of Scotland's
most powerful men.

With a tendency to break every rule in the book,
this time these Highland lords might have to break
their *own* rules to claim the women who try
to tame them!

Read Lachlan and Frances's story in
The Highlander and the Governess

And Dalton and Lady Regina's story in
The Highlander and the Wallflower

Available now!

Author Note

The Highlander and the Wallflower is a friends-to-lovers story that I hope you'll enjoy! Dalton St. George is a bold Highlander who's in love with Lady Regina, but she is betrothed to his best friend. Honor compels him to hide his feelings, but he sees that her shy wallflower demeanor is nothing like the outgoing girl he once knew. Instead, Lady Regina is hiding secrets—and when trouble strikes, Dalton won't hesitate to become her hero.

Did you miss Lachlan MacKinloch and Frances Goodson's prequel story? If so, then you might enjoy reading *The Highlander and the Governess* next. Last, if you'd like me to email you when my new books come out, you may subscribe to my author newsletter at michellewillingham.com/contact. I always love hearing from my readers.

MICHELLE WILLINGHAM

—

The Highlander and the Wallflower

HARLEQUIN
HISTORICAL

HARLEQUIN®
HISTORICAL™

Recycling programs
for this product may
not exist in your area.

ISBN-13: 978-1-335-50563-7

The Highlander and the Wallflower

Copyright © 2020 by Michelle Willingham

This edition published by arrangement with Harlequin Books S.A.

For questions and comments about the quality of this book,
please contact us at CustomerService@Harlequin.com.

Harlequin Enterprises ULC
22 Adelaide St. West, 40th Floor
Toronto, Ontario M5H 4E3, Canada
www.Harlequin.com

Printed in U.S.A.

RITA® Award finalist and Kindle bestselling author **Michelle Willingham** has written over forty historical romances, novellas and short stories. Currently she lives in southeastern Virginia with her family and her beloved pets. When she's not writing, Michelle enjoys reading, baking and avoiding exercise at all costs. Visit her website at michellewillingham.com.

To my new friends, the class of 46!
I have really enjoyed getting to know all of you,
and thanks to Tony, Frank, Jay and Laura
for the amazing leadership retreat. Thanks to
Elizabeth, Kathryn and Edna for your help as
I've begun this new journey, and for patiently
answering all my questions.

Prologue

Scotland—1806

His brother was dead.

Dalton St George walked out of the church, feeling as if his guts were frozen within a block of ice. His parents were in shock, grieving at the sudden loss of their heir, only two days ago. For him, it was a sense that nothing was real. He could almost imagine his responsible brother opening the casket, sitting up, and apologising for the inconvenience of dying.

His guilt churned in his stomach, and he slipped away from the mourners, not wanting to see his brother buried. No one noticed that he'd left.

Then again, no one ever really noticed him. Brandon had always been the beloved son, whereas Dalton was the black sheep of the family. He hadn't cared. There was glorious freedom in being able to do whatever he wanted. He was eighteen years old—independent and carefree.

He had lived a lifetime of unbridled sin over the past year, indulging in whatever he wanted. No one cared if he disappeared at midnight and didn't return until dawn.

Once or twice, he wondered if they would notice if he didn't come back at all. But then again, he'd been the spare son, hardly of any importance. He'd spent most of his time in Scotland while Brandon had been fulfilling his duties as Viscount Camford and the future Earl of Brevershire.

Dalton trudged through the tall summer grasses, loathing the blackcloth coat and waistcoat he'd been forced to wear. He unbuttoned them both and tossed the garments on the ground, still walking towards the loch. The morning sun was hotter than usual, and it blazed across a brilliant blue sky. The day was flawless—except that they were burying his brother.

A raw ache spread through his heart. His saintly brother *had* paid attention to him, though Brandon had never understood Dalton's intense need to cast off the trappings of nobility and wander through the Highlands. And now, he would never again hear Brandon's calm voice, chiding him not to do something reckless.

Right now, he wanted to be reckless. He wanted to tear off the rest of his clothes and swim in the loch until his muscles burned. He needed the frigid water to punish him as he churned through the surface.

His face was wet, though he didn't know when he'd begun to weep. Strange, that he could feel so numb inside, and yet, he had managed to grieve.

From behind him, he thought he heard footsteps. He didn't turn around, not wanting to see who had followed him. But a moment later, his foxhound, Laddie, pressed his nose against Dalton's leg.

The animal's compassion was his undoing. He knelt

on the ground, clutching the dog's smooth body as the loss roared through him. He was utterly alone. And God above, he wished that it had been *him* who had died. It should have been his heart that had stopped beating, not Brandon's. He could never be the man his brother had been, selfless and kind.

He heard the whisper of moving grass behind him, and Laddie barked a warning. This time, he did turn around. A young woman, hardly older than himself, stood behind him, her red hair slipping free from her braid. Clear blue eyes the colour of the sky's reflection stared at him with sympathy. She had an otherworldly beauty, as if she'd been conjured from the water.

'Are you all right?' she asked. His dog went to sniff at her feet, and his tail wagged in approval.

Dalton didn't even know how to answer that. No, he wasn't all right. But she could do nothing to help, so there was little point in answering. He swiped at his eyes, not wanting her to see him like this. All he could do was nod.

'I am Regina Crewe,' she said quietly. 'My father is the Earl of Havershire. We were visiting friends at Locharr when we heard about your brother's death. My father thought we should stop and offer our sympathies.'

Dalton nodded. Vaguely he recalled seeing Tavin MacKinloch, the Laird of Locharr, among the guests, along with his wife. 'Was Lachlan gone, then?' he asked. If Lachlan had been in Scotland, he would have attended the funeral. They had been schoolmates and friends for years.

'He was, yes. But the laird thought we should come.'

He nodded again, not really knowing what to say.

The heaviness of grief had stolen away his ability to hold a conversation.

'I don't think you and I have met before,' Lady Regina continued. 'I would have remembered.' A faint blush stained her cheeks, and then she added, 'You still haven't told me your name. Though I think I know who you are.'

'I am Dalton St George,' he told her.

'Then I was right,' she answered. 'I guessed who you were, after I saw you leave.' Her face turned soft with sympathy. 'I know I should have stayed for the burial, but… I didn't think you should be off alone.' Her words trailed off. 'I am sorry you lost your brother.'

He gave a third nod, feeling like he was made of stone.

'I'm not supposed to be here without a chaperon,' she said, but there was a tinge of irony in her tone. 'My mother would be furious. You won't tell, will you?'

'No. I won't tell.' It was strange to be so tongue-tied around this beautiful creature. He'd flirted and laughed with many of the village girls before he'd stolen kisses or enjoyed their charms. But the earl's daughter reminded him of a princess, so far out of his reach. Around her throat she wore an amethyst necklace on a silver chain. She couldn't be older than sixteen.

Lady Regina walked towards the edge of the loch, where several large limestone boulders lined the shore. His dog scampered at her side, and she laughed, leaning down to ruffle his ears. Laddie rolled to his back for her to rub his belly, and she glanced back at him. 'I've always loved dogs. They seem to know people better than anyone.'

He watched as she picked up a stone and hurled it as far as she could. It sank beneath the water with a loud splash.

'Why did you follow me?' he asked.

'Because I saw your grief, and it bothered me. So I came.'

Her words seem to reach deep within him, and he stared at her in disbelief. This girl had noticed his sorrow and wanted to console him. He hardly knew what to say or do. But her presence was an unexpected balm.

Before he could say another word, she added, 'Show me how far you can throw a rock.'

'Why?' he asked, feeling stupid at the question.

'Because it's a good distraction. We'll stay a little while, and we won't go back until it's over.'

Until his brother was buried, she meant. Numbly, he nodded and picked up a stone. He threw it as far as he could, and it landed deep in the loch. Then he found another and threw it hard. This time, it didn't travel as far, but the splash was stronger.

'It's all right to be angry,' she told him.

And with that, cold rage came rushing out. He *was* angry. Angry that someone as good as his brother should die so young. It wasn't right or fair.

Dalton let the next rock fall from his hands, and suddenly, she reached for his hand. Though she wore gloves, he could feel the warmth of her palm in his.

He gripped her hand, as if she were a lifeline. This girl's quiet strength was what he needed right now. And as he stood beside her, he felt that, for the first time in his life, he wasn't alone.

Chapter One

Seven years later

Dalton St George, Viscount Camford, was in love with his best friend's fiancée.

Oh, there was no doubting that it was wrong. He knew that. But trying to shut off his feelings for Lady Regina was like trying to stop breathing. *She* was the reason he'd stayed in London, instead of retreating to his grandfather's country estate in Scotland.

Some called her the Lady of Ice because she refused to speak with most men. Others called her a wallflower, for she rarely danced or conversed in public. They mistook her painful shyness for a haughty demeanour. But Dalton knew her better. There were secrets behind those deep blue eyes, as if she had suffered humiliation and wanted to remain in the shadows. Something had happened to her since the day they had met, years ago, but he could not say what it was.

Right now, she was standing at the back of the ballroom, watching over the crowd of people. Her straight red hair was pulled into a tight arrangement at the base of her nape, and she wore a light grey gown the colour of a pearl. Around her throat hung a sapphire necklace with another teardrop pearl suspended. She fluttered her lace fan, but her attention had drifted elsewhere as if she were dreaming.

Look, but don't touch, his brain warned. *You're not the right man for her.*

He knew she was meant to marry Lachlan MacKinloch. Their meddling fathers had planned an informal betrothal a few years ago. Sometimes he imagined what it would be like to steal her away. But he would never do that to a friend—especially his best friend. And more than that, he didn't believe he was the sort of man she'd want anyway. He wasn't the honourable viscount who always knew the proper way to behave. Despite his efforts to fill his brother's role, nothing he'd ever said or done had been good enough. And so, he revelled in impulse, hardly caring for the consequences any more.

He took a few moments to indulge in the sight of her beauty. Just being near Regina brought out his protective nature, though she knew nothing of his feelings. If anything, he'd done his best to drive her away, to ensure that she never suspected the truth.

It was safer if she didn't like him at all.

When she glanced up, her eyes met his. Dalton winked, knowing it would make her blush. And indeed, it did. His conscience warned him to leave her alone, but when had he ever listened to good sense? Instead, he crossed the ballroom to stand before her. He bowed lightly. 'Lady Regina.'

'Lord Camford.' She gave a slight nod of acknowledgement but said nothing else, not even looking at him. He didn't speak for a time, simply enjoying her nearness. Her skin smelled of flowers and a hint of rose. What he wouldn't give to press his mouth against that silken skin.

When he continued to stand before her, at last she enquired, 'Was there something you wanted?'

Aye. He wanted *her*. Preferably upon a bed, wearing nothing except a smile. But since he couldn't actually say that, he remarked, 'I heard that Lachlan is coming to London within a fortnight.'

'He is, yes.' The flush deepened across her cheeks, and he didn't know what that meant. Was she happy about it? Or afraid?

Jealousy speared his gut, and Dalton waited for her to say more. When she didn't continue, he couldn't stop himself from asking, 'Are you happy about the betrothal?'

She didn't answer at first. But when he studied her expression, he saw a hint of sadness. He couldn't quite understand what that meant, but he wanted to believe she held reservations about the marriage.

And yet, what good was it, even if it were true? It wasn't as if she would transfer her affections to him.

Eventually, she answered, 'The laird hasn't asked me to wed him yet, though it's what my father wants.'

'And what is it that *you* want, Lady Regina?'

She stiffened. 'I want to be left alone. By everyone.' Her mouth tightened, and she added, 'I would like nothing better than to be away from London and the rest of the world.'

'Shipwrecked upon an island?' he suggested.

That did soften her frustration. 'That sounds wonderful.' A slight smile curved at her lips. 'With nothing but sand and seashells all around me.'

He didn't tell her that it sounded lonely or that he wished he could be in a place like that with her. Instead, he changed the subject. 'Sadly, there is no sand to be found here. But we could stroll around the room and avoid everyone, if you like.'

She placed her hand on his arm. 'I suppose.'

As promised, he kept to the edges of the room and took the conversation lead, allowing her to relax. He spoke in a continuous stream about this person and that, so she wouldn't have to speak unless she wanted to. A few moments later, a gentleman stepped in front of them. He couldn't recall the man's name, but Dalton thought he was a baron or a knight.

'You'd better be careful, Camford,' the man remarked. With a glance towards Dalton's arm where Lady Regina's hand rested, he added, 'Your fingers might freeze off.' He laughed heartily at his own remark and then stepped aside. Dalton considered shoving the man against the wall and bloodying his nose, but Regina pressed her fingers against his arm and shook her head, leading him past the man.

'Ignore him,' she said softly. 'It's nothing I'm not already used to.'

Dalton's mood darkened, for she deserved better than to be treated so cruelly. 'He has no right to speak of you in that way.'

She raised an eyebrow at the insult and shrugged. 'I refused to let him pay a call on me. He's only bitter.'

'He wasn't good enough for you.'

She shrugged. 'I saw no reason to let him believe he had a chance at marrying me.'

'Because of Lachlan?' he asked quietly.

'He was only interested in my dowry. I've known many men like him. They're all the same.' She kept her gaze fixed ahead, but he touched her fingers lightly with his gloved hand.

'You don't want to be married, do you?' he said. He didn't truly expect her to answer, but she surprised him when she did.

'No.' Her voice was soft, with a fearful edge. 'But I have no choice.'

An invisible pain seemed to cloak her, and he couldn't stop the surge of protectiveness that rose over him. When he'd first met her, she had been adventurous and bold, throwing rocks into the loch to see how far they would go. But now, all that had changed.

He wanted to demand who had done this to her. Who had stolen her smile and her confidence? But he had no right to confront her.

'Why do you have to wed?'

'It is my father's wish,' was all she would say. 'I know my duty, however, and I will obey.' Beneath her dejected tone, he sensed fear. And though he could do nothing to assuage her sorrow, he could offer a distraction.

'Dance with me, Lady Regina,' he said quietly. He wanted a forbidden moment to hold her in his arms.

'Lord Camford, I must decline. I've no wish to dance just now.' Her voice was heavy, as if she had the weight of the world pressing down on her.

He hated seeing her in pain, and he wanted to see an emotional response other than the resignation in her eyes. Even anger was better. If that meant provoking her, so be it.

'Or you could stand there, feeling sorry for yourself and being melancholy.'

Her blue eyes flashed with irritation. 'I am not feeling sorry for myself.'

That was better. At least now, she was no longer caught up in her misery. He regarded her and slipped into a Scottish brogue. 'Aye, you are, lass.' He deliberately exaggerated the words, though he'd lived in England most of his life. His mother was a distant cousin of the MacKinlochs, and he had spent many summers in the Highlands. To his father's chagrin, Dalton had embraced his rebellious Scottish ancestry.

She tightened her mouth in a line and remarked, 'If you're trying to cheer me up, it's not working.'

'There are three gentlemen approaching us,' he said quietly. 'Your father is one of them. The other two will ask you to dance, and when you refuse, your father will force you to pick one of them. Is that what you're wanting?'

She glared at him. 'Fine. I'll dance with you once. But in return, I want you to leave me alone for the rest of the night.'

Even in anger, she was stunning. Her blue eyes flashed with annoyance, and he hardly cared at all. Were it possible, he would steal her away from this ballroom and indulge in his own improper fantasies.

Instead, Dalton offered his arm and led her towards the dance floor. 'God forbid if you were to enjoy yourself.'

She took her place across from him and curtsied as he bowed. 'You are not very nice, Camford.'

'No. I'm verra wicked.'

Regina took his hand as he spun her around in the

country dance, a false smile pasted on her face. 'Being wicked is not something to boast about.'

'I don't suppose you've ever done anything wicked in your life,' he teased. His words struck a nerve, and her expression grew stricken. He immediately regretted what he'd said and took it back. 'My apologies. I didn't mean to offend you.'

'You didn't. It's nothing.' She took his hand, and this time, he studied her expression. There was vulnerability in her eyes, and he wanted to know what had happened to cause the pain. She had her secrets and the inner thoughts she hid from everyone else.

Although he'd known Regina for years, he had been careful to keep his distance, maintaining the boundary of friendship when he'd travelled to London. But as the years went on, he'd spent more and more time in Scotland, avoiding his responsibilities.

Dalton touched his hand to hers as they turned in a slow circle. 'After the dance is over, I will keep my bargain and leave you in peace. But if you should like to be rescued from a gentleman who is bothering you, simply close your fan and place it by your side. I will find a reason to make him leave.'

Her expression turned amused. 'And what reason would you have to help me?'

'Because that's what friends do.' He kept his tone light, though he wanted to be far more than her friend. Regina was a beautiful woman, and he'd never forgotten her kindness after his brother's death.

The dance ended, and he bowed. As he escorted her back to her father, he rested his hand upon the small of her back, savouring the forbidden touch. She was the sort of woman his brother might have married, had

Brandon lived. And though a part of him wanted her still, he knew better than to think it would ever happen. It was only a matter of time before her engagement to Lachlan became official. And what kind of man tried to steal his best friend's fiancée? A traitor, that's who.

Let her go, his mind warned.

But as he walked away, he knew just how difficult that would be.

Three days later

'Are you ready, Regina?' Ned Crewe, the Earl of Havershire, held out his gloved hand. For an older man, her father looked rather dashing. His beaver hat covered his dark hair, which was slightly tinged with grey. He wore a black coat, waistcoat, and tan breeches, along with Hessian boots.

'I suppose,' she replied. 'Though I would much rather remain inside.' Her father had suggested a walk, in order to converse privately. She didn't know why he wanted her to discuss the night when she had been attacked—it was a memory she preferred to forget.

'Unfortunately, there are too many eavesdroppers if we are at home.'

They continued down the stone stairs, walking in silence through the streets. The earl led her towards a secluded pathway in the direction of the Serpentine, and once they were completely alone, her father's expression turned grim. 'I know you would rather not speak of this. But I need you to try to remember what you saw that night. Or whether anyone else saw it. It's important, Regina.'

She didn't understand why it mattered. 'It happened

nearly five years ago. It's over and done with. No one knows about it, except us.'

His discerning gaze reached beneath the surface of her courage, and she looked away. 'You're still afraid.'

Of course, she was afraid. She had faced her attacker and had barely survived. The memories were scarred inside her mind, and now, the very thought of being close to a man terrified her.

'I have every reason to be afraid,' she shot back. 'But I live with it, just as you do.' He had been there that night and had helped her cover up the truth. If anyone had learned about the attack, her name would have been ruined, and worse, her father would have been implicated. Thus far, they had kept everything hidden for years. And the last thing she wanted was to dredge up the horrifying memories.

'I wish I could have protected you better.' His words were an apology, but they couldn't change the past. 'But I will do everything in my power to keep you safe now. It's why I need to know if you saw anything.'

'Did something happen? Did anyone say anything to you?'

Her father sighed. 'Just…try to remember. Was there anyone you saw that night when you were returning home? Or did you see anyone afterwards?' He reached for her gloved hand and tucked it in his arm.

He hadn't answered her question, which meant that there *was* something he wasn't telling her.

'I saw no one beforehand. And afterwards, I couldn't—' Her voice broke off, and a chill caught her skin.

'I understand,' he said softly. But his face remained

uncertain. It looked for a moment as if he wanted to tell her something, but he was holding it back.

'What is it, Papa?' she asked.

He sighed and shook his head. 'It's only that I want to keep you safe. I pray that no one saw you that night. I need you to remember every detail, so I can protect you.' His face grew pained, and he reached for his handkerchief. A racking cough claimed him, and he used the handkerchief to cover his face, turning away from her.

'Are you all right?' she asked, touching his shoulder. His shoulders shook as the coughing fit continued. She waited until it passed, but her worry lingered. Over the past year, her father had lost a great deal of weight, and the coughing seemed to be worse recently. He claimed that it was nothing more than a lingering illness, but his skin pallor was quite pale.

'It's nothing. Let us continue our walk,' he said, while he folded his handkerchief and put it away. 'I understand that Locharr will be arriving soon. How do you feel about the marriage?'

As if I want to avoid it, she thought inwardly.

'He hasn't asked me to wed him yet,' she pointed out.

'No, but he will. It was his father Tavin's dying wish.' He mustered a smile. 'And mine, if the truth be known. The pair of you make a handsome couple, and I have no doubt he will keep you safe.'

Regina wasn't entirely certain of that, but she didn't want to argue. Instead, she feigned a false smile to push back the fear. She bit her lip hard and murmured, 'No doubt.'

Earlier, they had both agreed that it was best if

she left London altogether and married the Laird of Locharr. Lachlan MacKinloch could protect her, if any remnants of her past resurfaced. The Highlands would become her sanctuary, where no one would know of her secret scandal.

A wild part of her wished she could run away, disappearing from the outside world. Being shipwrecked on an island, as Lord Camford had suggested, sounded very nice indeed. But instead, she had to play the role of the dutiful daughter who was braver than she seemed. Especially now that her father was hiding something.

He led her back towards their house, and her skin grew cold. The earlier conversation suddenly brought back memories she didn't want to face. She stood at the entrance to the narrow street beside the house, her stomach churning with nausea. Her limbs had gone numb, and the horrifying visions washed over her. She had been seventeen, filled with dreams and naivety.

It had been late at night when the baron had escorted her home from the ball. The carriage had stopped near the narrow street and he had taken her there to walk for a moment. She had strolled down this very lane, her arm linked with his.

'I am going to ask your father for your hand in marriage tonight,' he'd promised. 'I want to speak with him now.'

The thought had been so thrilling to her girlish dreams she had laughed and agreed. Though a part of her had known that her father would never approve of a lowly baron, Lord Mallencourt had been daring and so very handsome. He had a way of convincing others to indulge his impulses, and at the time, it had been romantic.

'I don't know if Papa has returned from Scotland,' she had said. 'He might be at home, but it is far too late for him to receive visitors.'

'We simply must speak with him, regardless of the hour. I cannot wait any longer to call you my fiancée.'

Lord Mallencourt had made her laugh, pressing her close to the wall for a stolen kiss. His mouth had been heated, filled with sinful promises. She had been overwhelmed by the rush of feelings.

And then he had led her inside.

Mother had still been at the ball, and most of the servants were in the kitchen, cleaning or banking the fires. Aside from their footman, no one else had known of their late arrival.

The tremors shook her hands, and Regina tried to find the courage to push back the dark memories.

'Regina?' her father asked. 'Are you all right? Did you…remember something?'

She tried to think, but the only memories were of rough hands tearing at her gown. And then, the pain and horrible humiliation that followed. God above, she didn't want to recall anything, much less speak of it.

'I am sorry. I can't.' She wrenched her hand from her father's grasp, picking up her skirts. Bile gathered in the back of her throat, and she ran for the stairs, shoving open the front door.

She bolted up one flight of stairs and then another before she reached her room. Scalding tears ran down her cheeks and she barely reached the basin before she started retching.

Her impulsiveness had cost her everything, and she

could never bear the thought of a man's touch again. Papa had promised that the Laird of Locharr was a good man, and that he would take care of her. But a husband would expect her to share his bed, and that was something she could never do.

She laid her head down on her dressing table, wondering how in God's name she could ever endure a marriage ceremony or what came afterwards.

Dalton sat on the opposite end of the table from his father at luncheon. John St George, the Earl of Brevershire, dined precisely at one o'clock each day, and they ate in silence. It was as if he had created a wall of invisible stone around himself. He hardly spoke, and he only went about his daily tasks out of a sense of duty.

Dalton had no idea how to break his father out of the spell. But John had been like this for as long as he could remember. Dalton had accepted his status as the Invisible Son for years. His brother, Brandon, had been the good son, the heir his parents adored. Whereas Dalton was the spare they'd ignored.

After Brandon's death, it had become far worse. His parents had fallen into a deep despair, and nothing he said or did could break them out of the sorrow. If anything, his presence seemed to darken his father's mood. They still blamed him for what had happened. And nothing he ever did could atone for it.

'I think I'll return to Grandfather's estate during the Season,' Dalton offered. 'Someone should look after Cairnross.' He received only a nod from his father, as the earl's silver knife scraped the edge of the china plate.

He could easily have said that he was going to cut

off his right hand, and the reaction would have been the same. But still, he would try to make a conversation.

'Do you want to come with me?' Dalton ventured.

His father jolted, and a sudden flare of emotion caught his face. 'I—no. That is, no. I don't think so. And, well, Parliament is in session.' He set his knife down and added, 'But I should be grateful if you would go and see to the estate matters.'

Just like that, the conversation died again. Dalton thought about bringing his plate closer to his father. John had eaten only a little, and his face appeared ravaged with hunger. His father was naught but a shell of a man any more. He had begun fading after the death of his son seven years ago. It had worsened with the death of his wife, two years ago. He might as well have climbed into the grave beside them.

'Father, I am concerned about you,' he said to the earl. 'You never leave the house any more. You ought to go out, attend a few gatherings.'

'I don't want to go to a ball or a supper party. I'd rather remain here.'

Where I can bury myself in work and forget about the rest of the world, his expression seemed to say.

'You're dying here,' Dalton pointed out. 'There are too many memories in this house.' Before Brandon's death, his mother had decorated the house with bright colours and roses in every room. She had been like a whirlwind, constantly moving about and talking endlessly. They had all adored her.

But after his brother died, she had withered. Brandon's empty room had become an untouched shrine. Ailsa had gone inside each day, as if she could feel her

son's presence. Everything had been left as it was before. Even his clothes remained.

And while he understood their grief, he hadn't
known how to ease their pain. They rarely spoke to
him, and they were so caught up in the past, they could
not seem to fathom a future besides the one they had
planned.

'I am happy as I am,' the earl said quietly. 'Let me
be, Dalton.' He folded his napkin and peered down the
length of the table. 'I would rather concentrate on our
family's investments and continue building our wealth.
Someone has to see to it that our expenses are paid.'

Dalton didn't like the sound of censure in his father's voice. He had worked just as hard as his father,
ensuring that the estates were profitable. He had even
invested money in shipping ventures, expanding their
interests in India.

John's face held weariness. 'Go to Scotland if that
is what you wish. I will be fine here.'

Dalton's shoulders lowered when he realised that
there was nothing he could do. The sense of loneliness descended, making him feel like an intruder in his
own house. His father was unable to overcome his own
grief, and it was the same as it always had been before.

He departed the dining room and one of his dogs
trotted out to see him. Dalton leaned down and petted the foxhound's head. 'And what advice would you
give me, Laddie, if you were my father?' He went to
sit on the stairs, and the dog rested his head on Dalton's knees. 'Perhaps I should take my own advice.
Live my life as I please. Find a bride and settle down.
Have children of my own.'

In response, the dog slumped to the ground and

rolled to his back, exposing his belly. Dalton smiled and petted the dog until he squirmed with delight. 'And what about Lady Regina? What should I do about her?' The dog stood and shook himself before he circled the floor and curled up.

'It hardly matters, I suppose.' After their last conversation, he knew that Regina believed she had no choice but to wed the laird. Although he didn't understand her reasons, he hadn't pressed the matter. After all, she hadn't seen Lachlan in nearly ten years, and the arrangement had been suggested by her father, after Lachlan's father Tavin had died a few years ago.

He thought of her earlier vulnerability and wondered if there was aught he could do to ease her uncertainties. Aye, Locharr was the man her father had chosen for her. But he couldn't help but think that both of them were making a mistake.

His conscience warned that it wasn't his place to interfere or to pry in her affairs. Moreover, it would harm his friendship with Lachlan. He'd hidden his true feelings for years, teasing her relentlessly. If she pushed him away, it was easier to keep the boundaries between them.

Laddie went to the door and pulled down the leather lead with his teeth, bringing it to him. There was no denying that the dog wanted a walk.

'It is a fine day,' he agreed with the animal. 'But I don't know if Lady Regina would want to come walking with us,' he said. She tended to stay at home, away from prying eyes.

She might not accept his call, much less help him walk a dog. But it was an unconventional way of spending time with her. It might lift her spirits in some small way, and he could learn whether she needed his help in escaping the marriage.

You shouldn't do this, his brain warned. *It's wrong.*

He knew that. But he intended to try, even so.

Chapter Two

'My lady, you have a caller. Viscount Camford has asked if you are receiving.' The footman, Louis, was holding a silver salver with the card upon it.

Regina was about to refuse, when she heard the unexpected sound of barking. She regarded the footman. 'Is that a dog?' Surely, she was hearing things.

'It is, my lady. Two of them, in fact.'

A sudden flare of mirth caught her by surprise. 'Really. Lord Camford brought dogs with him?' She could hardly believe it. Why on earth would he do such a thing?

The footman's expression turned pained. 'Yes, he did, my lady. Would you like me to send him away?'

That would be the appropriate thing to do, considering she was promised to another man. But curiosity warred with her love of animals. She needed to see the dogs, regardless of Camford's intentions.

'Don't send him away,' she told the footman. 'I will receive him in the parlour. And the dogs, of course.' She had a weakness for them, since her mother had never allowed her to own one. Arabella believed that the animals were filthy creatures who would destroy the household. Although she had no idea what Lord Camford was up to, she was eager to see the dogs.

'Yes, my lady.' Her footman departed, and Regina put her book back upon the shelf of her father's bookcase. She walked towards the parlour, still wondering why he had brought the dogs. The barking noise increased, and she sat in a chair, waiting impatiently.

When Lord Camford entered the parlour, she could not stop the soft cry of delight at the squirming dogs. One was a pug and the other, his foxhound Laddie.

'Good afternoon, Lady Regina,' he greeted her. 'I've brought other callers with me. You know Laddie, and this is Hubert. I saw Worthingstone's footman walking him just down the street, and I offered to take him along with us.'

'So I see.' She knelt down to welcome his dog. Laddie was ageing, but he was still as sweet and affectionate as she remembered. Then she turned her attention to the other dog, and the pug began licking her gloves. 'Aren't you a darling?' she cooed, taking the animal. Hubert was wiggling in her arms, and she sat upon the sofa, bringing him to her lap. Lord Camford sat beside her so she was able to pet both dogs.

'Do you like them?'

'I adore them.' Regina lifted the pug for a kiss, and he licked her face. 'It's a good thing my mother is out paying calls. Else she would force you to take them away.' She wondered what exactly Lord Camford was up to and decided to ask. 'Why did you bring them to me?'

'I remembered you told me years ago that you loved dogs,' he said.

She didn't know quite what to think of that, but she was too distracted by the animals to care. The pug settled on her lap while the foxhound was darting between Lord Camford and her, sniffing furiously.

'They have a lot of energy,' he said. 'I thought you might like to go for a drive, and then we could walk with them near the gardens. I brought the leads.'

The instinct to refuse came to her lips, but then, it was a lovely spring day. The dogs clearly needed the exercise, and the idea of spending time with them was delightful.

'All right,' she said. 'But only for a little while.' She removed her glove and ran her fingers over the pug's head, smiling at his wrinkled face. He turned towards her touch and licked her palm. She laughed at his antics, and then glanced up at Lord Camford to see what he thought of the animals.

His eyes seemed greener just now, and he was staring at her with undisguised interest. His dark blond hair framed a strong jaw, and there was a faint stubble of beard on his cheeks. A rush of sensation flooded through her, for he looked as if he wanted to kiss her. Although the thought should have evoked terror, instead, she found herself captivated by his gaze. Her heart beat faster, and she turned away, feeling her cheeks flush.

The last thing she needed was a man's interest. She was ruined for marriage, and while Dalton St George was a titled gentleman whom any woman might desire, he was not for her, nor she for him. Were it possible to avoid all men, she would readily do so.

Lord Camford reached over and pressed a leather lead into her hand. His fingers lingered upon hers for a moment, and once again, she felt the surge of nervous energy rising. 'For Hubert,' he said, before he let go of her hand. There was a faint smile on his face, as if he was aware of her discomfort and was trying to reassure her.

Regina attached the leather lead on to the animal's collar and then put her glove back on before she lifted the pug into her arms. Hubert was heavier than she'd expected, but he seemed content in her embrace.

'You can put him down if you'd rather,' Lord Camford said.

But right now, the dog felt like a shield against her own distracted feelings. She preferred holding him close, and she pressed a kiss upon his furry head.

Instead of marriage, she decided it would be much nicer to live alone, surrounded by dogs. The thought made her smile.

Lord Camford was still watching her, but he set the foxhound on the floor, lightly gripping the lead to keep the animal from running away.

'Shall we?' he asked, offering his arm.

Regina took a deep breath, wondering what she had agreed to. 'I'll ring for my maid to chaperon.'

It took less than an hour before they were in Lord Camford's carriage. Her maid, Nell, sat on the rumble, and they began driving towards Kensington Gardens. The day was bright and sunny, though there was a slight chill in the spring air. The trees lining the gardens were still bare, though a few brave buds were starting to form.

All the while, Regina was very aware of Lord Camford's presence beside her. Although he sat on his side of the phaeton, sometimes his thigh inadvertently bumped against hers. It was disconcerting to feel the rush of embarrassment, and she didn't know what to think of it. Despite the accidental touch, he made no move to cross the boundary. He knew it made her uncomfortable, and she was grateful that he understood.

After a time, she grew distracted by the dogs. They licked at each other and tried to play, whimpering with their heads down and their tails in the air. She started to relax, laughing as they frolicked amid her skirts.

'We should stop soon, in case they get overexcited,' Lord Camford suggested. 'I wouldn't want them to soil your gown.'

She nodded in agreement. 'I hadn't thought of that, but you're right. They *are* excited, after all.' When the pug rolled on to his back, she stifled a laugh.

The viscount smiled back, but it wasn't a casual smile between friends. No, it was the smile of a man who liked her a great deal. She sensed it in the warmth of his eyes, and the underlying instinct that if she softened towards him, he would indeed want more from her. This carriage ride might not be a good idea, in light of that.

But even more concerning was that she didn't find it easy to freeze out his interest in the same way she could with other gentlemen. Most of the time, she could tell them no, or she could ignore them, and they would go away.

Lord Camford was different. When she tried to refuse him, he somehow managed to talk her into spending time with him. Even now, she was so very aware of how handsome he was. His dark blond hair had a rakish appearance from the wind. His broad shoulders filled up his coat, and he was a tall man. Despite his clothing, she sensed a wildness beneath it all. Perhaps it was his Highlander heritage. Her instincts warned that this proper English viscount was not as proper as she'd imagined.

There was far more to Dalton St George than anyone could guess. It unnerved her to realise that she was not entirely immune to his charm. Right now, she needed to strengthen the invisible walls around her emotions, ensuring that he understood there could never be anything between them.

She decided to be blunt. 'What are you doing, Lord Camford? Why did you arrange this carriage ride and the dogs?'

He paused a moment. 'Would you consider me a friend, Lady Regina?'

'I'm not certain,' she answered honestly. 'I am suspicious of your intentions, to be frank.'

The viscount drew the horses to a stop, pulling lightly on the reins. His face turned serious, and he said, 'If we are being frank, then I will tell you that I am worried about you. You've changed a great deal from the girl I once knew.' He gentled his voice. 'Is everything all right?'

No, she would never answer that question. Her heartbeat quickened, and she couldn't bring herself to speak a single word.

'I know that you've been unhappy,' he continued. 'You've not smiled in years, it seems.'

Because she didn't have a reason to smile. It felt as if her future had been stolen from her. And though she understood that he was concerned, she could never let down her guard. Even when she was with Lord Camford, whom she trusted, her nerves betrayed her. She tensed, always uneasy of his intentions, though he had never done anything wrong.

'My father has been ill,' she said at last, fumbling for an excuse. 'It has been difficult for our family.'

He nodded in understanding, though his eyes seemed to distrust her answer. 'I thought the dogs might make you smile,' he continued. 'You need a reason to smile, Lady Regina.'

His eyes warmed, and she felt her shyness returning. Though she knew he would never trespass on their friendship, she recognised the glimmer of interest. But even if she were not betrothed, a man like Lord Camford ought to have an outgoing, friendly young woman who would welcome him into her heart and give him an heir. Not someone broken, like her.

'I've made you uncomfortable, and that was not my intention,' he said lightly. 'Shall we take these two beasts for a walk?'

The pug had fallen asleep on her lap and Regina picked him up, cuddling him close. The animal continued to snooze while Lord Camford brought the foxhound down to the pathway. The hound began sniffing at the trail, and Regina smiled at his antics.

'Yours seems to be more awake than mine.' She walked with the sleeping pug, hardly caring about his weight. The innocent trust of the animal warmed her heart.

'He's a braw lad.' He exaggerated a brogue while keeping a firm grip on the lead. She'd noticed over the years that he sometimes slipped into his mother's ancestry from time to time. Though his father was English, Lord Camford seemed to enjoy behaving with a bit of Scottish flair.

The foxhound spied a butterfly and tried to chase it. Lord Camford allowed the dog to explore, but he kept his pace slow while they walked.

'I've heard that Locharr will arrive any day now,' Lord Camford said.

She nodded, though the thought filled her with dread. Not because she disliked the laird, but it was the idea of an impending betrothal. More than anything, she wanted to refuse.

And yet, her father was set upon the match and would brook no refusal. Every time she spoke of her reluctance, he insisted that it was necessary—now, even more so. Not only because he wanted to see her wedded, but it was for her own protection. He claimed that it was better if she travelled far away from London, and Scotland was perfect.

He had also sworn a promise to Lachlan's father that their families would join in marriage. Tavin had been Ned's best friend, and he intended to honour that vow, regardless of her own hesitance.

But what bothered her now was why her father had suddenly wanted her to recall the night of her attack. He'd been probing for more information, and he would not say why. If anything, she wanted to put it behind her and never think of it again. But something was troubling her father. She could see the worry nagging at him, and it made her wonder about the reason for it.

The viscount was waiting for her to speak, but truthfully, she had nothing at all to say. They turned a corner along the walkway, and out of nowhere, a young man came hurtling towards her.

A flash of fear made her nearly drop the pug. Before she could react, the viscount stepped in front of her and pushed the man away. 'Have a care and watch where you're going!'

Lord Camford kept himself in front of her, and the young man blurted out, 'I am so terribly sorry. We were just having a footrace, and I didn't see you.' He apologised again and beat a hasty retreat. The viscount turned back to her, but Regina's heart was still racing.

'Are you all right?' he asked. 'I'm so sorry he frightened you.' Though there was no harm done, she could not bring herself to speak.

'Come and sit down,' Lord Camford offered. He picked up the lead, and thankfully the foxhound had not wandered far. He brought her over to a bench, and she sat gratefully. For a time, he simply sat beside her while she calmed her fears. The pug was scrambling to get down, but she didn't dare move. Lord Camford took the dog from her and simply waited. He did not try to fill the silence with mindless conversation but let her take the time she needed.

When she could finally gather her thoughts, she said quietly, 'Thank you for defending me.' In truth, she had not expected him to respond so swiftly. Because of it, the young man had not stumbled over her.

'I will always keep you safe, Lady Regina,' the viscount answered. His voice was quiet and undemanding. In his eyes, she saw not only the promise of protection, but also an undisguised longing.

And she simply didn't know what to do about it.

Dalton watched from across the ballroom as Lady Regina pressed her hands against her white-silk gown.

He could sense her nerves, for Lachlan MacKinloch, Laird of Locharr, was finally here. Her father had a broad smile on his face, as if his greatest wish was about to come true. It took every shred of control for Dalton to push back his frustration. He had known this moment would come, when Locharr arrived to claim his promised bride.

But he'd not expected the surge of dark jealousy. There was no reason for it, for no promises had ever been made. He and Lady Regina had been friends, and that was all. It was his own fault for wanting more.

Instead, he walked to her side, and she turned to look at him. Dalton bowed in greeting and said, 'You look beautiful, Lady Regina.'

'Thank you,' she answered softly. Her white gown made her face paler than usual, but it accentuated her blue eyes and fiery red hair. She was like Aphrodite, a benevolent goddess whom he wanted to worship and adore.

'Have you spoken with MacKinloch yet?' he asked. He wanted to see her reaction when he spoke of the laird, for he didn't know if she was still considering the betrothal.

'Not yet.'

Again, her voice was so quiet, almost fearful. He knew he ought to leave her, to let her meet her future husband alone. But it felt as if he were leaving her among the wolves. So many men and women were staring at her—the men with knowing gazes and the women with bitter jealousy. The need to protect her, to shield her from gossip, overcame all common sense.

'Would you care to dance?' he asked. It would grant

her a distraction, and it gave him the chance to hold her hands and offer a silent reassurance.

'No, thank you.' Her voice remained cool, like ice. He could understand why other men would view her as frigid, but he knew the truth. It was fear beneath those deep blue eyes. Fear of what, he didn't know, but he wasn't about to leave her side.

Before he could speak, he heard a slight buzz of conversation, and the crowds of people parted. Beside him, Lady Regina seemed to shrink back in alarm. There was no mistaking the appearance of Lachlan MacKinloch, though he was wearing English attire instead of his Scottish tartan. His long hair was tied back, and he stared at the crowd until at last he saw her.

Dalton eyed his friend, wondering what exactly would happen. Locharr wasn't known for being a man of ceremony, and he cared little for manners. But it did seem that he was trying to blend in somewhat.

Regina, in contrast, looked as if she wanted to flee. Her blush suffused her face, and though he ought to leave her alone with her intended, something told him to remain here. She appeared almost grateful by his presence.

'Lady Regina,' the laird greeted her. 'It has been many years, has it no'? Do you remember me at all?'

She nodded but said nothing. When Dalton studied her surreptitiously, he noticed how she was gripping her gloved fingers together. She appeared vastly uncomfortable, and he didn't know what he could do or say to help her.

Lachlan eyed him with a genuine smile, though it held a wariness. 'I see you've been keeping the lady company, Camford.'

What are you up to? his gaze seemed to ask.

'Protecting her from the blackguards and rakes.' Dalton gave a mischievous smile to ease the tension. 'Though some might put me in that category.'

The laird replied, 'If you bother her, Camford, I'll skin your hide and leave it for the crows.' Although his words were teasing, there was a note of warning in them.

Dalton only shrugged as if he didn't care. Lady Regina knew he would never harm her, and he would not make demands of her.

She was still pale, and Locharr cleared his throat. 'I suppose that wasna a very polite thing to say. I beg your pardon, Lady Regina.'

Before she could answer, their hostess, the Duchess of Worthingstone, arrived. Dalton and Locharr both bowed in greeting to Her Grace while Lady Regina sank into a deep curtsy.

'Are you enjoying yourself?' Her Grace asked the laird. Dalton knew that Locharr was staying with the duchess and duke within their household. The ball had been arranged to give him the chance to see Lady Regina again.

'I've only just arrived, but I am, aye,' Locharr agreed. It was clear that the laird was trying to adapt to his surroundings, but he appeared uncertain. He glanced at Dalton as if wondering what to do now.

'Good.' The duchess smiled. 'There is someone I've been wanting you to meet. Forgive me, Lady Regina, but I must steal the laird away for just a moment.'

'It's no trouble at all,' Lady Regina murmured. In fact, she seemed rather relieved by it.

The laird bowed to her and said, 'I will only be a

moment.' Then he turned back to Dalton. 'You should ask the lady to dance.'

He already had, but he recognised the look of discomfort on Regina's face. It was as if all the attention overwhelmed her, and she was eager to be away from everyone's notice.

As soon as the laird had gone, she murmured, 'Thank you, but I still don't wish to dance,' she murmured. She opened her fan, as if the ballroom had suddenly become unbearably hot. Though she tried to mask it, she appeared miserable. Dalton refused to stand back and ignore her.

'Are you all right, Lady Regina?' Dalton kept his voice calm and quiet. He wanted her to know that he was still her friend, and there was nothing he wouldn't do for her. But though she tried to smile, he could see through her mask of emotions.

'I am fine,' she remarked.

He didn't believe that at all. 'Liar,' he said beneath his breath. 'You'd rather be anywhere than here.'

She jerked to surprise. 'Why would you say that?'

He continued as if she hadn't spoken. 'You'd rather be sitting on a stone bench in the morning sunlight, with a puppy in your lap.'

At that, her frozen expression seemed to thaw a little. 'Wouldn't everyone prefer that?'

'I think so, yes.' He offered her his arm. 'Are you certain you don't want to dance?'

'Very certain. I would rather watch from the shadows.'

'No matter how hard you try, you will never be a wallflower, Lady Regina,' he said quietly. 'There is not a man here who doesn't notice you.'

Or desire you, he thought.

It wasn't only her beauty that attracted notice—it was her vulnerability and shyness. While some thought it was hauteur, he knew better. And he would try any means of making her smile.

'I'll go and bring you lemonade, if you'd like.'

'I don't like lemonade at all,' she admitted. 'I find it too sour.'

'Then perhaps something else to drink,' he offered. Before she could refuse, he bowed and took his leave. As he walked towards the refreshment table, he paused and saw the duchess returning from another room. She had brought Lachlan to meet another guest, and Dalton's curiosity was aroused. He waited until Her Grace was gone, and then slipped into the narrow hallway. It seemed that the laird was meeting with someone in the music room, and he took a few cautious steps closer. Soon, he overheard the voice of a woman.

'You have to go back, Locharr.' The woman's voice held yearning, as if she didn't truly want the laird to leave.

'I ken that.' But Lachlan's voice held a gentleness that caught Dalton's attention. The laird genuinely cared about this woman, and he sounded as if he had no desire to leave.

A sudden flare caught him with the realisation that the duchess had brought this woman to Locharr in secret, because she did not want anyone else to see her. Who was she? And why was the laird speaking as if he held affection towards her?

'Don't make this any more difficult than it has to be, Lachlan,' the woman said. There was no doubting the emotion in her voice. And though Dalton wanted to know who she was, he didn't dare show his face. Instead, he remained hidden from view and waited until the laird emerged from the room. Locharr didn't see him, but the expression on his face was of a man who was grimly accepting his duty.

It sounded as if the laird didn't want to marry Lady Regina. Yet, this conversation was a farewell, not a secret liaison. And for a brief moment, Dalton sympathised with his friend.

For he knew exactly what it was to love a woman he couldn't have.

Chapter Three

It was early in the morning when Regina rose. She'd been unable to sleep, worrying about the laird. Though Locharr had been nothing but kind, he was indeed a large man. The thought of sharing a marital bed with him was terrifying, despite trying to convince herself that he would be gentle.

I cannot do it, she thought. He would crush her with his weight, bringing back the vicious memories.

There was no sense in trying to push back the fear, so she abandoned all thoughts of going back to sleep. With the help of her maid, she donned a long-sleeved blue morning gown with a high waist, embroidered with green leaves along the hem. Nell had suggested a looser hair arrangement, but Regina had refused. She wanted it tightly bound, but she had allowed her maid to adorn it with a pearl comb. Then she went downstairs to join her parents at breakfast.

She went down the first set of stairs but paused on the landing when she saw the door was open to her father's study. Sometimes he rose early, so she decided to greet him. But after she reached the doorway, she saw

that he had already gone. Regina was about to depart
when suddenly, she spied something beside the desk
on the floor that took her aback.

It was a handkerchief stained with blood.

A sinking feeling clutched her stomach, for she immediately thought of his coughing. Papa had never
wanted to admit he was ill, but his coughing fits had
grown more frequent. Had he even seen a physician?
She needed to speak with him, to make him seek help
for his ailment. She didn't want to think about what
could happen if his condition continued to go un-
treated.

Regina closed her eyes and sat down at the desk, her
heart aching at the thought of him being ill. She had
grown closer to her father during the past four years,
and they had an understanding between them. He loved
her and only wanted what was best. She knew that he
was only trying to arrange a marriage for her protection, so that no one could ever threaten her again.

But if Papa was dying, his time might be running
out. He had only ever had one wish—for her to marry
his best friend's son, Lachlan. And in doing so, he believed it would keep her safe.

Tears pricked at her eyes, and the harsh ache in her
gut tightened.

You cannot avoid marriage for much longer.

She wiped the tears before they could fall and resolved to take care of her father and help him as much
as she could.

Regina was about to leave, when a letter on the desk
caught her notice. It was not signed, and the handwriting was scrawled hurriedly. The note demanded three

thousand pounds and gave instructions for where to deliver the amount and when.

She frowned at the letter, wondering if she had read it correctly. Was this a jest or an unpaid bill? It seemed almost unreal to imagine such a demand. Could it be blackmail? Her heartbeat quickened at the thought. Who would do such a thing?

Her mind slipped back to her father's questions. He'd wanted to know every detail of her attack before their drive the other day. Was this why? Had someone witnessed Lord Mallencourt entering her house at a late hour, believing that she'd been seduced or ruined? That would explain her father's desire to marry her off to Locharr. A blackmailer could not destroy her reputation if she were married and living in Scotland, far away.

A heaviness settled in her stomach as another fear took hold. Or was it something else? Could anyone have witnessed the rest of it? She swallowed hard, feeling queasy at the thought.

No. She refused to dwell on it, for the attack had been nearly five years ago. Instead, she folded the letter and tucked it into her reticule. She would ask her father about it later.

When she entered the dining room, her mother was sipping a hot cup of tea. Arabella beamed at the sight of her. 'Regina, good morning! You look lovely, my dear.'

'Good morning, Mother.' She chose a seat, and the footman brought her a plate of eggs and sausage. Though she tried to eat, her thoughts remained troubled. She decided to voice her concern. 'I wanted to ask you…is Papa feeling well?'

'Of course, he is,' Arabella said brightly. 'Why wouldn't he be?'

But as she looked at her mother's face, she saw past the words. There were shadows beneath her mother's eyes, and she appeared pale.

'He has been coughing a lot,' Regina said. 'Has he seen a physician?'

Her mother's smile faltered, but she tried to dismiss it. 'It's just a spring cold. There's no reason at all to worry.'

She thought about confronting Arabella about the bloody handkerchief, but it was clear that her mother wanted to deny the truth. Likely, her own fears were preventing her from facing reality. Regina decided to quietly contact a physician and have him examine the earl.

'I am glad,' she answered. She decided not to mention the note, for it was unlikely that Papa had told her mother. Ned took great pains to avoid upsetting her, for Arabella tended towards dramatic behaviour. Regina didn't want to imagine how her mother would respond if she knew of the blackmail.

Her mother finished her tea and regarded her. 'I heard that Locharr is planning to pay a call upon you this afternoon. It would mean a great deal to your father if you would accept the laird's proposal.'

The very thought unnerved her, although she'd known it was coming. She wasn't at all ready for an engagement. Instead, she preferred friendship between them while they grew reacquainted. 'Last night was the first time I've even seen the laird in years. He's a stranger to me.'

'To you perhaps, but Locharr's father was Ned's best

friend,' Arabella said. 'Our families aren't strangers.' Her mother folded her napkin into a perfect square. 'And truly, it did seem that the laird was trying to behave like a perfect gentleman last night. Don't you think?'

'Yes, of course,' she said softly.

But inwardly, she couldn't help but think, *I'm not ready.*

A desperate panic roiled within her at the thought of marriage. She needed to leave the house, to take a few moments to herself. She didn't dare go alone, but she could ask her friend, Lady Anne, for advice.

Hurriedly, she finished eating while her mother extolled the praises of Locharr and how it was Regina's duty to wed him as soon as possible.

'I will allow him to pay a call upon me,' she promised, 'but it is too soon to decide upon marriage.' She stood from the table. 'I should go. I am meeting with Anne today.' It was stretching the truth, for her friend had no idea about it.

Regina made her excuses and ordered a carriage. Then she asked her maid, Nell, to accompany her. Once they were inside, she withdrew the folded paper from her reticule to study it. She didn't understand who would threaten her father. No one had seen anything that night, she was certain. The only witness had been their elderly footman, Frederick, who had died two years ago. No, the footman would never have betrayed them. He had worked in their household since her grandfather had been alive.

And Frederick had done everything in his power to help them.

'Is something wrong, Lady Regina?' Nell asked.

The maid's expression grew concerned, but Regina would never share the details with her. Although the young girl had proven herself trustworthy since she'd been hired a year ago, Regina had no intention of sharing her father's troubles.

'It's nothing,' she said, managing a smile. They continued driving through the city streets until they reached Anne's house on the outskirts of Mayfair. Her father, Lord Blyton, had died six years ago, and her mother, Judith, had not remarried. Although Lady Anne was an earl's daughter, she had not received any offers of marriage, due to her modest dowry and the fact that she had four older sisters, three of whom were unmarried.

Regina had offered to help her, but Anne was proud and refused to accept money or gowns. Her friend had the obstinacy of a stone wall and was determined to stand on her own feet.

As they arrived, she saw Anne walking down the stairs with her mother and two of her sisters. The look on her friend's face was dogged, as if she were trying to avoid an execution.

When the driver opened the door to her carriage, Regina stepped out. Offering a light smile, she said, 'Did you forget our outing today?'

Anne's face brightened. She spoke to her mother, and before Regina could say a word, her friend had seized her hand. 'I am *so* terribly sorry, Lady Regina! I had quite forgotten. Do forgive me.' She squeezed her hand tightly in a silent warning not to undermine her. 'Mother, I must go with Regina, for we made our plans a week ago.'

Lady Blyton gave a weak smile and waved them

on. Regina lifted her hand in farewell, and within moments, Anne spoke to the driver, then climbed inside the carriage.

'You are the answer to a prayer, my friend.' She sighed in thanksgiving and settled back against the seat. 'I was very nearly trapped into paying calls. Mother had a list of friends, and I thought I was about to perish of boredom.'

'Where are we going?' Regina asked. 'I saw you speaking to the driver.'

'We are going to enjoy ices at Lady Hardwicke's,' Anne informed her. 'That is, if you have your pin money. And I will entertain you with all the latest gossip.'

'I do have money,' she agreed, knowing that Anne had no money of her own for ices. But she didn't mind paying, though her friend might protest at first.

'Wonderful. I shall sit and watch you enjoy the ices while I regale you with delicious tales.' Anne beamed at the idea. 'I know something about your laird.' She offered a wicked smile and a wink.

'You can tell me more after we arrive,' Regina said. 'I will arrange a table for us.'

They arrived at Lady Hardwicke's, and there were several small tables with ladies seated together. Against the opposite wall, there were a few gentlemen, and the sight of a taller man gave her pause. It was Lord Camford, wearing a bottle-green coat with a cream waistcoat and buff trousers. He was bringing a fruit-flavoured ice to a fresh-faced blonde debutante. The young woman smiled brightly at him as he joined her.

A flare of irrational annoyance caught her, though it

was foolish. Camford could spend time with whomever he wanted. It wasn't jealousy, she told herself. They were friends, and it was better if he found a young woman to court. As she stole a quick look at them, she saw that the debutante was spellbound by him, while the viscount remained polite. A curious ache caught up within her gut, almost a faint note of regret—and she couldn't say why.

'You're not listening to a word I've said, are you?' Anne interrupted.

'I'm sorry. I was distracted,' she said. 'You said something about a knight you met?'

'Yes. Sir Roger is *very* handsome, though he doesn't say much. He seems shy,' Anne said, sighing with happiness when she spoke of him. Regina smiled, and a moment later, a young man delivered a variety of ices—vanilla, strawberry, and lemon—to their table, along with spoons.

'I don't believe these are ours,' Regina said. 'We haven't ordered yet.'

'They are from Lord Camford,' the man answered.

Regina stole a look back, and the viscount smiled at her. What was he thinking, doing such a thing while he sat across from another woman? 'I am sorry, but I cannot accept these.'

'Yes, we can,' Anne answered, dipping her spoon into the vanilla ice. She took a hearty bite and said, 'Oh, dear. Now we cannot send them back.'

She nearly laughed at her friend's mischief, though she knew the true reason was that Anne didn't want her to pay for her ices.

'You should thank him,' Anne said. 'It was very kind.'

'He has a young lady as his guest,' she countered. 'I wouldn't dream of interrupting them.' Yet, she couldn't help but wonder why he had done this. It might have been a whim or a friendly gesture, but it made her slightly uncomfortable.

She turned her attention back to her friend. 'Why don't you tell me the gossip you've heard about the laird?' She needed to concentrate on Lachlan MacKinloch instead of being distracted by Lord Camford.

'Of course. Did you hear about last night when Miss Brown fainted?'

Regina shook her head. She knew that there had been some sort of commotion, but she hated crowds and had remained against the wall before quietly slipping away to return home.

'You missed quite a scene,' Anne informed her. 'After she fainted, the laird tried to help her. *Then,* Miss Goodson pulled him back and warned MacKinloch that if he touched Miss Brown, he'd have to marry the girl.'

'Who is Miss Goodson?' She vaguely recalled hearing something about a woman with that surname, but it had been a long time ago.

'She was ruined by scandal years ago and became a governess. That's the most delicious part,' Anne said. '*I* heard that she was hired to give the laird lessons in manners. His mother arranged it in Scotland, months ago. Can you imagine?'

'A governess?' The very idea was shocking. No one would ever hire a governess for a grown man. And if a ruined lady had given him lessons, it made her wonder whether Locharr could be trusted.

'Yes. They returned to London together.' Anne

frowned a moment and added, 'I'm sure it's nothing. But they do say he will ask for your hand any day now.'

Regina took a taste of the lemon ice, trying to avoid an answer. The tart taste mingled with the creamy flavour, though she could hardly enjoy it.

'Are you going to say yes?' Anne prompted.

'I'd rather wait until I know him better,' she admitted, even though she knew her father's illness made that difficult. She was supposed to say yes and be grateful for it. Yet, her mind was in turmoil, between her worries about Papa, the strange note she had found, and the idea of having to marry so soon.

Anne's gaze drifted back to the viscount. 'Well. It looks as if *someone else* wants to know you better. Careful, Regina. The viscount is coming this way.' Then she smiled slyly. 'Since you're already promised, do remind him that I am quite available.'

Regina wanted to groan, especially since the young lady was accompanying Lord Camford. His companion was beautiful, and Regina had the sense that she had seen her before. Her blonde hair was artfully arranged with a few curls to frame her face, and she did seem to be much younger. Lord Camford smiled at both women, but his green eyes were fixed upon her. 'Lady Regina, I hope you enjoyed the ices.'

'It was kind of you,' she said carefully, 'though unnecessary.' Her attention drifted towards the other young woman in a silent warning to Camford that he had overstepped.

Lord Camford cleared his throat. 'Forgive me, I've neglected introductions. Lady Regina and Lady Anne, this is Miss Amelia Andrews, the youngest sister of Her Grace the Duchess of Worthingstone. I agreed to accompany her on an outing today. Miss Andrews, may I present Lady Regina, daughter of the Earl of Havershire, and Lady Anne, daughter of the Earl of Blyton.'

Miss Andrews smiled warmly. 'I am glad to meet you. My sister, Toria, was supposed to join us, but she was not feeling well. Lord Camford knew how much I adore ices, and he offered to escort me.' She glanced at another woman standing a short distance away and added, 'And my maid, of course.'

'I am pleased to make your acquaintance,' Regina answered. Anne murmured a hello as well, and she eyed the viscount with her own undisguised interest.

'Were you at your sister's ball last night?' Anne asked Miss Andrews. The young woman nodded. Then Anne's expression turned sly. 'What do you know of Miss Goodson? Did you see her there?'

It wasn't something Regina wanted to truly know about. She barely listened to the two gossiping women, and Lord Camford eyed her with concern. She was thinking more about the blackmail note and what to do about it.

'Lady Regina, might I solicit your help?' the viscount asked. 'I wanted to ask your opinion on a gift for my father.'

She wasn't at all certain of it, but she did want to escape the gossip. Miss Andrews and Anne were still chatting, and she stood from the table, following him towards a display of cakes and confections.

'Miss Andrews is like a younger sister,' he explained. 'I escorted her as a favour to the duke and duchess.'

She nodded, and her annoyance eased when she re-

alised he was telling the truth. 'I thought you were behaving like a wicked rake, courting one woman while
sending ices to us.'

His mouth twitched. 'I may be wicked, but I'm not
that bold.'

She sent him a sidelong gaze. 'I wouldn't put it past
you, Lord Camford.'

'Not at all.' He shook his head and then eyed her
more closely. 'Are you well, Lady Regina?' he asked.
'Is something troubling you?'

She hesitated, not wanting to say anything at all. It
wasn't his concern, and there was an inherent risk of
Camford discovering the truth.

Her father had been so careful to hide the scandal.
Years had passed, and no one knew what had happened
that night…at least, she didn't think so.

The demand for money might have no connection
at all. But what if it did? She couldn't seek the answers
without help, and she wanted to trust Lord Camford.
Perhaps the risk was worth it.

Discreetly, she withdrew the folded note from her
reticule and handed it to him. He read it, and his gaze
turned serious. 'Have you spoken to your father about
this?'

'No.' She turned her attention to the cakes. 'He's
not well, Camford. His handkerchief had blood on it,
and I worry about him. I don't want to upset him further if I confront him.'

'Would you like me to find out more for you?' he
asked gently. 'I could make discreet enquiries.'

'I would be grateful.' She ventured a slight smile. It
was easier to trust Camford than to ask for help from

the laird. Especially if this blackmail involved her own past. 'I only want to know who sent it.'

Camford placed the folded note inside his waistcoat pocket. 'I would be glad to help you.' But although his words were kind, she didn't miss the worry in his eyes. He looked like a man determined to find answers for her, ready to fight off her foes. And despite the inner warnings of her brain, she trusted him. Camford had been a friend for years, and she believed he would discover the answers.

He glanced around as if suddenly aware of his surroundings. Then he changed the subject by turning his attention to the cakes. 'What flavour should I buy for my father? Lemon? Strawberry?'

'Vanilla custard,' she said. 'It's my favourite.'

He ordered two of them and directed the clerk to wrap one of the cakes for him. Then he told her to wrap the second one and send it to her residence.

'You didn't need to do that,' she said softly. 'But thank you.'

He nodded and accepted the wrapped cake from the clerk. As they started back to the table, Regina admitted, 'I didn't realise you were being serious about a gift for your father. I thought you were merely trying to rescue me from gossiping women.'

'Of course. God forbid I should return home from Lady Hardwicke's without something for my father. He and my mother used to spend time together here when they were young. It's a fond memory for him.'

It surprised her that he would be so considerate. Her smile deepened, and she remarked, 'You are a kind and loyal son.'

There was a faint response that shadowed his face

before he masked it. 'I am indeed. And one who will be travelling soon enough. I'm returning to the estate in Scotland.' He lowered his voice and affected a Scottish brogue. ''Twill be grand to be returnin' to the Highlands, lass. They've been missing me so dearly at Cairnross.'

'You are not a Highlander in the way Locharr is,' she corrected, still unable to stop her smile. When he was behaving with such mischief, it was hard to take him in all seriousness.

'Nay, but I've lived in Scotland since I was a wee laddie. I may be half-Scots, but the important bits are all Highlander,' he boasted, glancing downwards.

She flushed with shock at his innuendo. Though she knew he had meant it only in teasing, the sensual tilt to his smile made her nervous. It took an effort, but she managed to ignore the remark.

'I haven't been to Cairnross in a long time,' she said. But she didn't elaborate, for he knew why she had been there on the day of his brother's burial.

'I visit often,' he said. 'It feels more like home than London.' Then his hand reached towards his waistcoat where the note was hidden. He tapped it lightly and added, 'I will try to have answers for you about this matter before I leave for Scotland.'

She thanked him and then asked, 'Lord Camford, am I wrong to keep this matter from Locharr? Should I talk to him about this?' Her instinct was not to mention it while they were getting reacquainted. The laird was still a stranger to her, and it would feel quite awkward to solicit his help. 'I know that my dowry was a matter of concern for him, and this…complicates matters.'

'I wouldn't,' the viscount answered frankly. 'It's too soon for that.'

Regina agreed with him. And yet, she worried about the note demanding money. Until now, she had never imagined that there was a financial threat to her father. But now, she was beginning to wonder. A cold spiral threaded through her nerves.

'Find out anything you can,' she said, 'and let me know if you learn who sent the note.' It was likely impossible to discover the truth, but she had faith in Camford.

He inclined his head. Then he paused a moment and said, 'You don't have to wed Locharr, you know—even if your father wants you to. We're past the era when a woman could not refuse.'

'I know it.' But even so, it was her father's greatest wish to see her married to his best friend's son. It had never been about money or social standing. Ned wanted their families to be joined, and he wanted her to live in Scotland, far away from the terror of her past. It would be a new beginning, and she was willing to give the laird a chance.

Camford studied her intently for a moment, his green eyes growing shadowed. There was an unspoken emotion beneath them, and she suddenly realised that she had never once considered his feelings in all this. He had always been a friend to her, and it was unkind to ask favours of him—selfish, really.

Against her better judgement, she asked, 'What of you? Are *you* all right, Lord Camford?'

He regarded her for a long moment, before the corner of his mouth tilted upward. 'Aye, lass. I'm well enough.'

As he escorted her back to the table, it made her realise that Lord Camford had always been there when she'd needed him. The burden of guilt pressed down, for she shouldn't have asked this of him, despite their friendship.

But as she looked into his eyes, she somehow wondered if there was more he hadn't shared.

Chapter Four

Getting drunk sounded like a fine idea that night. Dalton sorted through his cards, though he hardly cared whether he won anything. His mind was fixed upon Regina, and he sat across from his enemy.

No, not his enemy. His friend Lachlan MacKinloch, the Laird of Locharr, who intended to ask Regina for her hand. And it was quite likely that she would say yes.

The very thought made him want to shatter the glass of brandy in his hand. Instead, he attempted a conversation with Locharr. 'So this…marriage was arranged when you were children, is that it?'

He already knew all about it, but he was trying to gauge whether Locharr had any real desire to wed Regina.

The laird nodded. 'Our fathers were friends for years, you ken? Regina's father told mine that he wanted us to wed, but she had to agree to the marriage. In return, her dowry will help my clan.'

So Locharr had agreed to the match, in order to provide for his people. It was a marriage of convenience, as he'd always suspected. Dalton took a sip of brandy, wondering whether another heiress could possibly take Regina's place.

He pretended to be interested in the cards. They were playing whist with the Duke of Worthingstone and Gabriel MacKinnon. The four of them had been school mates, long ago, and their friendship had remained strong over the years.

The duke's demeanour seemed almost gleeful, so likely he would win this round. Gabe was scowling at his own hand. He had travelled down from Scotland, though Dalton had no idea why. MacKinnon had been widowed two years ago, but he attracted women easily. They were happy to flirt with him, and he smiled enough to gain their full attention. Yet, he seemed uninterested in marrying again.

'Does she want to marry you?' Gabe asked, leading off with an ace.

Locharr laid down a three, following suit. 'I dinna think she wants to wed anyone, truth to tell. She doesna seem like any of the other ladies. It's almost as if she's scared of something.'

Dalton tightened his grip on the brandy glass. Though his mood had darkened, he forced himself to lighten the atmosphere. 'Scared of you?' he teased. 'With that scar, I can't think why.'

'There's no reason to be.' But Locharr did relax somewhat, tossing another card on the table.

'What of your governess?' Gabe prompted. 'She's a bonny one.'

That *did* elicit a reaction. Locharr's mouth tightened and his eyes flared with anger. 'Leave her alone, Gabe. She's no' for you.'

MacKinnon only smiled, as if he'd got the reaction he'd expected. Interesting. Dalton hadn't imagined such a possessive air from someone intending to wed another lady. It made him recall the night he had discovered Locharr with Miss Goodson, when they had said goodbye to one another.

Despite what he'd overheard between them, Dalton recognised the truth. Locharr would never choose a governess over Lady Regina. Her dowry of twenty thousand pounds wasn't something he could walk away from, given his clan's poverty. But there was a yearning in the man's face, along with grim determination that he would obey his duty.

Worthingstone took the next trick and then said, 'Toria asked me to find a post for her. I am sorry if Miss Goodson was embarrassed the other night by idle gossip.'

Now why would the duke care about the reaction of a governess? His wife had tried to hide Miss Goodson in another room. Did Worthingstone know something? Dalton hid his reaction by studying his cards.

'What happened to her?' Locharr asked. It was clear that he was not speaking of the other night—he was asking about the prior scandal surrounding the governess. Dalton knew little about it, for he'd been in Scotland at the time.

Worthingstone arranged his cards and paused. 'It was years ago. She made her debut, and Viscount Nelson was quite taken with her beauty. He gave her all his attention, and she was overcome by it. He seduced her and disappeared.'

The black look on Locharr's face startled Dalton. His friend looked ready to murder the man, which was not the reaction of a man who had let go of his feelings for this governess. It didn't bode well for the marriage.

'Where did she go afterwards?' Locharr demanded.

'I cannot say,' Worthingstone finished. 'She never showed her face in society again. Her father left, and I don't believe she's had any contact with her family.' He cleared his throat. 'There was a rumour of a child, but no one knows.'

All throughout the duke's revelation, Dalton kept his gaze fixed upon Locharr. He was trying to understand the truth of the laird's intentions. The man's expression was tightly strung, as if his anger were held back by a single thread.

At last, Locharr answered quietly, 'She deserves better than the life she has now. Thank you for finding a post for her.' Though his words were calm, there was no denying the emotions behind them.

They tried to ignore it, but there was an invisible tension lingering. The duke inclined his head and placed another card on the table. The game was a welcome distraction, and they played another round. This time, Dalton took the trick with his king. Though he knew he ought to drop the subject, he couldn't stop himself from voicing his greater concern. As he pulled the cards across the table, he asked, 'Will you ask for Lady Regina's hand in marriage?'

'Soon,' Lachlan answered.

It was the answer he was expecting, but in his friend's eyes, he could see the same sense of helplessness, the realisation that he could not have the woman he wanted. Locharr's pain mirrored his own, and Dalton grimly tossed another card down.

He was starting to wonder if there was anything he

could do. Though he shouldn't interfere, neither did he want to see both of his friends miserable. Both were marrying out of duty, and the thought of it was an invisible blow to Dalton's gut.

If there was a way to help them, he had to try.

Her father had spent most of the day in bed, coughing. Earlier, Regina had summoned a physician, who had given him medicines to help him sleep. She had planned to watch over him, but after the Laird of Locharr came to call, her mother had practically dragged her into the parlour after arranging for tea.

'Regina, I cannot tell you how fortunate you are.' Arabella sighed with happiness. 'Now promise me, you will be a model of ladylike behaviour.'

She simply nodded, for what else was there to say? Her father was determined that she should marry Locharr, and it felt as if a trap were closing in around her. She had seen the physician's grave expression after he had tended her father, and though he had tried to remain hopeful, she sensed that the worst lay ahead.

How could she entertain a guest when her father might be dying? It took all her years of training to compose her emotions and hold them back. Right now, she wanted to curl into a ball on her bed and weep. Instead, she had to accept Locharr's call and remain polite and serene.

Her mother squeezed her hand, beaming when they reached the parlour. Then she stepped back and allowed Regina to go in alone.

Inside the small room, Locharr appeared quite uncomfortable. He was a large man, and the gilt chair seemed as if it might crack apart beneath his weight.

This was not a man accustomed to delicate furnishings. He greeted her quietly, and she tried to muster a smile.

'Would you like tea?' she asked. 'My mother sent for refreshments.'

'Aye,' he answered. 'That is, if you're wanting a cup.'

At the moment, anything she might drink or eat would taste like dust, but she nodded. The silence between them was an invisible weight, and try as she might, she couldn't bring herself to speak. The worry over her father was suffocating, and she couldn't think of a single thing to say. Even Locharr appeared unsettled by the lack of conversation.

Regina was grateful when the footman brought in the tea cart. She poured the laird a cup, but the fragile porcelain appeared as if it might shatter in his large hands.

She tried not to overreact to the laird's physical size. *You're being ridiculous,* she tried to tell herself. Lachlan MacKinloch had never done anything to threaten her. She glanced at the window, trying to press back the fear.

'The weather seems fair enough,' he said at last, breaking the stillness.

Weather. Yes, that was a safe topic for conversation. She ought to say something. Anything. But the words tangled up in her throat, and she could only manage a nod. Good heavens, she was behaving like someone who was too scared to speak. Which wasn't entirely true, but just a little bit.

He was asking her something else, but she missed it. 'I'm sorry, what did you say?'

'I asked if there was anything you enjoyed in your spare time. Whist, perhaps?'

He really was trying to make conversation, and she was being a terrible hostess.

Give him a chance, she told herself. *Be honest.*

She took a sip of her tea. 'Cards aren't my favourite pastime, I fear.'

'Then what? Watercolours? Reading? Hunting boar?'

She choked on her tea at his last suggestion, and laughter caught in her throat. Boar? What had prompted that question? She bit her lip, trying to keep her mirth under command. His humour was entirely unexpected. 'I cannot say that I've ever hunted boar.'

'Wolves, then?' he offered. 'Or dragons, perhaps.'

The laird's dry teasing did ease the tension between them. A slight smile played at her lips. 'I have been known to hunt down my cat when she refuses to come in at night. Unfortunately, Belinda believes in staying out all night when she finds mice as her prey.'

'Is she here now?'

Regina shrugged, not knowing if he truly held an interest in her cat. 'I imagine she is asleep on my father's papers in the study.' The thought of the large feline sprawled across the earl's desk made her smile deepen.

Now that she was smiling, the laird appeared more relaxed. 'I thought we could have a word about our meddling fathers.'

And with a single sentence, her mood shifted to wariness. If he had called their fathers meddling, then he was about to discuss their potential marriage. Regina wasn't at all ready for this conversation. She couldn't possibly consider a proposal. Not this soon. She hardly knew the man, despite her father's wishes.

Panic boiled inside her, and it took an effort not to blurt out no. Instead, she forced herself into a voice of calm. 'What do you mean?'

'You ken that our fathers wanted to arrange a match between us,' Locharr said. 'They were good friends, and it was my father's dying wish that we be married.'

She knew that, but she couldn't imagine marrying anyone just now. Why should it matter what their fathers wanted? She was a grown woman, capable of deciding for herself whom she wished to marry.

But your own father may be dying, her conscience warned. *Would it not grant him peace if he knew you would be cared for?*

The earl alone knew the truth about what had happened that night. He wanted her to be protected, far away from London society. And he was willing to pay a high dowry to ensure that she was wedded to a man who could guard her from all harm.

Lachlan MacKinloch certainly met those terms. The man was large enough to intimidate anyone who dared to threaten her. His very size dominated the room, but it also evoked all the terrible memories she had wanted to push away. Marriage to him might create a sanctuary—but it would also bring back the terror she had spent almost five years trying to forget.

And for that reason, she wanted to refuse. She wasn't ready to even consider being bound to a man. 'No,' she answered hastily. 'I do not intend to marry.'

Instead of arguing with her, the laird's face turned thoughtful. He paused for a time, choosing his words carefully. 'I ken that you have your life here and that you dinna wish to change it. But if you would consider a life in Scotland, I swear to you that I would make no demands upon you as a wife. We would live as friends, and you'd have your own room.'

She stared at him, wondering if she had heard him correctly. Her own room? And…was he implying that he did not intend to touch her? He couldn't be serious.

'What about children? What if I don't wish to—that is, what if—?' She felt her cheeks flushing with embarrassment, but he seemed to understand her meaning.

'It could wait several years,' he promised. 'We are both young enough, and my first concern is to my clan. The winter was harsh, and they've no' had verra much food. I need to provide for them.'

In other words, he needed her dowry. And he was willing to consider a celibate marriage in return.

For the first time, she studied him, wondering if this was even a possibility. Could she live with this man, far away in Scotland, where no one could threaten her with the scandal of the past?

She decided to clarify the issue. 'Are you saying that it would be a marriage where you would…allow me to be alone?'

'No' precisely,' he answered. 'You would live with me at Locharr and help me look after the people. I would expect you to be mistress of the household and take on those duties. But consummating our marriage could wait until later.'

Well, that was clear enough. There was no question that this was the strangest marriage proposal she'd ever received. And yet…it was something to consider. If he was being serious and would not expect a true marriage, it might be a possibility. Still, it was entirely too soon to accept.

'I will think about it.' Then she added, 'Would you care for more tea?' The moment she spoke, she realised what a foolish question it was. His cup was still full, barely touched.

Locharr shook his head. 'In truth, I dinna care for tea. But I'll have another sandwich.'

She offered him the plate, and he took a sandwich with buttered bread and minced ham. Regina poured herself another cup of tea and took a biscuit from the tray. She nibbled at it, and admitted, 'I must say, I was not expecting this conversation. At least, not so soon. And not from someone who used to play such terrible tricks on me.'

'I was an angel,' he teased. 'I dinna ken what you are talking about.'

From the mischief in his eyes, he knew exactly what she was talking about. 'You tied my hair in knots. My maid spent most of the day trying to untangle it. You were a horrid boy.' Whenever her family had visited the MacKinlochs, Lachlan had teased her mercilessly.

Locharr only smiled and ate. But as they dined in silence, she saw his demeanour beginning to shift. Instead of being hopeful at her consideration of the proposal, his mood dimmed. He eyed her as if he wasn't certain what to think of her as a bride. Certainly, he didn't have the hopeful anticipation of a bridegroom. Instead, there was a sense of regret, though she couldn't understand why. If he didn't want to marry her, then there was no reason to ask. Likely he didn't mean to be rude, but he wasn't exactly enthusiastic.

In the end, he said, 'Thank you for the tea. I would be glad if you'd think about my offer of marriage.'

He might as well have spoken about the weather again, for all his lack of eagerness. Out of habit, she rose from her chair, and he did the same. She held out her hand, and he squeezed it gently.

'I will send word when I have made a decision,' she said.

He nodded and then departed from the room. After he'd gone, she sank into a chair, not knowing what to think. She ought to be grateful that Locharr had offered a celibate marriage. It was what she'd wanted, wasn't it? A life to live as she chose, with no man to threaten her.

Her thoughts drifted to Dalton St George. In her mind, she compared the two men. Dalton would never have agreed to such a marriage. Although they were friends, even the slightest touch of his hand upon hers evoked the heat of anticipation. Among the ladies of the ton, he had a rather wild reputation—indeed like a rake. But with her, he had only ever been kind and gentle.

And yet, was that not just as dangerous? With a man like Lord Camford, it would be more difficult to maintain a cool distance. He was one who might lure her into trusting him, slowly breaking down her boundaries.

Unlike the laird, who wanted to maintain them. There was no question she ought to be delighted by this offer. And yet, she could only feel a numb emptiness.

The door opened, and her mother entered with barely concealed excitement. 'Well? What did he say? Did he ask you to marry him?'

'He did,' Regina admitted.

Her mother's smile lit up her face. 'Oh, my darling, how wonderful! And you accepted his suit?'

'I told him I would think about it.'

Arabella's smile faltered. 'What is there to think about? Our families have been friends for years. And we both know that this marriage is very important to Ned.'

She studied her mother for a time and then voiced the question she had been wondering. 'But *why* is it so important to him? I know they were friends, but I feel as if there's something more. I don't understand why Papa and you want me to marry Locharr so badly.'

Her mother took a chair, and she seemed to be choosing her words carefully. Then she regarded Regina and admitted, 'When he was alive, Locharr's father loaned Ned money during a time of great need. He never asked for repayment, but instead, he wanted our families to be joined in marriage.'

'So *I* am to be given as repayment,' Regina said. It felt rather mercenary, as if her father had offered her up in sacrifice. 'How much did he lend to Papa?'

Arabella shook her head. 'I never asked. But he will never allow you to marry anyone else, regardless of rank. Even when I suggested that the money could be repaid, he outright refused. It's a matter of honour to him.'

It might be honour, but to her, it felt like all choices had been taken from her. She didn't want to marry any man at all.

And yet, Locharr had offered the only sort of marriage she would consider. He appeared to have little interest in her as a woman, which gave her a sense of relief. No other man would agree to such an arrangement—so what choice did she have?

'I don't have to give him an answer right away,' Regina insisted. 'And I will think about it.'

Her mother brightened and clasped her hands together in hope. 'I am so glad.'

But Regina couldn't feel the same way at all.

Dalton stared at the handwritten note from Lady Regina. Only six words were written by her hand, but they struck a fist into his heart.

I am sorry for your loss.

Today marked the anniversary of his brother Brandon's death. And she had remembered. Out of all his friends and acquaintances, she was the only person who had sent him a note of sympathy. Though it was a simple gesture, it meant a great deal to him. He had been close to his brother, and Brandon's death had created an emptiness that could never be filled.

A heaviness settled into his throat, for their entire household seemed shrouded in darkness. His father had secluded himself in his study, and Dalton knew he would not see him the rest of the day. It was early afternoon, and he needed a distraction.

His gaze centred upon a stack of invitations, as he turned over the possibilities in his mind. He sorted through the cards, and when he saw the garden party hosted by Lady Anne's mother, he hesitated. Regina would be there, for she was Anne's best friend. The thought of seeing Regina was a welcome one, and it would give him the chance to thank her for the note.

He hadn't written a reply to his own invitation, but he didn't suppose Lady Anne would mind if he arrived late to the party. He had to escape this prison of melancholy within this household, or he would drown in difficult memories.

Dalton ordered a carriage and made a cursory attempt to seem presentable. He didn't bother to change his attire, but instead waited impatiently for the vehicle to be brought out.

On the way to Lady Anne's residence, he thought about the blackmail note Regina had showed him, demanding three thousand pounds from her father. He had no answers yet, but he had paid a Bow Street Runner to learn more. Surely something would turn up within another day or two.

When he arrived at the Blyton residence, the guests were already out of doors. The flowers were blooming cheerfully, and several guests were indulging in a game of croquet. He greeted Lady Blyton and Lady Anne, making casual conversation while he discreetly searched for Regina.

She wasn't among the others, and it took some time before he eventually discovered her standing near a stone fountain. Her red hair was pulled back from her face, tucked beneath a green bonnet. Her gown was a matching shade of green apple, and the sight of her made him stop to appreciate her beauty. Her maid was nearby, but Regina was otherwise alone. When she saw him approaching, her face appeared troubled.

'I didn't expect to see you here today, Lord Camford.'

He drew closer and took her gloved hand, raising

it to his lips. 'It's been a difficult morning,' he admitted in all seriousness. 'I appreciated your note. And then I found it impossible to stay at home. There were too many memories. My father refused to see anyone, and... I needed to get out.'

He knew he ought to let go of her hand, but he couldn't quite bring himself to do so.

'I'm glad you did,' she answered. 'No one should be alone on such an anniversary.' There was warmth and sympathy in her voice, but she extricated her hand from his.

'I wanted to see you,' he said.

'Because you learned something about the threat to my father?' Instantly, she drew closer, bringing her voice to a whisper. 'Who sent the note?'

He shook his head. 'I've made some enquiries, but I don't know yet.' Keeping his voice low, he said, 'I will find your answers, I promise. But today, I just... wanted to see you.'

He didn't care that his words were trespassing into forbidden territory. Lachlan had been so withdrawn last night, and it didn't bode well for the future. Dalton knew he had no right to even be here with Regina, not with the direction his thoughts had wandered. He imagined what it would be like to take Lachlan's place.

'Camford, don't say that,' she whispered. And yet, though her words were a warning, he was spellbound by her blue eyes and soft skin. He wanted to take her face between his hands and kiss her until she could no longer stand.

You can't, his conscience reminded him. *She doesn't want you in that way. She never has.*

And if he trespassed and claimed what he truly

wanted from her, it would end their friendship. She was already hesitant, eyeing him with wariness.

Regina flushed, but she didn't turn away. The tension stretched between them, and he said nothing more. There was no sense in speaking of feelings when she didn't feel the same way. Better to bury the thoughts and never say them.

'Locharr asked me to marry him yesterday,' she said at last.

Her words stopped him cold, for he'd never imagined that Lachlan would ask so soon. It meant that his friend was resolved to go through with the union, setting aside the governess. He should have expected it, but it seemed far too early.

'And did you give him an answer?' The words came out more demanding than he'd intended, but it unnerved him to realise that he was losing her so soon.

Regina dipped her hand into the stone fountain, cupping the cool water. 'I told him I would think about it.'

He breathed a little easier since she had not said yes. And yet, he recognised that he had no right to court this woman. She belonged to his best friend. What right did he have to interfere? None at all.

Before he could say another word, Lady Anne appeared. '*There* you are. We are playing another game of croquet in teams. Both of you, stop being wallflowers and come join us.'

Though he didn't truly want to play, the idea of striking a ball with a mallet might relieve some of his tension.

'Very well,' Regina answered. 'If I must.'

'There are prizes for the winners,' Anne added.

Dalton regarded Regina and asked, 'What do you think? Will you join me?'

Her eyes held a warning, but she nodded. 'I will.'

Regina was well aware of Lord Camford's dark mood. His demeanour appeared restless, and when it was his turn to play, he struck the ball with too much force. It ricocheted off the metal wicket and rolled to the far end of the grass.

It couldn't be jealousy, could it? She hadn't actually agreed to marry the laird, but even if she had, Camford had known of the long-standing promise between her father and Tavin MacKinloch.

There was no denying that the laird's offer of marriage suited her. She would have the chance to leave London as his wife, live in a safe place, and their union would have no intimacy. The thought of the wedding night terrified her, but Lachlan had not even tried to kiss her hand. They had known one another for many years, and she was aware of his need for her dowry. It was an excellent offer, one she was strongly considering.

But something made her pause. There had been a strong change in Lord Camford's behaviour, ever since she'd told him of the proposal. Though it should not have come as a surprise, he seemed on edge. The air between them seemed charged, like lightning during a storm.

Once, he turned to look at her, and his green eyes revealed an intensity that stole her thoughts. Though he had never spoken of anything between them, she sensed that he had considered it. Her skin warmed, tightening at the unexpected vision of his mouth upon hers.

She sensed that a kiss from Lord Camford would be demanding and heated. The blood seemed to rush to her face as she wondered how she would respond. It was forbidden to even imagine it. She turned to meet his gaze and saw the hard line to his jaw and the bold stare in his eyes.

But it was her own response that frightened her. For it felt like a sudden awakening.

He had been her friend, a calm presence beside her who had made her feel safe. Never had she considered what it would be like to be courted by him. His wicked teasing had been a deterrent—or was that really true? She was starting to wonder.

He excused himself to walk across the lawn towards his wayward croquet ball. His long strides revealed his unspoken annoyance, and she suspected it had nothing to do with the game. He took careful aim, and she watched as he struck the ball back on to the course. As he returned to her side, she tried not to be too blatant in her observation of him. But the truth was, she couldn't quite help herself. She was aware of the way he moved, the purposeful strides when he followed the path of his ball.

I just...wanted to see you, he'd said.

The words had held an ache that now touched her heart. No one had ever spoken to her in such a way, as if he needed her. And she could not deny that the words had affected her deeply.

She moved closer to him, not even knowing why. His frustration had shifted into a shadowed emotion, and she wondered if she'd misread him. Perhaps he was only remembering his brother's death. His expression had turned solemn, and she asked softly, 'Are you all right, Lord Camford?'

'What do you think?' He leaned against his mallet like a cane, and there was a darkness in his tone.

She couldn't understand whether it was the game that had turned his mood or the bad memories, but she refused to respond with anything except understanding. 'I'm sorry,' she responded. 'You came here for a distraction, and I think I've only made your day worse.'

'No. You haven't.' His eyes softened, and she felt a pang of warning. In his face, she saw the bitter sadness, the raw intimacy of a man who was hurting. She faltered, feeling as if she ought to take his hands in hers and offer her sympathy.

But her imagination took it a step further, and she imagined holding him. She felt the urge to console him, to wrap her arms around his neck.

Such thoughts were foolish. More likely, the past fears would overwhelm her with such terrible memories, she would shrink away. And that wasn't what either of them needed.

'Camford, I—'

'It's all right, Regina. I'm fine.' He took a breath and eyed the others. No one had even noticed them, it seemed. And perhaps that was because they were losing so badly, there was no reason to pay them any heed.

'Perhaps we should return to our game,' she hedged. 'Even if we are losing, we might still manage to catch up.'

He nodded in agreement. But as she was about to strike her ball, he interrupted. 'Are you going to accept Locharr's proposal?'

A chill broke over her skin as she hit the ball with her mallet. She didn't want to give an answer just yet.

But then, Camford caught her by surprise when his gloved hand touched the small of her back. The unexpected contact made her jolt, but what startled her more was her response. Heat flooded through her, and she was fully conscious of his touch. Regina didn't know why he had conjured such a reaction, and she felt the sudden need to push him away.

She blurted out, 'Yes. I think I will accept the laird's proposal.' It would help her to lock away the past for ever. Her father would have his wish, and she could live in peace, away from the rest of the world. She had no feelings towards the laird, and that was for the best.

Camford drew his hand away from her back, and his eyes had turned cool. 'You said that you didn't want to marry anyone. Why did you change your mind?'

Because he will never touch me, she thought.

But she couldn't ever say that. Lord Camford would never understand. 'I have my own reasons.'

She never intended to lie with a man. Not ever. And for that reason, she had turned down suitor after suitor. It wasn't fair to lead a potential husband to believe that theirs would ever be a true marriage.

Unlike the previous gentlemen, Lachlan had promised to wait as long as she desired.

But she intended to wait for always.

'You don't love him,' Camford pointed out.

'I don't have a choice,' she answered. 'And besides that, love isn't necessary to be content within a marriage. Afterwards, I will leave London and never return.'

He looked as if he wanted to say more. His eyes had turned stormy, like a jealous man. But he said nothing at all, silencing whatever thoughts he had.

Chapter Five

Dalton drove swiftly through the streets, wishing he hadn't delayed his trip to Scotland. He'd rather be anywhere else than tangled up in this mess.

Locharr had returned to Worthingstone's residence in a foul mood. He'd got quite drunk and had revealed that Regina had accepted his proposal of marriage. It had taken every ounce of control for Dalton to congratulate him. But inwardly, he'd wanted to drive his fist through the glass window.

Because you *want her,* a voice inside reminded him.

He pushed back the thought, for he knew better than to consider it. Regina didn't want him, and why should she? All his life, he'd never been good enough to please his parents. He was the black sheep, the ne'er-do-well who could never truly take his brother's place as heir. If his own family didn't care for him, neither would she.

But even so, he hadn't liked her insistence that she didn't have a choice in the marriage. He wanted to be certain no one was forcing her into this decision. He already knew that it wasn't Lachlan's desire—the laird was in love with the governess, Miss Goodson.

This was naught but an arrangement for the sake of a twenty-thousand-pound dowry that would save the MacKinloch Clan.

Though he understood why Locharr had agreed to the match, Dalton didn't truly understand Regina's reasons. It seemed as if she was trying to run away. Her last words, her claim that she would not return to London again, seemed to emphasise it.

And so, he had decided to pay a call on her. He wanted to be absolutely certain that no one was forcing her into the betrothal. For Locharr could marry any wealthy heiress to save his clan; it didn't have to be Regina.

He knocked on Lord Havershire's front door, and the footman sighed. 'My lord, Lady Regina is not receiving guests.'

He paused a moment, wondering if he ought to leave. 'Is she all right?'

The footman cleared his throat. 'That is none of your concern.'

'Actually, as her friend, it *is* my concern if she's not feeling well.' He was about to offer his calling card, but it was then that he saw Lord Havershire approaching. The man's face was ghastly pale, and he clutched a handkerchief. The earl coughed and straightened. 'What's all this about, Camford?'

He didn't want to have this conversation in the hall with half the servants listening. 'I came to pay a call upon your daughter, Havershire.'

'Why?' The earl eyed him and said, 'You've heard about my daughter's betrothal to the Laird of Locharr, haven't you?' The man's face reddened, as he stared hard at Dalton. 'Do you somehow believe she might change her mind and wed you instead? Is that why you're here?'

'No, that isn't the reason,' he started to say.

But the earl took a step forward and glared at him. 'I promise you, it will never happen. Regina knows that Lachlan MacKinloch is the only man she is permitted to marry.'

Permitted? Dalton's suspicions tightened, and he chose his question carefully. 'Why would you take that choice from her? Is there a reason you won't allow her to wed anyone else?'

The earl shrugged. 'The agreement was made years ago. And I am not a man to go back on my word.'

Dalton was about to argue, but then, it occurred to him that the earl was speaking about the marital contract as if he owed a debt. And perhaps that's what this was—he was selling his daughter into an arrangement, in order to repay Locharr's family. He could think of no other reason why the earl would demand that Regina marry one man, and a laird at that.

Dalton pulled out the crumpled note demanding three thousand pounds. 'Does this have something to do with your reasons for the betrothal?'

The earl took the paper and paled. 'Where did you get this?'

'From your daughter,' he answered. 'Is this why you would never allow her to marry anyone else? Because of a scandal you're being blackmailed about?'

The older man's face grew stricken, as if Dalton had predicted too much of the truth. 'Get out.' To the footman, he added, 'Lord Camford is not welcome in this house again.'

A racking cough came over the earl, and he covered his mouth with the handkerchief. His shoulders shook from the effort, and he turned away, clutching the note in his fist.

'She deserves better than this,' Dalton said. 'You shouldn't force her into marriage.'

Especially when Locharr is in love with someone else.

'Out,' the earl repeated.

This time, Dalton went to the door, though he made no effort to hide his frustration. It seemed there was nothing he could do, and he wasn't so certain that it *was* her choice.

Dalton walked down the stairs towards his waiting carriage, when suddenly, he saw Regina arriving with her mother and her maid. Her face grew guarded, and she hesitated while they approached.

'Lord Camford,' the countess greeted him. 'What a surprise to see you. Did you hear of Regina's good news? She has accepted a marriage proposal from your friend, the Laird of Locharr.' The woman smiled brightly, though he recognised the hidden warning in her words.

'Yes, I spoke with Lachlan last night,' Dalton agreed. 'I thought the news was rather sudden.' He sent a direct look towards Regina, who didn't flinch at all.

'I am so pleased by it,' Lady Havershire continued. 'As is my husband. We've already begun our wedding plans, and we will host an engagement ball very soon. As Locharr's friend, you will certainly be invited.' She smiled warmly, though Dalton had no desire to see the pair of them together.

'I will be glad to attend,' he said. Though he would

rather be tortured than watch Regina stand with another man.

'Mother, may I have a word alone with Lord Camford?' Regina asked. 'I will only be a moment.'

'It would not be appropriate,' Lady Havershire argued. 'I am sorry, but I must refuse.' Her mother gave an apologetic smile. 'You *are* betrothed to the laird, after all.'

Regina eyed him, and then nodded. 'I suppose you are right.' To Dalton, she added, 'Do you remember the letter from my friend? Another note arrived only a day ago. I thought you might like to know.'

So, the danger was still there. He wondered what the newest threat had been and tried to discreetly enquire about more.

'Thank you for telling me,' he said. 'I hope all is well with your friend.'

'I fear that her health is getting worse,' Regina answered. 'But thank you for your kind words and the assistance you offered. Please let me know if you hear anything more.'

So, it was indeed bad news. And she wanted him to continue the investigation.

'Of course,' he answered.

'Who is ill?' Lady Havershire demanded. 'I've heard nothing of this.'

'You've never met her,' Regina said. 'She is a distant cousin of Anne's.' To Dalton she said, 'Thank you for your assistance. Perhaps I will see you at the ball.' With a murmured farewell, she ascended the steps with her mother.

Now he knew the reasons why she had accepted Lachlan's proposal. She didn't feel safe here any more.

Her father's insistence on the marriage suggested that he was desperate to send her away, as if she needed the laird's protection.

The only question was why.

Three days later

Regina stood at the dressmaker's feeling as if she'd been poked and measured and prodded for hours. Her mother had chosen the wedding gown, and she was eager for it to be finished. The colour was sky blue, and the dressmaker was holding up different patterns of lace. 'Which of these do you like best?'

'I don't know,' Regina murmured, eyeing her mother. 'Whatever you prefer.'

Arabella was happy to make the choice for her, just as she had chosen everything else. It didn't matter. The earl's health was worsening, and the wedding plans were a welcome distraction for her mother. Though the physician continued to visit him, he had cautioned them to keep a safe distance from the earl. Arabella had been ordered not to share a bedchamber with him, and the maids were instructed to burn the earl's soiled handkerchiefs. The physician had prescribed a medicine to help him sleep, but it slurred her father's speech and made it difficult to wake him.

Regina was trying not to think of it, but each day, her father seemed weaker. He kept his spirits up by talking of her wedding. It seemed to be his reason for living, and she tried to behave as if she were excited by the forthcoming nuptials.

'I am so happy for you, my dear,' Arabella said with a warm smile. 'I know this wedding will be perfect.'

Regina managed some sort of response, but she didn't truly believe it would be a perfect wedding. It was a ceremony and a means to her escape; that was all. Bleakly, she finished the dress fitting, and then departed with her mother.

They started driving through the streets, and her thoughts wandered back to the second blackmail note. A part of her wished she could have waited at the lamp post near Bedford Street last night, to learn who was demanding money. But it wasn't a safe part of town, and she doubted if the true blackmailer would show up—more likely a hired person. Still, she would send another note to Camford, telling him the details.

In the meantime, she had more questions for her mother. Perhaps she could find the answers in a different way. 'Mother…there's something I've been worried about. You said that Papa borrowed money from the Laird of Locharr, years ago.'

Arabella stiffened and glanced out the window. 'It was a long time ago, Regina. And this is not the time or place to discuss it.'

'Five years ago?' Regina ventured, wondering if that was when the blackmail had begun.

Her mother shrugged. 'I don't remember. But the debt will be repaid when you marry Lachlan MacKinloch. As I said, it was a long time ago.'

Her father would only allow her to marry Lachlan, so he could pay back the debt through her exorbitant dowry. And it made Regina feel utterly trapped. The walls of the room seemed to close in on her, and she needed an escape desperately.

On the journey home, her mother continued to converse about plans for the wedding breakfast and her trousseau. As she described the gowns, Regina interrupted. 'Are you certain we have enough to pay for all this, Mother?'

The countess appeared shocked that she would even voice concerns. 'I will never allow my daughter to be married and leave home dressed like a pauper. The very idea is insulting.'

Regina lifted her hands in a silent apology, though she had a feeling her mother knew nothing about the blackmail. 'If you say so.'

The carriage arrived back at the house. When the driver opened the door, Regina was surprised to find Lord Camford waiting nearby. Her mother stiffened at the sight of him. 'I thought your father told him not to return.'

'Is that why he's waiting outside?' she wondered aloud. Did he have news regarding the blackmailer?

'It doesn't matter,' Arabella answered. 'You shouldn't be accepting male callers any more. What would people say?'

'The viscount is a friend of mine and has been for years,' Regina said. 'He is also a good friend of Locharr's.'

'But what would your fiancé think of this?' her mother warned. 'It doesn't look good, Regina.'

'I would hope that my fiancé would trust me,' she said. 'But if you would prefer, I could stand outside on the stairs and speak to him in public where everyone can see us.'

'You shouldn't speak to him at all,' her mother warned.

Regina dismissed the thought, for her mother was only concerned about propriety. Her greater concern was about the threat against her father. If Camford knew anything at all, she had to see him. But in order to get past her mother's doubts, she would have to redirect Arabella's suspicions.

'Had you thought that perhaps he brings news from Lachlan?' she suggested. 'I want to hear what he has to say.' When her mother was about to protest further, she added, 'If it makes you feel better, I will receive him in the kitchens, so Papa doesn't know he's here.' She saw, from the look on her mother's face, that this was the true reason for her discomfort.

'He won't know,' she reassured her mother. 'And Camford will not stay long, I promise you that.' As another distraction, she said, 'I think we should begin addressing the invitations, don't you?'

Her mother's expression wilted, and she sighed. 'Ten minutes. Nothing more than that, and your father must *not* know that he's here.'

'Thank you, Mother.' She reached out to squeeze Arabella's hands. 'Why don't you go and see how Papa is feeling? I'll join you soon.'

The carriage pulled to a stop in front of their town house, and Regina climbed out with the help of the coachman. Lord Camford nodded in greeting and tipped his hat to both of them. 'Have you brought any news?' she ventured.

'I have.' He smiled politely to the countess and said, 'Good afternoon, Lady Havershire.'

The countess looked pained and simply said to Regina, 'Ten minutes,' before she ascended the stairs and spoke quietly to the footman.

'Ten minutes?' Camford repeated, his expression revealing his confusion.

'Follow me, and we will speak in private,' Regina said. She opened the door and touched a finger to her lips when she walked past the footman. 'Papa mustn't know you are here.'

'Where are we going?' he murmured, following her down the winding stairs towards the servants' quarters.

'To the kitchens. Just for a moment,' she said. 'I am allowed ten minutes to speak with you, no more. Let me send the servants away first.' She guided him down a narrow hallway and then into a large kitchen. A huge wooden table rested in the centre of the room, and two of the kitchen maids gaped at her. Regina couldn't remember the last time she had ever ventured into the kitchens.

'Will you excuse us for a moment,' she asked softly. When the cook eyed her hesitantly, Regina added, 'You may return within a few minutes.'

No one moved at first, but the cook finally said to the kitchen maids, 'You heard Lady Regina. Out! All of you.'

Only then, did they set aside their cooking utensils and scurry out the door. Regina waited a moment, and then glanced down the hallway to ensure that no one was eavesdropping. She leaned against the table and asked in a low voice, 'What did you learn?'

Lord Camford drew closer, and murmured, 'The Bow Street Runner believes that your blackmailer is likely female, from the handwriting. He waited at the lamp post the other night to see who arrived. It was a man, and he spoke to him. The man was hired to pick up a delivery, but he didn't know what it was or for whom. The Runner gave him a package filled with blank paper, and he took it. He was discreet in following the man, but it was delivered to another address in Cheapside. Whoever it was is not a member of the nobility.'

Her heart sank, for it was possible that one of the servants, other than Frederick, had witnessed her shame. But who?

A sinking suspicion clenched her stomach as she wondered about her maid. Nell was Frederick's granddaughter. He wouldn't have told her anything, would he? She couldn't imagine he would betray them like that. The young woman had only come into their employ within the past year, but Frederick had died two years ago. And if the notes had been sent over the past five years, she didn't think it was possible that her maid would have anything to do with them. Moreover, she wasn't entirely certain Nell knew how to read or write.

'What should I do?' she asked Camford.

His steady gaze met hers. 'You don't need to do anything. The Runner will watch the house and learn who it is. Then we will alert the authorities and have your blackmailer arrested. It will be over soon.'

He seemed convinced that it would be so, and she wanted to believe him. 'Thank you, Camford.'

He gave a nod and then asked quietly, 'How are you, Lady Regina? The last time I came to pay a call on you, your father ordered me out.'

She thought of lying and telling him that she was fine, but instead, she said, 'I feel as if my life is a spinning wheel that won't stop. My mother is making all the wedding plans, and my engagement ball will be soon. I ought to feel something about the wedding, but all I can feel is panic. I'm overwhelmed.'

'Then don't marry him,' he said quietly.

She said nothing about the debt or their family obligation. Instead, she turned away from him. He didn't understand that her life was not her own. She was being sold into marriage for her father's sake, and Lachlan had agreed to leave her untouched. It was the best she could hope for. But being around Lord Camford unnerved her with unexpected feelings. Even looking into his eyes made her skin tighten, as if he had drawn his fingers over her skin.

'I have to wed the laird,' she insisted. 'And though I am grateful for your help with this blackmailer, I cannot walk away from this marriage. It's for the best, Lord Camford.'

'I'm not so certain about that,' he said. 'He's in love with another woman.'

Regina nearly flinched at his words but suppressed the instinct. 'It doesn't matter.' If Locharr cared for someone else, it was likely that he would leave her alone. And that was necessary to surviving the marriage. She took a step backwards and glanced at the door. 'My father is dying, and he wants to see me married. I intend to keep my word.'

With that, she straightened and regarded him. 'Thank you for your help, Lord Camford. I will see that you are repaid for hiring the Runner.'

'I will not accept any repayment,' he countered. 'You know this.' The look in his eyes held a hint of frustration, but it was the softer tone that bothered her.

He cared. And the more she spent time in his presence, the more she was starting to falter in keeping up the wall around her feelings. For so long, they had been friends. She trusted Camford, knowing he would never,

ever hurt her. Over the years, he had proven himself, and she was grateful for his friendship.

But during the past few weeks, it was as if something within her had shifted. She could not deny that she was attracted to his handsome face, but it was his kindness that was her undoing. There was a yearning within her and the knowledge that she would miss him when he was gone. And that was entirely too dangerous.

'Please accept my gratitude for your assistance, Lord Camford,' she said with all formality. She was careful to keep all warmth or friendliness from her voice. Despite her traitorous feelings, she needed Camford to leave and not see her again. 'I bid you farewell.'

With that, she left the kitchens, only to nearly stumble into her maid, Nell. 'It is not polite to be lurking around corners,' she told the young girl. 'Especially after I asked you to leave.'

'Forgive me, my lady. It's only that Lady Havershire ordered me to remain close by as a chaperon.'

She wasn't surprised at her mother's interference. But as Lord Camford departed, he never said a word to her, nor did he look back. His stony silence cut her heart, despite her attempts to remain frozen to any feelings.

It was better this way, she told herself. And it was the only way she could protect herself from unwanted emotions was not to see the viscount again.

It was the night before his engagement ball, and Lachlan MacKinloch looked terrible. Never had a man seemed more reluctant to wed. Dalton, Gabriel, and the laird were gathered around a bottle of brandy. It was meant to be a celebration, but Locharr appeared troubled.

'You're looking rather glum for a man about to be married,' Gabriel MacKinnon said. He took a sip of brandy, eyeing their friend.

An understatement, if there ever was one.

'He looks as if he's about to be strung up,' Dalton remarked, trying to keep his tone light. He knew, all too well, the reason for his friend's misery. 'Though it's wise to let the bride and her family make all the plans.' He had heard that Lady Havershire had thrown herself into the wedding plans, delighted at the idea of their match.

Lachlan poured his own glass and didn't answer. He looked as if he wanted to call it off. But then, Gabe MacKinnon intervened, saying, 'I didna love my wife when I first married her. I'd never seen her before, you ken? It was arranged, and I hated the thought of wedding a stranger. But I learned to care for her.'

You're not helping, Dalton wanted to say but didn't. It seemed that both Lachlan and Regina intended to go through with a loveless marriage. The laird sipped at his brandy and stared outside the window, though Dalton knew he'd heard every word.

MacKinnon came to stand beside him and reminded Lachlan, 'Your father wanted this. And you said that you wanted the match as well, to save Locharr from ruin.' There was a slight question in his voice, as if wondering if it were still true.

'I did say that,' Lachlan answered. But his voice held a numb quality, almost toneless.

Dalton was torn about what to say. He wanted the laird to call it off—and yet, Locharr needed her dowry to save his people. The laird would not hesitate to sacrifice himself for their sake.

'Have you arranged for the special licence?' MacKinnon asked. 'Or are you having the banns read?'

'Lord and Lady Havershire are wanting me to get a special licence. I'll take care of it on the morrow.'

Dalton's gaze narrowed. Locharr hadn't procured the licence yet? It seemed that he was quite the reluctant bridegroom.

Gabe said quietly, 'All will be well, Lachlan. You'll see.' He clapped Locharr on the back as he departed the room.

But likely, it wouldn't be.

Dalton stayed behind, wondering if he dared ask Locharr the truth about his feelings. His friend appeared resigned to the marriage as if it were an execution. 'You don't want this marriage any more, do you?'

Lachlan shook his head. 'I thought I did. I thought I should wed her for the sake of Locharr. But it's no' the right thing to do. She doesna deserve a man like me.'

Dalton chose his words carefully, hiding his own thoughts. 'What will you do? Withdraw your offer?'

It would embarrass Regina, but was that not better than a lifetime of unhappiness?

Lachlan shrugged. 'I dinna ken what I should do. I suppose I should talk to her. Tell her the truth.'

But Dalton wasn't so certain that confronting her in person was wise. Lord and Lady Havershire would be furious if Locharr tried to call it off with Regina. 'It may already be too late. They've set the date, haven't they?'

'They have, aye.' He set down the brandy snifter

and stared at the window again, almost as if searching for a way out.

And there was a way out—if Locharr ended the engagement. By now, Dalton knew that Regina would not walk away from the wedding. Not unless she had no choice.

'Write her a letter,' he suggested. 'I'll deliver it on your behalf. Tell her that you no longer wish to marry her—tell her whatever you want. Then take your woman and go to Scotland.'

For the first time, there was a glimmer of hope in Lachlan's eyes. 'What of the engagement ball tonight? I canna just leave.'

'Go to the ball, then. And leave afterwards. Give me the letter, and I'll make sure she reads it after a day or two.'

Lachlan appeared hesitant. 'I should tell her before the ball. I dinna want her to be humiliated.'

'It's too late to send word to all the guests,' Dalton reminded him. 'Just attend the gathering tonight and tell her afterwards.'

'I suppose she could delay the wedding,' he hedged. 'The wedding invitations have no' been sent yet.' He brightened at the realisation. 'You're right. I'll go to the ball tonight, but afterwards, I'll leave. You give her the letter, and it can end quietly.'

Dalton nodded in agreement. The gratefulness in his friend's eyes matched his own feelings. Calling off the wedding might infuriate the earl and the countess, but it was the right thing to do.

Regina felt sick to her stomach. Her engagement ball had been dreadful. Lord Camford had tried to warn her about Lachlan's feelings for another woman. She hadn't wanted to believe it—but once she'd seen it for herself, she had been torn by confusion and hurt.

She wanted a man to look at her in the same way Lachlan looked at Miss Goodson. Never had she seen a man more in love, and though she had no feelings towards the laird, she was starting to see that it could be a problem. She had initially believed that it didn't matter if he kept another woman on the side, for he would stay out of her bed.

But now, she was starting to realise the complications. He would resent her for being his wife when he wanted someone else. The marriage might turn to bitterness, and she didn't want that.

Yet was there any other choice but to go through with the wedding? She didn't see a way out, for it would break her father's heart.

On the table beside the fire lay a third blackmail note demanding three thousand pounds. This time, she could no longer ignore it.

Don't try to avoid payment any longer. I saw what happened that night. If you do not send the money I will inform Mallencourt's family that his death was not an accident.

The scrawled words made her swallow back the bile rising in her throat. Thus far, her father had not paid the blackmail—and she didn't want it to continue any longer. Likely his worsening illness had prevented it, besides her attempt to keep the notes from him. She didn't want anything to upset him, for his physical health was waning.

And even more, she wasn't entirely certain about the state of their wealth. Did he have the money to pay the blackmailer? Or even her dowry? Her worry deepened, and she understood how grave their situation was.

No one could ever learn what had happened that night, so many years ago. Her father had done what he could to silence the idle gossip. But more than anything, she needed to escape London, to avoid suspicion and quietly disappear.

Lachlan had sent over his own note last night. Most likely it was an apology she didn't want to hear. She closed her eyes, calming herself. It was better to let the past go.

She couldn't change his feelings for the governess, but she could become a good wife to him. Although their own marriage would be an arrangement that neither truly wanted, it would grant her the escape and the protection of the laird's clan.

Regina moved close to the fire, warming herself. Her mother had advised her to move the wedding date up, and she agreed with the decision. It no longer mattered when this wedding took place. They could have a quiet ceremony with only a few guests, and then she would go to Scotland.

With that, she tossed the blackmail note and Lachlan's letter into the fire. The last thing she wanted was to hear reasons why he loved someone else. The edges of the paper curled up, and she felt better after both papers burned into ashes.

A knock sounded at the door, and she glanced up to see her mother. Arabella's eyes were red as if she'd been crying, and she asked, 'May I come in?'

'Of course.' Regina gestured for her to sit down. 'Are you all right?'

Her mother's mouth tightened, and she shook her head. 'I would like to tell you yes, but it wouldn't be the truth.'

'What is it?' She moved to sit beside Arabella and touched her hand.

'Your father…the physician says that he has consumption. He—he's dying, Regina. And I can't bear to think of living without him.' Her mother's sobs broke through, and Regina could only embrace her. Her throat ached with her own tears, but someone had to be strong. There were no words to ease the sorrow, so she let her mother cry.

'I wanted him to be there for your wedding,' she wept. 'I wanted it to be special. With flowers and food and guests to celebrate with us. But I worry that he doesn't have much time.'

Regina pulled back and held her mother's shoulders. Though she didn't personally care what sort of wedding it was, she now understood that Arabella was using the plans as her own way of escaping the pain.

'I've sent word to Lachlan about having the wedding in three days,' her mother said. 'At least then your father can be there and try to enjoy it.' Her lip trembled, and she wiped her eyes with a handkerchief. For a moment, she seemed to be gathering her courage. 'We will celebrate as if he is well and whole. And I know it will bring him joy, despite his illness.'

Regina took her mother's hands in hers, pushing back her own doubts. With effort, she summoned a smile. 'I know it will be a beautiful wedding.'

Arabella mustered a smile through her tears. 'I was

more eager than I should have been, I know. Your gown is ready, and it will be easy to have all the flowers. Mrs Fitch will make the cake and all the food. I will begin changing the invitations today. Perhaps you could help me?'

'I would be glad of it.' She smiled and squeezed Arabella's hands.

And she realised that she needed the distraction of writing out invitations as much as her mother did. It would keep her thoughts away from the fear that she was making a terrible mistake.

Three days later

'What are we going to do?' Gabriel demanded. 'You need to tell Lady Regina what happened.'

'I already tried yesterday and the day before,' Dalton said. 'Her mother refused my calls.' And after Lord Havershire had ordered him out the last time, he wasn't entirely surprised. But this was a problem beyond anything he'd ever anticipated.

The bride didn't realise that her bridegroom had run off to Scotland and married someone else. Dalton had sent several notes to Regina, but it didn't seem that she had paid them any heed. And now, a more dire meaning had become clear. He had received a revised invitation to the wedding only a day ago. Lady Regina was under the mistaken impression that Lachlan still intended to marry her this morning.

'I will go there now,' Dalton said. 'I'll find a way to speak with her.' He would climb into Regina's bedchamber if he had to. She didn't deserve to be left stranded at the altar—not if he could stop it.

He hurried to his carriage and then checked his pocket watch. There were two hours before the ceremony. If the guests were planning to arrive, so be it. He couldn't stop the wedding, but he could save Regina.

After he arrived at his father's residence, he hurried up the stairs to his room. There, he sorted through his clothing until suddenly, he stopped short. He stared at the kilt in the colours of his mother's clan. They were similar to Lachlan's colours, since they were neighbouring clans.

He didn't know why he was considering wearing it. There was no reason. But a sixth sense prickled at him.

It's a terrible idea, his conscience warned him. *There's no need.*

But what if there was? What if Regina was waiting for a Highlander bridegroom who never came?

He had delivered Lachlan's note calling off the engagement, as promised, but he wondered if Regina had read it. He was beginning to think she hadn't. And if she didn't know her bridegroom wasn't coming, it would mean public humiliation.

He finished getting dressed and stared at himself in the mirror. What he was about to do went beyond all civilised manners. It was the actions of a Highlander, not a gentleman. But Regina needed to be rescued, and he would do anything necessary to help her. He opened a small chest and perused its contents of silver cuff links and a gold pocket watch until he found what he was looking for and tucked it away.

A sudden rush of nerves caught him. Never had he imagined such a reckless plan. And if she refused to let him save her, he didn't know what he would do.

Dalton glanced outside the window and saw that the

streets were crowded from an overturned cart. Carriages and coaches were stopped, while several men tried to turn the cart upright. There was no means of driving to the wedding now; he would have to walk and hire a hackney cab further away.

Dalton stared at his attire, wondering if this was a mistake. His intention was to help Regina, but she might refuse his aid. He gathered his sense of resolution and walked downstairs. Then he ventured out into the streets amid the chaos. There was still time to reach Regina.

And when he reached her house, he intended to offer her the choice—a chance to escape…or he would marry her himself.

Regina could not stop her sense of foreboding. Her maid finished helping her dress, but despite the gardenias in her hair and the sky-blue wedding gown trimmed with lace, she felt that something was very wrong. There had been no answer from Lachlan over the last day or two, and she questioned whether he was aware of the new wedding date. Her mother had assured her that of course he knew and that he would be there. Arabella had sent a servant to his father's house to ensure it.

But there was no sign of him yet, and it was time for the ceremony.

'You needn't go downstairs yet,' her maid Nell offered. 'We can wait until he arrives.'

But Regina felt the need to see for herself what was happening. She could not hide in her room like a frightened mouse. 'No, the wedding is supposed to be at ten o'clock. It's nearly a quarter after the hour.'

She opened the door to her room and stepped into the narrow hallway. Her mother had wanted them to be married at the house, so the clergyman was waiting. There were nearly fifty guests standing, and her father's face softened with joy when he saw her. He crossed the room to offer his arm, and she took it. He looked dashing in his double-breasted black cloth coat and silk waistcoat. 'My dear, you are a vision,' he said. With a slight laugh, he added, 'If only your bridegroom were here to see it.'

He lowered his voice to a whisper. 'I sent one of the footmen to fetch him. He must have been delayed, but do not worry. Some of the guests mentioned that the streets were more crowded because of an accident with a cart. But be reassured—the laird is a man of honour, and he will be here.'

She wanted to believe it but could not be certain. 'Then I will wait.' She went to stand before the minister, but she could feel the sympathetic gazes from the wedding guests. A quarter of an hour passed, then another. She remained standing, not looking at anyone.

But when an hour had passed, she could not ignore the guests whispering. Her father's face turned thunderous. 'I will go and fetch him here myself.'

Regina wanted to tell him no, but her insides felt like ice. He wasn't coming. She knew it in her heart.

But then, she heard a door opening, and the guests began to murmur. She turned to the door and saw a bold blue and green pattern, and a Highlander crossed to her side. But it was not Lachlan MacKinloch—it was Dalton St George, wearing a kilt. Lord Camford reached for her hand and kissed it. 'I apologise for being late.' To the guests, he said, 'Grant me a moment alone with my bride to grovel at her feet.'

A few women laughed quietly, while other guests who recognised him appeared confused. Before her parents could intervene, Lord Camford took her hand and led her away. 'Allow me to rescue you,' he murmured under his breath.

'Gladly,' she whispered, following him into the hall. He led her into the music room and closed the doors behind them.

Regina sank into a chair, burying her face in her hands. She didn't know whether to weep or groan with frustration. 'Why did you come, Lord Camford?'

'Because you didn't read Lachlan's note, nor any of mine. You refused my calls, and I had no other way to tell you that the laird married someone else.'

'His governess,' she predicted, feeling as if the bottom had dropped out beneath her. She had burned his letter without reading it. And he had been trying to call off the wedding. Dear God.

'Aye,' Camford answered. 'I am sorry to be the bearer of such news.'

Her emotions gathered into a tight ball of humiliation, but she managed to say dully, 'The wedding is off. We'll send the guests away and be done with it.' She already felt miserable, and the last thing she wanted was to face everyone else or see the sympathy in their eyes.

But then, this was what she deserved. She had been using the laird as a means of escaping her problems. She hadn't wanted to marry him, and it was now quite evident that he hadn't wanted to wed her either. If only she had opened his letter or allowed Camford to pay a call, she would have known the truth.

The viscount came close and knelt at her feet. 'I know that you wanted to marry him to escape London. Because you're afraid of your father's blackmailer.'

She didn't look at him, so afraid she would break into tears. He took her hands, and she felt her heart begin to pound. 'But there is no reason why *I* cannot give you what you're wanting.'

What did he mean by that? Regina stared into his green eyes, uncertain. Then Lord Camford said, 'Marry me, instead. I will take you to Scotland, and you can escape London as you wanted to. I will also ensure that no one ever blackmails you or your father again.'

Marry Camford? She blinked at that, a denial rising to her lips. She couldn't just marry him. Did she think he could just substitute himself as the bridegroom and no one would notice or care? Her father would be furious.

Shock prevented her from answering, though she gaped at him. Camford continued holding her hands, and then she met his penetrating gaze. 'I know I'm not the man you want. But perhaps you can still be content.'

His words held such gentleness, she felt tears in her eyes. 'I don't know.' She didn't want him to hold regrets, and certainly a marriage to her would cause him to resent her.

He released her hands and took her face in his hands. The touch of his palms warmed her cheeks, and she felt a flutter within her skin. Every logical thought in her brain simply fled.

'I've stood in Lachlan's shadow for too long. I won't be doing so again.'

With that, he leaned in and claimed her mouth in a kiss. His lips were inviting, and heat roared through her. She could hardly breathe as he gently took her mouth, showing her what he wanted. There were no demands, only an offering of himself. When he pulled back, she was trembling, unable to grasp a single thought.

'I would never force you against your will,' he said. 'But I cannot promise not to tempt you.' With that, he released her and stepped back. 'Marry me, Regina.'

Chapter Six

Dalton returned to the room of wedding guests, behaving as if nothing had gone wrong. There was outright confusion from many of the onlookers, along with a low murmur of conversation. Some recognised him and were unsure of what was happening. Others were elderly with failing eyesight, and he suspected they didn't even realise he wasn't Lachlan MacKinloch. Since he was dressed as a Highlander, they hadn't looked too closely.

Lord and Lady Havershire appeared stunned by his presence, but neither dared to say a word in front of their friends. The countess seemed if she were about to faint, while Lord Havershire looked ready to call him out with pistols at dawn. The earl was about to say something when his wife suddenly touched his arm and shook her head.

Instead, Dalton waited near the clergyman. He had done everything he could to help Regina save face. And if she did not want to go through with the ceremony, then that was her choice.

It was strange, standing here to wait for her. He'd

never dreamed of anything like this—and yet, the stares and whispers didn't bother him at all. He was here to rescue Regina, whether that meant stealing her away…or speaking his vows in a marriage that he'd hardly dared to imagine.

Within another minute, she opened the doors and walked through the crowd of people to stand before him. Slowly, she extended her hand to him.

He couldn't stop the smile that broke over his face. Aye, there were so many things wrong with this day— her shame at being left at the altar. Her parents' fury at a switched bridegroom. The fact that he didn't have a wedding licence, which made this entire ceremony illegal. But this was about saving her from humiliation. And when he glanced at her mother, Lady Havershire seemed to understand.

The Earl of Havershire was another matter. 'Regina—' His voice was razor-sharp, but she interrupted him before he could protest.

'Everything will be fine,' she said. 'We will be married.'

He started to shake his head, but she sent her father a sharp look of warning. Then her mother leaned in and spoke softly to the earl. Dalton didn't know what she had said, but it seemed to pacify the man.

The clergyman's expression was concerned, but Regina muttered beneath her breath, 'Continue the ceremony, if you please.'

'But, my lady, without a—'

'Just say the words,' she interrupted. 'We will worry about the rest later.'

He knew the clergyman was speaking about the lack of a licence. But Regina had effectively silenced him, implying that they would correct the matter at another time.

Dalton nodded in agreement. And when the clergyman began the words to the wedding ceremony, he no longer cared about anything else. He was speaking vows to the woman he desired above all others, the woman whose heart he wanted. Regina had, by some miracle, agreed to marry him in front of guests. He didn't know what had convinced her—and he knew she had no feelings for him beyond friendship—but for now, it was enough. He pushed back the rising doubts that warned him she would regret this. After a few weeks of living in Scotland, she might wish she'd never gone through with the false marriage. Regina deserved a true English gentleman as her husband, and Dalton could never be that for her. The wildness of Scotland burned in his blood, and he could never be a proper viscount.

When the minister asked if there were any reasons why they should not be wed, Regina turned to her parents and sent another silent threat. Her mother's face was pale, but she said nothing at all. Neither did the earl.

It surprised him that they'd listened to their daughter, for he'd expected her parents to raise any number of objections. But he supposed they were trying not to cause a scene in front of so many guests. It was bad enough that Lachlan had cried off, but Regina had clearly made her choice. She spoke her vows in a voice loud enough to be heard by all.

Dalton, in turn, promised to love and cherish her, forsaking all others. When it came time for the ring, she appeared worried for a moment. But he had come prepared for that, and he reached into his waistcoat for his grandmother's wedding ring. It was a simple silver ring, engraved with roses, and he slid it on her finger. The clergyman blessed their marriage, and Dalton leaned in to kiss her. It was only a slight meeting of lips before he pulled back.

'This isn't a true marriage,' she whispered.

'Aye,' he agreed. 'But they don't know that.'

'My father very well might murder us both,' she said against his ear. 'What shall we do? There will be so many questions. People will want to know why I married you. And why my parents didn't put a stop to it.'

Dalton cupped the back of her nape and whispered back, 'I think I should carry you off, as a Highlander would. It would save us from answering questions.'

Her expression turned thoughtful, and she nodded. 'I agree with you. We've already created a scandal. We might as well make our escape.'

He reached down and lifted her into his arms. Regina let out a startled gasp before she tossed her posy of flowers to one of the women. To the crowd of guests, Dalton called out, 'Enjoy the wedding feast!' He strode out of the room, taking her away. And from the way she clung to him, he suspected that Regina didn't mind it at all. Several of the shocked guests began to applaud, and a mood of good humour rose among everyone.

He took her to his waiting coach and lifted her inside. Regina still had amusement on her expression, even after he spoke to the coachman and closed the door.

'What have we done, Lord Camford?'

'I believe we've caused the scandal of the Season,' he said. 'And I, for one, am glad of it.'

* * *

Regina had never done anything this spontaneous in all her life. It felt strangely good to be rebellious. Her bridegroom had run off, and in return, she had married someone else. Sort of. Without a licence, it wasn't *really* a wedding or a marriage. But somehow, it had been empowering to take command of her situation and ensure that she wasn't abandoned at the altar.

Before their coach could drive away, her father was banging on the door with his fist. Camford didn't open it. 'We can leave if you don't want to talk to him.'

She didn't, but somehow it seemed even worse to turn her back on her father. He was likely in shock after what she'd done, and she did owe him an explanation.

'No, it's all right. We should open the door.'

The moment Camford did, she regretted the decision. Her father wasn't in shock—he was livid with rage.

His face was practically purple, and his greying hair was in disarray from where he'd raked his hand through it. 'Regina, what have you done?'

She could tell that her new husband was about to intervene, but she lifted her hand, silently asking him to wait. 'Lord Camford offered to stand in for Locharr when he didn't arrive.'

'But Lachlan agreed to marry you. Something must have happened,' her father argued. 'I cannot understand why you felt the need to go through this…sham of a ceremony.' He stopped to glare at Lord Camford. 'It is not a legal marriage, and it will be annulled.'

Her father started to tell her all the reasons why she'd made such a mistake, and Regina bit her lip, wondering how to best proceed. He appeared intent upon stopping them from leaving, and she glanced over at Camford in a desperate plea for help.

The viscount understood her, and he interrupted the earl's tirade, saying, 'Your daughter received another blackmail note just the other day, threatening to tell everyone her secrets. Is that something you want?'

The earl blanched at his words. 'Wh-what do you mean?'

'I mean that your daughter is afraid of the threat. Since Locharr cried off and married his governess, I offered to take Regina to Scotland myself. You needn't worry, because I will protect her.'

'But—I swore to Tavin on his deathbed that my daughter would wed his son. They were promised.' He reached for his handkerchief, fighting back another cough.

'That promise is over now,' Camford said. 'But the blackmail must stop. I am taking Regina to Cairnross in Scotland, and I have an investigator searching for the culprit. They will be apprehended soon and prosecuted.'

With that, the earl grew more agitated. He shook his head. 'No. You cannot investigate this.' He stepped back and turned his face as a coughing spell overtook him. When he had finished, he insisted, 'The past must be left alone.' Then he turned back to her. 'Regina—I promise, I will take care of you. I will talk to Locharr. Make him see what a mistake he has made.'

She could see how upset he was, and she felt the need to reassure him. 'Write to him if you wish. But Papa, this was my choice. It may not be a true marriage, but I believe that Lord Camford will protect me.

He has promised to bring me to Scotland, and that is what I want.'

Her father didn't appear to be listening. He was muttering to himself about talking to Lachlan, and without saying farewell, he turned around and went back to the house. His behaviour was so unlike him, she didn't know what to do. But Camford gave orders to the driver and closed the door.

'Do you still want to go to Scotland?' he asked.

She nodded. 'I think it's best if I go away for a while. Then maybe my father will calm himself, and I can decide what I want to do next.'

They travelled through the London streets, and Lord Camford moved to sit beside her. She didn't truly know what he wanted, but he said, 'We need to talk about this marriage and come to our own understanding.'

His voice was calm and reasonable. He was right on that account, and she turned to face him. 'Thank you for helping me save face today. I don't know how I made such a mistake about Locharr. I truly thought he would come.'

'He called off the engagement in the letter I gave you. He said he spoke to you about it at the ball, but I think there was a misunderstanding.'

She thought about it and recalled that they had spoken about his governess. 'I told him I knew he was in love with Miss Goodson. It didn't matter to me because we were never going to have a marriage based upon love. I said that we needed to move on. But perhaps he thought I meant we needed to end it.'

Camford nodded. 'He did. And he asked me to give you the letter to ensure it. When I realised you were still making wedding plans, I tried to call upon you several times. Your parents and the servants refused to let me see you.'

And she hadn't answered his notes either, feeling so caught up in worry for her father. 'It was my fault about ignoring everyone. I just…didn't want to think of the wedding, aside from wanting my father to be there. He's been so ill, I fear that he doesn't have much time.'

Camford reached out to take her hand. His palm was warm, soothing against hers. 'I understand. But I also need you to understand that…there are complications now.'

She was fully distracted by his touch, knowing she should pull her hand away…and not wanting to. 'What sort of complications?'

'Even though our ceremony was not legal, we are bound together. Just by travelling alone together to Scotland, your reputation will be ruined if we part ways. I would rather wed you again legally so that does not happen.'

She turned to look outside the window. So much had happened, she hadn't had time to consider the long-term consequences of this impulse. To stall him, she asked, 'Why did you help me today? I never imagined you would do such a thing.'

He reached out to take her hand. 'Because you needed it.' Though he did nothing more than hold her hand, shivers erupted against her skin. She was torn between wanting to pull back and knowing that he was not threatening her.

It was as if her mind and her body were separate beings. She knew that he desired her, but why? This went beyond friendship. 'Camford, I don't think—'

'You needn't worry that I will ask for more than you can give,' he interrupted.

Her cheeks flamed at the mention of intimacy. Even now, just the touch of his hand upon her palm, was enough to unnerve her. Regina calmed herself and took a deep breath. 'That—that's good,' she agreed. To calm herself, she pulled her hands back and folded them in her lap.

But her mind was spinning with the true consequences of what she'd done. Camford was right. Even without a legal marriage, the rest of the world would believe that she given herself to him. 'I am grateful that you came to my aid today.' He had done everything in his power to save her, and she *was* thankful for the farce.

He inclined his head and then asked again, 'So what do you want to do about…us?'

Regina drew in a deep breath. The last time she had made choices freely, her rebellion had resulted in disaster. For the past five years, she had retreated into herself, allowing others to shape her life. It had been a means of survival, of pushing back the harsh memories and falling into a pattern of obedience.

But now, she wanted to emerge from that shell, to begin making her own decisions again. And to do that, she needed time.

She tried to keep her voice gentle and calm. 'Camford, please don't force me into another marriage. It doesn't matter what anyone else thinks.'

His green eyes remained steady, but she saw the slight hurt within them. This marriage had been a heroic act, and she was grateful for it—but she could not let him believe that she would submit to him as a proper wife should.

'In time, the gossip will die down,' she said. 'And it's not truly necessary for me to remain in their social circles. I would be quite content not to return to London.'

His expression revealed that he didn't believe that at all. 'And what about my servants? What do you intend to tell them?'

She raised her chin. 'Tell your staff whatever you wish. Let them believe we are married, if you like. But you and I will know the truth.'

It was evident that he didn't agree with her at all, and he tried again, lightening his tone. 'You were prepared to wed Lachlan in an arrangement. Why not do the same with me?'

Because it would never be the same with him. Every touch, every moment was heightened in his presence. Dalton St George was so very dangerous to her heart, for she could not remain indifferent. Even now, she was remembering the stolen kiss and the way it had moved her.

He tried again. 'They're naught but words spoken with a licence. We gave the words already. All we need is the legal paper.'

She couldn't truly explain her reluctance, for she didn't want him to know of her hidden feelings. All she knew was that marriage to this man would shatter the walls of ice she had so carefully erected. She wasn't able to risk a true marriage. Not yet.

She took a breath and straightened in her seat. 'I will gladly compensate you for the inconvenience of being your house guest for a while.'

'You're not a house guest.' His voice turned dark, revealing his frustration. And she simply didn't know how to ease his anger.

'Yes, I am, Lord Camford. It's all I can be.' Her heart was pounding as she tried to maintain a brave front of prim behaviour. Year of behaving like a proper lady were her only weapon against this man. She still hadn't forgotten his kiss, and there was no doubt that he wanted more.

For a long moment, he studied her. His gaze moved over her hair, to her face, and at last, he turned away. There was a grim tone in his voice and he said, 'Very well. Then I swear, I won't touch you again. You will be a house guest, nothing more.'

The words should have been reassuring. Instead, it felt like a judgement, and a sudden loneliness descended over her.

He is doing the right thing, her brain insisted. *He's behaving like a gentleman.*

But I don't know if I want him to be a gentleman any more, her heart answered.

She longed for the bold Highlander who had carried her away.

'It has been a long day. I am so tired,' she said. It was a temporary means of ceasing their argument, and she hoped he would understand.

'Then lie down and rest,' he offered. 'I will let you know when we stop for the night.'

Regina curled up to try to sleep, though the coach was not at all comfortable. But as she started to close her eyes, she caught him staring at her as if he couldn't quite believe what had happened this day.

Neither could she.

* * *

Dalton stopped the coach at an inn later that night and bought food for everyone to eat. Regina's demeanour held tension, and he knew she was nearly at her breaking point. Her refusal to have a true marriage with him had been clear enough. She didn't want him and never had. It felt as if she'd sliced him in half, ripping his heart from his chest.

You're not the man she wants. You never will be.

His pride ached, and he forced the pain away. He had known it was a risk to steal her away from the wedding, but a part of him had hoped that she might allow him to court her. Now he knew that would never happen. She wanted to be a damned house guest, not a wife.

So be it. He would take her to Scotland with him, and she could do as she pleased until the threat of the blackmailer was resolved. He would lock away his own feelings and never bother her.

'Will you take me to my room?' she asked Dalton softly. 'I would like to eat alone.'

Given how crowded the inn was, he could understand her wishes. But he hadn't yet told her that there was only one room available. And he didn't know where he would stay if she refused to let him share the space. Which, undoubtedly, she would.

Instead, Dalton gave a nod and took the tray of food from the innkeeper's wife. He led Regina upstairs before he unlocked the door and set the food down on the table inside. She was eyeing him as if she intended to dismiss him from her presence. Instead, he sat down in the other chair. 'Do you mind if I share a meal with you before I go?'

Her shoulders relaxed as she took a chair on the opposite side of the tiny table. 'Of course not.'

Dalton dipped a piece of bread into the hot stew and devoured it. He hadn't realised how hungry he was until now. 'I suppose we should have taken some food from the wedding feast,' he said. 'I'm starving.'

'I think you were too busy carrying me off.' But she ventured a slight smile and took a spoonful of her own stew. For a while, they ate in silence. She savoured the stew, sipping it slowly. 'It's delicious.'

'So it is.' But he was speaking of her, not the stew. She had removed her bonnet, and her red hair gleamed in the candlelight. Though several strands were escaping, she smoothed them back, tucking them away—as if she would never consider the idea of unbinding her hair. Her blue eyes were thoughtful, and her manners were impeccable. She was a lady in every sense of the word.

And yet, the taste of her lips haunted him. The softness of her mouth, the way she had yielded to him earlier today, made him want to kiss her again.

But she wouldn't want that. As the meal drew to a close, Dalton had no idea what to say to her. It was as if he were living in a dream, married to the idealised woman he'd loved for years. But the flesh-and-blood woman was so very different. Regina didn't feel the same towards him, and he was at a loss on what to do now.

When she had finished eating, his wife stood. 'Thank you for the meal, Dalton. I think I will retire now.'

She was waiting for him to leave, but there was nowhere to go. The servants were all crowded together on the floor of the inn downstairs, and he wasn't about to join them. Instead, he decided to guard her room from the outside. He stood and said, 'Goodnight.'

Dalton departed her room, closed the door behind him, and sat in the hallway. It was the strangest wedding night he'd ever imagined. And yet, she had been clear about her wishes. Making demands would get him nowhere, save to make her uncomfortable. He started to take off his shoes, wondering if he would get any sleep at all. It was highly unlikely. But the moment he lay down in the hall, the door opened. He stared up at Regina's confused expression. 'Dalton, what are you doing?'

'Finding a place to sleep,' he explained. 'There was only one room.' He crossed his arms behind his head.

Her face held consternation, and she shook her head. 'No, my lord. You cannot sleep in the hall.'

'The floor of the inn would be worse,' he countered. 'I'd rather not have our coachman and the other guests casting judgement over us.'

She opened the door wider. 'What I meant was that you should come inside.'

Worry knotted her face, and when he didn't move, she reached down with her hand. 'Don't stay out there.'

He took her hand and slowly rose to his feet. 'I won't be bothering you, lass. There's naught to be afraid of.'

'I—I know.' She turned and gathered a blanket and her own pillow from the bed. 'Take these, and you can sleep over there.'

'Thank you.' Though he still didn't think he would be able to sleep much at all, being in the same room as Regina. Her nerves were palpable, and he wanted a means of turning the conversation so she would not feel threatened. Upon the far end of the room, he spied a small shelf with a wooden chess set upon it. 'Would you want to play a game of chess to pass the time?'

She did turn around at that, and her brow furrowed. 'Chess? At this hour?'

Dalton shrugged. 'If you're wanting to sleep, go on then,' he said. But spread out the thin blanket upon the floor. There was no hearth, so he intended to make the best of what he had for bedding.

Regina's own bed appeared bare, with only a linen sheet and no pillow. He didn't want to take from her, especially now. 'You should keep the pillow. It will be more comfortable for you.'

'I have the mattress,' she answered. 'Keep it for yourself.' She sat down on the bed and tried to curl up, closing her eyes. He could imagine her discomfort, for she still wore her stays and petticoats. But he wasn't about to offer to undress her, given how skittish she was.

Dalton finished unpinning part of the tartan and folded it, setting it aside. Then he laid back against the pillow, staring at the cracked ceiling of the inn. He was starting to count backwards from one hundred when Regina suddenly sat up.

'I'm tired,' she admitted, 'yet, I do not think I can fall asleep just now. I feel…distracted.'

He couldn't have agreed more. But his reasons for being restless had nothing to do with distraction and everything to do with physical frustration. He sat up and turned to look at his bride.

'Perhaps one game would help to relax both of us,' Regina said. 'If you're willing.'

'Aye,' he agreed.

She crossed the room and brought the chess set over to the table. 'But I will confess that I am terrible at chess.'

'So am I,' he lied. He rose from his place on the floor and stretched. His shirt hung open, and she glanced at his chest before she blushed. It made him wonder if she had any interest at all, or whether it was merely embarrassment.

'I know a way to make the game more interesting,' he said. 'Would you care to place a wager on the outcome?'

She set up her pieces while he did the same. 'It depends on the wager.'

'If you win, what do you want from me?' he asked.

She thought a moment. 'I would like to go riding in Scotland. It's been a long time since I've been on a horse. I miss it.'

'Done,' he agreed. He had several horses at Cairnross, and she would enjoy riding across the fields.

'What about you?' she asked. 'What is it you want if you win?' From the suspicious tone of her voice, he knew he had to tread carefully.

At first, he wasn't certain he should admit it, but then he decided he might as well be truthful. She would likely refuse anyway. 'I want a kiss, freely given. Nothing more.'

Her face flushed, and she appeared wary. 'Dalton, I'm not certain that is a good idea.'

'If you win, it won't matter, will it?' He reached for his pawn and made the first move.

'I've already said that I am terrible at chess. And it's a bad idea.' Even so, she claimed his pawn as her own.

'Kissing you is never a bad idea,' he countered. 'But

I will not force you into anything. If I win, it's your choice whether to grant my request.'

She appeared unconvinced but turned her attention back to their match. As they began to play, he saw her strategy. Whether she would admit it or not, Regina was quite good. She sacrificed a few pieces to make bigger moves, and he found that the game was more challenging than he'd imagined.

It intrigued him, and when he placed her in check, she studied him with interest. 'You lied about your skill, Dalton.'

'So did you. But does it matter?' He watched as she considered her next move.

'I still want to go riding. I love horses,' she admitted.

He eyed her closely. 'You realise, we could both win this game. Even if I take the match, I'd be glad to take you out riding.'

After his answer, she eyed him, her head slightly tilted in consideration. Then she made her last move, putting herself in checkmate.

The game was his. And yet, it was only beginning.

Regina hesitated, waiting for Dalton to speak. But he said nothing to her—he only waited with infinite patience.

I can't do this, her brain protested. Not because kissing him was frightening—quite the opposite. The last time he had kissed her, she had felt a part of herself awakening. Yearning, even. She wasn't afraid of Dalton demanding more from her. She was afraid of her own response to him.

Her heart was thundering in her chest, and Dalton remained motionless. He'd asked for a kiss, freely given. And she could not deny that she wanted to kiss him.

His eyes were dark and hooded, and he waited for her to approach. She wasn't certain whether to lean down, but when she drew near, he pulled her to sit on his lap. Then he let his hands fall away, in a silent invitation.

She rested her hands on his shoulders, feeling uncertain. Restless emotions rose up within her, along with her own insecurities. Dalton's body was strung tight, as if he was barely hanging on to control.

And yet, she was drawn to this man.

He was handsome, with dark blond hair and green eyes that were sometimes blue, depending on the way the light played. His face was clean shaven, and she reached out to touch his cheek. The angle of his jaw and the strong face made him more masculine. He was waiting for her to kiss him, but she could not yet abandon her fears.

It had been years since she had been violated, and the harsh reality kept invading the present moment.

But he seemed to guess her hesitation, and he reminded her, 'I will never harm you, Regina. You are in command.'

She believed him, for in his voice, there was complete sincerity. And perhaps he would help her to move forward, to put the past behind her. She put her arms around his neck and leaned in for the promised kiss.

But when her mouth came to his, she felt a breathless longing. The moment she kissed him, he kissed her back. She tasted his lips, and there was a hint of ale upon them from their earlier meal. His mouth was heated, giving a sensual caress that reached deep inside her. She had only meant for it to be a brief kiss, but she found herself captivated. Against her hip, she could feel the hard ridge of his arousal, and panic rose up.

But he did nothing, except continue to kiss her. And when she drew back, his eyes were dark and filled with desire.

Regina waited for him to make demands, to press her, but he did nothing except drink in the sight of her. She felt breathless, unable to grasp the fleeting thoughts that went through her mind. She didn't know what to do now. She wanted to kiss him again…and yet, she feared it would only evoke temptation. She didn't want a true marriage with Dalton. It wasn't possible to forget the past.

But right now, she wanted to weep, for he had made the kiss so good. He made her feel things she'd never imagined she could feel. And it terrified her.

'Why did you marry me, Dalton?' she whispered.

'Because you needed my help.' He drew his hand over her, gently stroking the base of her spine.

'That doesn't truly answer my question. We've known each other for years, yes. But I never gave you any signs of…more.'

He kept his hands upon her spine while she remained seated on his lap. 'When my brother died, most people kept a respectful distance because of my parents' grief. You were the only one to notice that I was in pain.'

'I saw you leave the burial,' she argued. 'You didn't need to be alone.'

'No one else came but you.' He reached up and drew his thumb down the line of her jaw. The simple touch undid her, and she felt the heat down to her bones. 'To you, it was nothing. To me, it was everything.'

He kept his palm against her cheek. 'But I know I'm not the man you wanted.' With that, he pulled his hand away, giving her the chance to leave.

She knew she should get up from his lap, but she couldn't bring herself to move. His touch had made her crave more, and she didn't understand what he had evoked. The heat of his skin and the thrumming of her heart only heightened the sensations rising inside.

'We should go to sleep now,' she whispered. 'It's late.'

'It is.' He eyed her for a moment and asked, 'Do you want me to loosen your stays so it's easier for you to sleep?'

She shook her head, not wanting to take the risk. The thought of his hands unlacing her was a sensual promise that she couldn't bear to face. 'No. Just leave them.' Her face was burning with embarrassment, and she extricated herself from his lap.

'Are you certain?' he asked. 'I won't touch you more than that.'

She believed him, but that didn't mean she was ready to let him undress her. 'I'll be fine. Please… just don't.'

His eyes grew guarded. 'Regina, what happened to you? Who hurt you?'

She shook her head and stepped back, unable to deny his question. 'I don't wish to ever speak of it again.' She sat upon the straw mattress, lying on her side with her knees drawn up. But Dalton didn't return to his own bed. Instead, he knelt beside her, and she nearly flinched at the sight of his tension. He looked as if he wanted to tear the man apart.

'One day, you will tell me the truth,' he warned. 'And I will kill him for what he did to you.'

You can't, she thought to herself. She swallowed hard, the anguish rising within.

Because he's already dead.

Chapter Seven

It took a few more days of travelling before they reached his grandfather's estate in Scotland. Dalton helped Regina disembark from the coach, and he led her up the gravel pathway. 'Welcome to Cairnross.' He lifted her hand to his mouth, and she managed a smile, glancing up at the stone towers.

'It looks like a fairy-tale castle.'

'It has been around for hundreds of years, but its history isn't at all like a fairy tale,' he warned. 'There were a few unsavoury men among my mother's ancestors.'

'What did they do?' She kept her hand in his arm as he led her up the stone steps.

Dalton glanced at the courtyard on the far side of the castle. 'The Earl of Cairnross imprisoned some of the MacKinlochs for years.' He shrugged. 'But eventually, Cairnross passed into more benevolent hands.'

'Such as yours?'

'And yours,' he said softly. It was a risk to say it, but he wondered how she would respond to the idea. She had insisted on being nothing more than a house guest, but he wanted far more than that. Their friendship was on fragile footing just now, and he admitted to himself that he didn't know what would happen. She had given him the kiss he'd wanted. But now that he'd had a taste of her, he craved her with a fierce hunger. He wanted her naked skin upon his, and he wanted to watch her come undone with pleasure. But he knew better than to press her further. If he made demands of any kind, she would freeze him out.

It reminded him of the years he'd spent trying to please his father—being so careful to say the right thing or to behave in the way John had wanted him to. A part of him rebelled against trying to become the man she wanted, for he wasn't the sort of man who'd had any luck following rules.

But the rules didn't apply to Regina. She hadn't denied that *someone* had hurt her in the past. Fear ruled her emotions, and he could only win her heart with patience.

If he could win her heart.

They reached the main doors, and were greeted by Elliott MacLachor, the elderly butler. ''Tis good to see ye again, Lord Camford. You're very welcome.' He raised an expectant look at Regina.

'This is Regina St George, my wife and the new Lady Camford,' Dalton introduced. He didn't miss her wary response, but it was far easier to continue the ruse than to pretend she was a guest who had travelled alone.

MacLachor beamed with happiness and reached to shake her hand. 'I bid ye welcome, my lady. We are glad to hear of your good tidings.' The butler led them inside where a footman took her cloak and bonnet.

Dalton brought her into the parlour and gave orders for tea and refreshments.

After they were alone, Regina confronted him in a low voice. 'Why did you tell him I was your wife?'

'Because it gives you more freedom,' he answered. 'And because it's the truth. Licence or no', we spoke vows. I can't brush that aside or pretend it didn't happen.' He lowered his voice. 'But you will have your own room.'

Her tension eased, but she asked, 'Will it cause problems later?'

Not if he could help it. He was hoping she would grow accustomed to the idea. Instead, he gave a shrug. 'If it does, we will handle it then.'

She seemed to accept it. Then she remarked, 'I feel strange without having any of my belongings. I cannot even change my gown.'

'I can let you borrow some of my mother's clothes,' he suggested. 'If you don't mind wearing them, that is.'

'Will it bother you to see them?' she ventured.

He paused and shook his head. 'She would have liked you, and I believe she would want you to have them. I'll send a maid to help you with them.'

'Later,' she said. 'For now, I'm starving.'

Regina studied the room with interest. It was decorated in shades of emerald and cream, and she walked towards the window where there was a view of the estate grounds. To Dalton, she said, 'Cairnross is lovely. I look forward to seeing the gardens.'

He hoped that meant she was growing accustomed to the idea of being his wife. 'Then I will show them to you this afternoon.' He went to stand beside her, studying the landscape. For a time, he simply enjoyed being so near.

Outside, a female wren chirped, attracting the attention of a male. She let him get close, only to dart away in her own flirtatious mating dance. Intrigued, the male pursued her even more.

And suddenly, Dalton wondered if he'd been going about this all wrong. He had tried to remain patient and steady, slowly coaxing her towards affection, but Regina was still reluctant to get close. What if he attempted the opposite? What if he pulled back, still letting her know of his interest…but allowing her the freedom to choose? It made him wonder if distance— or even temptation—would kindle her own interest.

'The roses are lovely,' Regina whispered. She was staring outside at the wide stone terrace that led down into a walled garden with a fountain in the centre. His mother had planted the roses that climbed upon one of the walls, while other rosebushes lined the opposite terrace.

'My mother designed it.' It had been her labour of love, and he remembered exploring the gardens as a lad while she clipped and trimmed the bushes. There had always been roses in each of the rooms—red, pink, yellow, and white.

'Perhaps I could help your gardener take care of them,' she offered. 'I do love roses.'

'If you want to.' Their conversation was interrupted when the footman brought tea and refreshments. The housekeeper, Mrs Hughes, greeted them with enthusiasm and told Regina, 'I've arranged for Evina to tend your room. She can serve as your maid until yours arrives.'

'Thank you,' Regina said.

Before the housekeeper could leave, she asked, 'Will you be celebrating another wedding with us, my lady? We would dearly love to host a *cèilidh* and share in your happiness. I would be glad to make all the arrangements.'

Regina glanced at Dalton with a doubtful expression. He interrupted and said, 'Mrs Hughes, there is no need to worry about that just yet. We've only just arrived in Scotland.'

The housekeeper appeared disappointed, but she nodded as she departed the room.

Dalton poured her a cup of tea and gave her a sandwich. Time to see if his experiment would bear fruit. 'Was I wrong to say it's too soon?'

Regina shook her head. 'No, you're right. We shouldn't get their hopes up.' Even so, there was a faint trace of confusion on her face.

'You *did* want to merely be a house guest, yes?' He took a sip of his tea, drinking it black.

'Well, yes. If you think that's possible.' Again, her eyes held concern. 'But I am aware that the servants will think that I…that we—'

'That we've consummated the marriage,' he finished.

Her face coloured, and she nodded. 'Camford, what exactly do you expect from me while I'm here?'

He set down his teacup and rested his wrists upon his knees. For a moment, he studied her, drinking in her beauty. In spite of the rumpled wedding gown and her hair falling down from her bonnet, he desired her.

'I want to protect you,' he said quietly. 'We may not be legally wedded, but I don't want anyone speaking idle words after we've spent days travelling together. And I agree that you do need more time to decide what you want.' He rose from his chair and drew closer. Though there was room to sit beside her, he remained standing. She had to tilt her head up to look at him.

'Y-you're right,' she answered. 'I feel as if we hardly know each other, and I don't want to be forced into a marriage. If I ever marry, I want to feel a sense of happiness. I want the wedding I should have had.'

'You want to be courted,' he predicted.

'Not exactly,' she said, nibbling at a sandwich. 'What I want is to have choices. I agreed to marry Lachlan because it was what my father wanted. And now, I want to feel as if I can live my own life.'

He could understand her intense need for freedom. Nothing was worse than being forced into a life you didn't want. He had never wanted to be a viscount, much less an earl one day. Though it was a title most men desired, he hadn't wanted it at the cost of his brother's life. If he could bring Brandon back and surrender everything, he would do so without hesitation. His parents had never recovered from the death of their son, and Dalton knew he couldn't ever fill that role. He'd grown accustomed to not being enough.

He just wanted to be enough for Regina. And if that meant waiting, if it meant giving her the time she needed to feel something more for him, he intended to try.

Regina stood and faced him. She was so near, he could inhale the scent of her skin. More than anything, he wanted to steal another kiss, to make her crave him as badly as he wanted her. It took every ounce of his control to remain motionless.

'I just need time, Dalton,' she murmured. 'For so long, I expected to wed Lachlan. I feel as if you and I are still strangers.'

He'd thought they were friends, but it bothered him to realise that she hadn't considered it a true friendship. She really did see him in the same light as any other gentleman.

She reached out to take his hands in hers, and the sudden move made it that much harder not to touch her. 'Is that all right?'

He barely managed a nod. 'But there is something I want, in return.'

'What is that?'

'A chance,' he said softly. 'Don't close yourself away from me.'

Her cheeks grew rosy, and she didn't answer at first. Then she raised her blue eyes to his.

'All right,' she agreed. 'But Dalton—don't ask me to give more than I can.'

Gently, he squeezed her hands and was rewarded when she inhaled with a slight sigh. He murmured, 'One day, I hope you will trust me with your secrets.'

Regina spent the day with Dalton, but all the while, it felt as if he were chiselling her defences away. The gentle touch of his hands on hers had evoked strong feelings she didn't understand. He had hardly done anything, but somehow he'd begun breaking down the invisible walls that had guarded her for so long. She didn't know how to keep him at a distance...nor was she certain she wanted to.

Gone was the London gentleman she'd known for so many years, and in his place was a handsome Highlander. Dalton had taken her to the gardens, as promised, leading her to the roses.

'Choose, Regina,' he'd said. She selected a golden yellow rose and another that was a deep pink. He'd used a knife to cut them for her, stripping them of the thorns. But when he gave them, he had taken her other hand in his. Though it might only have been with the intent of guiding her through the grounds, she was aware of the heat of his palm. In his fingers, her hand felt small. His thumb grazed the edge of hers, and for a moment, her wayward mind imagined that he was caressing another part of her. She could almost envision him as his medieval ancestor, conquering her defences and tormenting her with unexpected desires.

If theirs had been a true marriage, she had no doubt that he would spend the entire day making love to her. But he didn't know the dark memories that resurfaced with every touch. She didn't want to remember that terrible night, nor what had followed.

One day, she would have to tell him the truth. But in the meantime, she was trying to make sense of this unexpected marriage.

'We should go back,' he suggested, releasing her hand. Though the sun had not yet set, she supposed he wanted to show her the rest of the estate. And when it was possible, she longed to change her gown. She had worn the same wedding gown for the past four days, and while she had washed her face and hands daily, she wanted to wear a clean chemise and petticoat.

'Will you take me to my room and send a maid to me? I should like to change my gown before dinner.'

'Aye,' he agreed. He led her back inside, and she absorbed the sight of her surroundings. There was an aura of peace in Cairnross, and she decided it would make a good place to hide from the scandal and blackmail shadowing her. Here, she could start a new beginning, forgetting all about the past. Perhaps she could bring her father here to visit, and the fresh air might do him good, as well as her mother.

'Would you care to play another game of chess later?' he asked.

'I am terrible at chess, remember?' She tried to hide her smile while they walked through the halls. Dalton was far better than he'd let on, and she had to be careful of his wagers.

'I remember that you're a beautiful liar. You only want me to believe that you're terrible.'

She laughed, and as they walked, his hand bumped against her fingers. The slight touch unnerved her with the sudden desire to take his hand again. This man was not her legal husband, but it startled her to realise how much she was enjoying his presence. She felt drawn to him, and though it should have frightened her, she took comfort.

They walked through the rest of the house, and he showed her the older wing that had once been part of a medieval castle. 'It burned to the ground, hundreds of years ago,' Dalton explained. 'When it was rebuilt, some of my ancestors created hidden passages.'

'The old Earl of Cairnross?' she mused.

'Indeed. His castle came into our hands through an arranged marriage between a Highlander's daughter and a Norman.' He shrugged. 'It's ours now.'

'How did your mother inherit the property?' she asked. He led her up a stone staircase towards the bed-chambers.

'In truth, it's not hers—my grandfather is still living. I'll introduce you to him tomorrow. But after he dies, it will become mine. My mother had no brothers, and her father wanted it to pass to her sons. After Brandon died, Granda named me the heir.'

She hadn't realised that his grandfather was still alive, and it occurred to her that she knew very little about Dalton St George. But she wanted to know more.

He stopped before one of the bedchambers and opened the door. 'This was my mother's room. I asked Evina to prepare it for you. You'll find gowns in the wardrobe and the trunk. Choose whatever you like.'

'Thank you.' Before she lost her nerve, she took his hand and squeezed it lightly. He held it for a moment, as if savouring the touch. His green eyes drank in the sight of her, and she sensed that if she offered more, he would tempt her beyond all reason. The invisible heat between them made her lose her courage, and she reluctantly released his hand.

She walked inside the doorway and found a modest room with a mahogany wardrobe, a small table with a basin and pitcher, a fireplace which the servants had lit, and a narrow bed with a canopy. A quilt rested upon the bed, and the colours were soft blues and greens. 'It's lovely,' she said. On the opposite side of the room, she saw a door. 'Where does that lead?'

'To my room,' he said. He closed the door behind him, to give them privacy. 'But you needn't worry. I won't intrude.'

Her skin tightened at the mention, and she wondered what it would be like if the door were open between their rooms. In her mind, she imagined him trailing a single finger down her cheek to her throat. She envisioned him cupping her chin and leaning in for another kiss. His mouth would be warm and inviting, making her crave more. She felt the colour rise to her cheeks, but she let the vision continue as she imagined him undressing her.

He would be gentle, she knew. And, God help her, she could feel an ache between her legs, the stirrings of desire.

She turned away, and another memory slammed into her, of being forced against the wall. Harsh lips ground against her, while Mallencourt's hand reached beneath her skirts.

Regina trembled, and pulled back, unable to separate the present from the past. Her heart was beating rapidly, and she reminded herself that this was Dalton, not her attacker. He would never harm her.

But he was unaware of her sudden panic. 'I will send Evina to help you dress for dinner. I hope to see you there.'

Then he departed, closing the door behind him.

Regina closed her eyes, trying to calm her fears.

You have to tell him, her conscience warned. *He needs to know the truth.*

As she reached for a green gown, she willed the thoughts away. He could only know part of the truth— otherwise, it would ruin everything.

Being married to Regina but being unable to touch her was slowly killing him. Dalton had kept his promise, but he longed for more. This woman had twined herself into his life, and he desired her with a desperate need. But he was resolved not to touch her until her fears receded. She had taken his hand twice yesterday, and it gave him hope that she was starting to feel more comfortable around him.

He hadn't realised how the loneliness had crept into his life until now. The house felt different with her here, as if she could somehow silence the ghosts that haunted him. Her smile gave him hope, and he didn't want to lose that. If that meant upholding the boundaries and the closed doors, so be it.

Dalton waited for her in the dining room, and when she arrived, he greeted her. 'Good morning.'

'Good morning.' Her red hair was pinned up, and she wore one of his mother's morning gowns in a shade of deep green. It brought out the blue in Regina's eyes, and though the gown was slightly loose and a little short, she was lovely. 'Will we go riding today?'

'We will. My grandfather lives a short distance from here, and I thought we could pay him a call.'

She sat at the table and chose a piece of toast to go with her egg. 'Why doesn't he live here, in this house? You said he owns the land.'

'His memory is failing him, and he grew overwhelmed by all the space. He lives with a caretaker in a small house, and it's easier for him.' Dalton sat across from her at the table and tapped into his soft-boiled egg.

'I look forward to meeting him.'

There was a silence that descended as they ate. He tried to think of what else to say, but she appeared lost in thought.

Then a moment later, she continued, 'But perhaps it's best if you do not tell him of our false marriage. We wouldn't want to upset him needlessly.'

Though her words were intended as compassion, it underscored a truth he didn't want to face.

She doesn't want to be married to you. This isn't real or permanent.

He revealed none of his thoughts or emotions, locking away his feelings. Her pity was the last thing he needed.

One of the footmen arrived and cleared his throat. 'My lord, the...um...wedding gift you requested has arrived.'

The man's timing couldn't have been worse. Dalton merely gave a nod and pretended as if the footman hadn't spoken. But Regina set down her fork. 'What wedding gift?'

'It's nothing,' he said. 'I shouldn't have sent for it.'

But he'd caught her curiosity now, and she asked, 'May I see it?' He shrugged, and she continued, saying, 'I'm so sorry I have nothing for you in return.'

'It's all right.' He wanted to say that being married to her *was* his gift. Simply seeing her each day, being with her, meant everything. But he held back the words, not wanting to seem desperate.

'Is there something you want?' she ventured. 'Something I can give to you?'

The words were innocent, but they awakened a storm within him. He couldn't tell her what he wanted, and he wasn't about to risk frightening her.

She stood from her chair and chose the seat beside him. 'Dalton?'

He met her gaze, letting her see the full force of his desire. His fingers dug into his chair to keep from reaching for her.

Her blue eyes were staring at him, and he didn't

miss her uncertainty. She looked like a deer, caught by the hunter, waiting to flee. And yet, she held steady, watching him.

'I'll give the gift to you after breakfast,' he promised. It was her invitation to go.

But instead, she reached to his face and rested her hand upon his cheek. Softly, she bent down and touched her lips to his. A yearning rushed through him, and he caught her hand, holding it. He wanted her touch everywhere, against his bare skin, exploring and caressing him. He was iron hard with need, but he managed to gather his control again.

'Regina, don't,' he warned, rising to his feet.

His words humiliated her, and she turned scarlet. 'I'm sorry.' She tried to pull away, but he held her hand steady, bringing it to his chest.

'You said you wanted this to be temporary, and I am doing everything I can to grant that wish. But I want more.'

He didn't know if she could feel his heart racing. 'I'm trying to give you that freedom of choice.' With her hand in his, he leaned in so that her mouth was a breath away. 'But unless you want this to become a permanent marriage, don't offer me anything at all. Because I'll take everything.'

Her eyes widened in shock, but she held her ground. 'You don't want a woman like me, Dalton. I'm trying to do the right thing by not trapping you into marriage. I know I'll have to let you go.'

'Why?'

She shook her head, avoiding an answer. 'It's in the past, and I won't speak of it. But be assured, you don't want to be married to me.' With reluctance, she lowered her hands to her sides.

He realised that he was starting to crack the surface of her fears. 'What happened to you, Regina?'

She stiffened at his nearness. 'It's in the past, and there it will stay.'

Her fear was palpable, and he didn't press for more. 'If that's what you want.' Though he wanted to hold her, to reassure her, he stepped away instead. She appeared miserable, and he steeled himself not to show a reaction.

Instead, he checked his pocket watch. 'We should go and meet Grandfather. He'll be wanting to see you.' Her face remained worried, but he thought it best to abandon the subject. 'Do you still want to go?'

She nodded. Dalton offered his arm and then after she took it, he said, 'I'll show your wedding gift to you, just before we leave.' As they passed MacLachor, Dalton murmured, 'Go and fetch the gift for my wife. She is ready now.'

Regina waited in the hall beside Dalton, feeling utterly bereft and confused. For so long, she had believed she could never be the wife he wanted. He would want children one day, and she didn't want to see his face transform with irritation or loathing. But she couldn't deny that he made her yearn for a different life, one where she could be whole again.

When she heard the patter of paws approaching, she turned and saw a dog that made her heart melt. 'This is your wedding gift,' Dalton said. 'He's still very young, nearly a year old.'

Regina could hardly speak, for she was overcome

by joy as she knelt down. The dog's golden fur was silken, and he licked her fingers as if searching for hidden treats. 'He's mine?'

'He is. I remember how much you enjoyed dogs when I brought you the pug in London.'

'I've always wanted a dog. I love him.' Happy tears came to her eyes, and she brushed them away. But more than that, she realised that Dalton truly did care about her if he had brought her such a gift. She stood, needing him to understand how very much this meant to her. Though she kept the leather lead in her hand, she reached out and squeezed his hand. 'I have never had a nicer gift.'

He continued holding her hand, his gaze intent upon hers. It evoked the memory of his mouth upon hers, and an unexpected yearning filled her. She wanted to kiss him again, but he had asked her not to touch him. Though she would respect his wishes, she rather wished she could embrace him.

'What will you name him?' he asked as he led her outside.

'You might laugh at me,' she warned. 'But when I was a little girl, I loved legends and folklore. I always wanted to name a dog after King Arthur.'

'Then Arthur he shall be.'

She was eager to enjoy time with the animal. It also gave her a way of occupying herself. Her emotions were all over the place just now, and she felt uncertain. This wasn't meant to be a true marriage—and yet, it was starting to change. With each day she spent at his side, she found herself softening. Dalton was a decent man, and he deserved a true wife, not her. If she had any feelings towards him, she should release him from this false marriage and give him the chance to win a woman who could love him in the way he deserved.

But selfishly, she didn't want to.

For so long, she had been a ruined woman, damaged and broken. Was it possible to change that? Could she somehow bury the past and try to be a stronger woman, one who could love this man? She didn't know.

The walk to his grandfather's house wasn't long, but along the way, Arthur sniffed at the ground and stopped several times to mark his territory. The dog was a welcome distraction from her tangled thoughts. 'It may take an hour to arrive at your grandfather's home if we have to keep stopping,' Regina remarked. 'I hope he won't be upset if we are late.'

'He doesn't know that we are coming to pay a call,' Dalton answered. There was a hesitation in his voice, and he added, 'Regina, I don't know if this will be a good day or a bad day for him. My grandfather often forgets many things.'

'How old is he?' she asked.

'He is eighty.' Dalton paused and then said, 'Sometimes he lives in a world of his own imaginings.'

She understood his unspoken request for patience and nodded. Though she had met many elderly folk who had difficulty with memories, she suspected that this was far more.

They continued to walk for another quarter of an hour before they reached the house. Regina was surprised to see that it was larger than she had imagined. The front of the house appeared tiny, but it stretched back farther and was all on the same level with no stairs.

Dalton approached the front door and rapped the knocker. A matron answered the door and smiled at him. 'Och, laddie, he'll be glad t'see you today. And I've heard from the Cairnross staff that this be your wife, Lady Camford? What a bonny one she is. His Lordship will be so glad.' The housekeeper bent down and ruffled Arthur's ears.

So much for keeping the news from Lord Cairnross, Regina thought. But perhaps it wouldn't matter in the end. Her nerves prickled at the thought of making a true attempt to be a real wife.

'What kind of day is Grandfather having, Mrs Howard?' Dalton asked.

Her mouth turned up in a smile. 'I canna say. I'll leave it to you to decide.'

Regina didn't know what to think of that, but she picked up the puppy to ensure that he didn't startle Dalton's grandfather.

'Is he too heavy for you?' he asked, but Regina shook her head.

'Arthur's not heavy at all. But I will need you to open the door.' The dog squirmed in her arms, licking her face with vigour. Regina tried to hide her amusement, but when she walked inside the parlour, she was startled at the sight of Lord Cairnross.

The earl had tacked up long sheets stretching from the curtains to the piano. Chairs lined the room, and he stood on the piano bench. He still had his hair, but it was snowy white. His beard was also white, and he wore a uniform that reminded her of the Royal Navy. In his right hand, he held a spyglass, which he turned to her. 'So, you've returned, Marguerite.'

Regina didn't know who Marguerite was, but Dalton took the dog and set him down on the floor. 'Just play along.'

Play along? She decided to greet the old man and extended her hand. 'Good morning, my lord. My name is Regina.'

'Well, now. Come aboard, lassie, and try not to fall in the water when you do.'

She was beginning to realise what Dalton had meant. The earl was lost in a dream world of his own making. And although it was only his fantasy, he was caught up in the vision.

'Where are we sailing, Grandfather?' Dalton asked, stepping on to a chair. He held out his hands to her, and Regina joined him to stand on another chair. She could hardly believe what they were doing, play acting as if they were children. For a moment, she felt foolish, pretending to be on an invisible ship.

'To India, laddie. We'll seek our fortunes and bring back our ship laden with diamonds and rubies.' The earl turned his spyglass towards the wall. 'We'll fight off the pirates on our journey. I hope you've brought your sword.'

Regina suppressed a smile as she watched her new husband listening to his grandfather's imaginary world. The old man's face held joy as he wielded his cane like a weapon. Dalton steadied his grandfather when he nearly lost his balance. 'The waves are rough tonight.'

'Aye, so they are. But you've a fair maiden to keep you on the right path. Your wife, is she?'

Dalton hesitated, but Regina answered, 'I am,' before Dalton could speak.

He put his hand upon his grandfather's shoulder and

ventured a smile at Regina. She returned it, and a silent understanding passed between them. He believed that she was humouring his grandfather…but the truth was, she didn't know what she wanted any more.

'I wish I could have attended your wedding, laddie. Was there dancing?'

Dalton eyed her with a questioning look. 'There was no time.' But he held out his hand. 'Will you dance with me now, lass?'

'How?' she asked, staring at the chairs. With a glance towards his grandfather, she added, 'Won't we fall in the water?'

'Nay. I'll keep you safe.' Dalton held out his arms, and she went to stand before him. Though she knew this was only for his grandfather's sake, she felt the tension rising between them. He placed his hand upon her waist, and she welcomed the simple touch. The warmth of his palm made her feel closer to him. She held his other hand while they swayed gently atop two chairs. His grandfather's face broke open with joy, and he clapped to the beat of a silent song. Dalton met her gaze, and she understood.

There was no reason to shatter his grandfather's dream by refusing to participate. The man had lived a long life, and if these elaborate visions brought him happiness, what was the harm?

But more than that, during this spectacle, she recognised Dalton's empathy and inner strength. He never belittled his grandfather or told him that there was no ship in the middle of the parlour. Instead, he gave the old man a moment of joy. And seeing his compassion utterly crumbled her heart.

You could fall in love with him, her head warned.

His green eyes held warmth and amusement, and he held her close as they danced.

You have to distance yourself. It will only be worse if you get too close.

Dalton would despise her if she ever told him the truth about that night. Instead, she forced herself to let go of his hands. She turned away and shielded her eyes from an invisible sun. 'Is that another ship I see?'

When his grandfather began singing a sailor's tune, Dalton said, 'I think it's time we went ashore, Regina.' His tone was calm, and she tried to push back her regrets. She was making the right choice for both of them, though it hurt.

He set her down from the chair, and the puppy ran to them, wagging its tail. Dalton was about to offer his arm, when suddenly, Lord Cairnross stepped off the piano bench. He pulled her into a fast-paced step, spinning her around until she began to laugh. The old man was surprisingly spry, and her skirts whirled as he danced with her down to the end of the room and back. When he'd finished dancing with her, the earl bowed, and Regina curtsied.

Lord Cairnross kissed her hands. 'Laddie, if I were fifty years younger, I'd steal her awa' from you. You're a lucky man.'

'I am indeed.'

Regina was about to take Dalton's arm, but he lifted the dog and handed it to her instead.

Her cheeks were burning, and she veiled her disappointment. Instead, she braved a smile and told the older man, 'It was a pleasure to meet you, my lord.' Then, to avoid Dalton, she took the dog with her and departed.

* * *

Dalton followed Regina as she set the dog down upon the gravel pathway leading from the house. She kept up a swift pace, and the animal appeared eager for the exercise. He watched as she kept up with the dog and wondered if he was doing the right thing by giving her the space she wanted. Right now, she seemed eager to escape him.

He trudged through the grasses, wondering what the hell he was doing. He'd tried to rescue Regina, and she had gone along with it. Yet, he had no idea how to win her heart. He didn't really know *her* any more, and she didn't know him.

They were strangers, bound by a false marriage that could dissolve at any moment. All his life he had put Regina up on a pedestal, imagining a future with her…but what if the young woman he'd loved was a dream? Like his grandfather, he'd been building up his life around shadows and images, wanting to believe that he could make Regina love him in return. Yet, love couldn't be forced.

He was struggling to be patient, to give her the freedom she wanted. But he didn't know if that would diminish her fear of marriage. He also didn't know if she could learn to love him. He'd spent his entire life trying to please others after his brother's death. He'd tried to be the heir his parents had wanted. But no matter what he'd done, it was never enough. And he recognised how pathetic he had been, trying to reshape himself.

Dalton trailed her until she made it home safely before he turned away and strode towards the loch. He needed some time to himself, to decide what to do next. When he reached the shores of the loch, he stripped off his shirt and tossed it to the ground. He needed the punishing water against his skin. After the remainder of his clothing lay on the ground, he walked into the frigid water. He didn't care that it was cold, for it matched his mood. He dived beneath the surface, pulling his arms through the water. His muscles burned from the exertion, but he continued to swim.

He was a fool to think that a few days would make her see him in a new light. Regina had been right. They didn't know each other at all, and he had no idea how to win her heart or even if she wanted him to.

The cold water washed over him, clearing his thoughts. It was time to stop feeling sorry for himself. He was weary of behaving like a gentleman. What had that ever accomplished for him? Nothing at all. Instead, he decided that it was time to live his life as he chose, not according to the dictates of others.

And if that meant letting Regina go, so be it.

Chapter Eight

~~~~~~~~~~~~~~~~~~~~~~~~~~

Regina waited for several minutes, but Dalton never arrived at the house. When she returned to the front door, she saw him walking in the opposite direction. Where was he going? Though she knew she ought to wait, she decided to follow him instead.

The groom saddled a horse for her and she rode in the direction she had seen Dalton walking. There, a silvery-blue loch stretched across the meadow. She found him swimming with a furious pace, his arms churning through the water. And he was naked.

You need to leave, her conscience warned.

But she could not help being interested by the sight of his strong body cutting through the water. He was angry, and it was her fault.

Again, her inner voice cautioned her to go away. But something made her come closer instead.

Regina dismounted and walked towards the edge of the water, letting her horse graze. Dalton could not see her yet, but she chose a spot upon an outcropping of limestone. She climbed atop the rock and tucked her skirts around her while she watched him swim.

You shouldn't be here, her brain reminded her. *He wants to be alone.*

But a part of her didn't really care. Instead, she watched him, marvelling at his strength. He looked like a medieval Highlander of old, a warrior who would defend her against all enemies. And although he could easily subdue her, she had never been afraid of Dalton.

Despite her claim that they barely knew each other, it wasn't entirely true. She knew that she was safe with him, more than any other man. And something about that knowledge emboldened her.

At last, her husband caught sight of her, and he slowed his pace. He stopped swimming and stood in the water staring at her. From here, she could see his bare chest. Water gleamed upon his skin, and she followed a rivulet trickling down his ribs to his waist. Dalton pushed his wet hair back, and his expression hardened. 'Was there something you were wanting, Regina?'

She didn't know. Right now, she was unable to tear her gaze away from him. Earlier today, she had seen him as a man with great compassion. But now, she could not deny that she was attracted to him. His broad shoulders were wet, his skin warmed by the sun.

And when he took another step forward, more of his body was revealed to her. She saw the ridges of his abdomen and the edge of his hips.

'Unless you're wanting to see all of me, you had best turn away, lass.' The words were a warning, she knew, and yet Regina wanted to give in to her curiosity. She had never seen a naked man before. Much less one she was almost married to.

She locked away all the fears of her past, dwelling

only on the man in front of her. Her cheeks burned with shyness, but still, she did not close her eyes or turn away. She wanted to overcome her fears, and this was her opportunity.

Dalton didn't seem to care, and he walked slowly from the water, revealing his full naked body. The heat in her cheeks grew hotter, but she watched him. Never had she imagined what he would look like, but instead of frightening her, she found him fascinating. It made her wonder if she'd been wrong about her fears. With Dalton, she was starting to feel a physical attraction she had never expected.

Without apology, he reached down and picked up the length of tartan. He wrapped it around his waist and drew closer to her. 'Did you enjoy the view?'

She hardly knew how to answer that. Her mouth had gone dry, but she nodded. 'Yes, I did.'

With that, a slow smile slid across his face. 'Good.' Then he picked up the remainder of his clothes and started walking away.

It startled her that Dalton had left her alone. She had half-expected him to kiss her or make a demand of some kind. Instead, she felt fully aware of his presence.

Quickly, she scrambled down from the large rock, and retrieved her horse, holding the reins. By now, Dalton had pulled his shirt over his chest, but he still held the length of tartan wrapped around his waist.

'Are you angry with me for watching you?' she asked, after she'd caught up to him.

'No,' he answered. 'But you're making it difficult for me to leave you untouched.'

Regina walked her horse alongside him, feeling the

rise of guilt. He was right, that she was trespassing into a forbidden realm. 'I'm sorry.'

He moved closer and took the reins from her. 'Are you? Or are you starting to wonder what it would be like between us?'

His presence overshadowed her, though he didn't touch her at all. It was his voice that had grown seductive, making her skin tighten with interest. 'Were you wanting to touch me?' he murmured. 'Do you want that power, to know how I would respond to your hands upon my skin?'

Her breath seized up in her lungs, and his voice slid over her in an invisible caress. She was aching in secret places, wanting him to kiss her.

'Do you want me naked in your bed?' he said softly, moving his mouth to her ear. His warm breath gave her goose bumps, and her mind could not push the image away. She could envision him lying upon the bed, his green eyes burning into hers. And if she touched him, she wondered how it would feel.

His mouth brushed against her cheek in an invitation. 'All you have to do is open the door between our rooms, Regina. You can have whatever you want from me.'

He gave back the reins to her horse and strode away. She was deeply shaken, uncertain of the feelings coursing through her. It was desire and need. God help her, he had awakened a temptation she'd never imagined. Her heart was racing at the thought of putting her hands upon him or kissing him.

She wanted that. When had he transformed her fear into need? She could hardly bear it, and as he ascended the stairs, she gave the horse to a groom and hurried to catch up with him. Instead of waiting on her, he continued up the stairs. 'Will I see you later, Dalton?'

'Perhaps.' From his demeanour, he didn't seem to care. 'Do as you please, Regina. The house is yours.'

But after the door closed behind him, she felt a sense of restlessness. The truth was, she had enjoyed his company. And now she was beginning to realise that there was more to Dalton than she had known. There was a wildness to this man, an untamed Highlander who was more at home in his beloved Scotland then he had ever been in London. It was difficult to reconcile the two sides of the man. And strangely, she found that she was far more intrigued by the Highlander than the gentleman.

Regina desperately needed a distraction right now, or else she might follow him up the stairs. Instead, she decided to spend the rest of the afternoon exploring the estate. She walked through the drawing room and the earl's library, which was full of books. In the dining room, a large table seated twelve, and upon the walls, she saw various oil portraits. One was of the earl and his countess. Another painting was of his brother Brandon. She turned to look, but there was no portrait of Dalton. Strange. Yet, on one wall, there was a bare spot…as if a portrait had been removed.

After she had finished exploring the rooms on the main level, she decided to venture upstairs. Temptation warred within her as she imagined her husband in his rooms, waiting for her.

But she wasn't ready for that yet. She pushed back her feelings and crossed the hallway beyond their bedrooms. At the far end of the hall, she spied a room apart from the others. She knocked first, and then opened it. The room held a faint aroma of sandalwood. In one corner, a portrait was covered with a cloth. She lifted it gently and saw that it was Brandon again. This must have been his old room.

The bed curtains hung open, and the coverings were dusty, as if they had remained untouched over the years. Inside the wardrobe, she found neatly hung clothes. On the bottom of the wardrobe was a crumpled handkerchief. It was embroidered—and from the looks of it, she guessed it had belonged to the countess.

Strange to see the pieces of a man's life left behind. Clearly Dalton's family had tried to keep the memory of their eldest son alive. But what about her husband's needs? She felt a rise of protective instincts. Where was *his* portrait? Did they even care about him?

She was about to leave when a stack of letters on the desk caught her attention. The first was addressed to Dalton. Regina knew it wasn't right, but she couldn't stop herself from reaching for it.

Dear Brother,
I hope this letter finds you well. I am trapped in London while Father insists that I learn every-thing about being an earl.

I would much rather climb trees or go fishing with you. I envy the freedom you have. I would trade everything I have if I could be invisible like you.

Regina stopped reading, uncertain of what Brandon had meant by that. Dalton could never be invisible. He was bold and daring, a man filled with zest for life. Everything she wasn't.

She put the letter down, and suddenly, she realised that she didn't want to be that woman any more. She didn't want to be a wallflower, letting life pass her by because she was afraid. Nor did she want a loveless marriage with a man she cared about. He hadn't touched her, and he'd done everything she'd asked of him, giving her a marriage in name only.

But was that what she wanted now? Earlier, he had issued an invitation, giving her permission to open the door between their walls. What if she dared to reach for a very different sort of marriage?

Regina set down the letter, wondering how to even begin. All she knew was that she couldn't continue living this way. It was time to change.

Dalton was startled to hear a knock upon his bedroom door. Right now, he was feeling restless and frustrated. But before he could speak, the doorknob turned slightly. 'Dalton?' came Regina's voice. 'May I come in?'

For a moment, he was struck speechless. He'd never imagined she would actually visit him, though he had invited her to do so. Before he could say anything, she opened the door a little wider, and he saw that she was carrying the chess board. 'I thought we could play a game.'

'If you want,' he answered. He wasn't entirely in the mood to play chess just now, but she opened the door and came inside.

There was something different about her. He couldn't say exactly what it was, but she was already setting up the game pieces on a side table. 'White or black?' she asked him.

'Black,' he answered. Her hair, he decided. That's what was different. Instead of being pinned into a neat chignon, it was pulled back from her face and hanging freely around her shoulders.

'I have a confession to make,' she said, after she made her first move.

'And what is that?'

'I don't wish to be...that is...' She struggled for a moment, trying to choose the right words.

Married to me, he almost said, but didn't. Instead, he claimed her pawn and waited.

'I've lived my life obeying the rules. Doing what everyone wanted of me. And I realised today, that it's no life at all.' Her face was flushed as she contemplated her next move.

He wasn't entirely certain where she was going with this. Then she continued to speak, adding, 'I want to learn to break the rules.'

His hand paused upon his knight. 'I don't understand.' What rules was she talking about?

'I've been a good girl. A perfect lady, really. And now I want to change.'

'You want to be a bad girl?' In spite of himself, his mouth twitched with humour.

'Well, not exactly. It's just that, I would like to be more daring. Perhaps I should climb a tree or learn to swim.' She lowered her voice and added, 'Or I could wear trousers.'

Now he did smile. 'God forbid that you should wear trousers.' But he envisioned her body wearing form-fitting clothes, and he could imagine the curve of her backside straining at the seams.

Definitely trousers.

'I want to experience freedom,' she said softly. 'And I thought you could help me.'

He still wasn't entirely certain what she was wanting. But the idea was intriguing. The Laird of Locharr had learned how to be a gentleman from his governess, Miss Goodson. And now, it seemed that Regina wanted lessons on how *not* to be a lady.

He needed to clarify this. 'So you're wanting me to give you lessons on how to be more daring?'

'Yes. That's it, exactly. Will you help me?'

The idea held merit, but he still didn't believe her. 'Why would you want to change who you are, Regina?'

She hesitated and gave the chess board her full attention. 'Perhaps I want to change back into the girl I used to be. I don't like the person I am now.'

Her answer sobered him, for he didn't understand why. But he pressed further. 'Who do you want to be?'

'A woman of courage,' she answered. 'Someone brave.'

And then he understood. She was trying to overcome her fear, and he did want to help. Though she had never revealed what had happened to her, he would do everything in his power to make her feel safe again.

'All right,' he agreed. 'But if I help you, there is something I want in return.'

'I know what you are going to say—' she began, but he cut her off.

'No. You don't.' He leaned forward and moved his knight. 'I want you not to be afraid of me.' He wanted to court her openly, to spend his days with her and find ways to make her smile again.

Regina's expression turned thoughtful. 'I'm not afraid of you, Dalton. I'm afraid of myself.' She made another move and met his gaze. There was fear lingering through her words, though she tried not to show it. 'I have a confession to make. I saw your brother's room and I read one of his letters.'

He felt on edge, as if she had trespassed into other memories. Guilt flushed her face, but she continued. 'Why did your brother say that he wished he was invisible, like you? You are one of the boldest men I've ever met. You could never be invisible.'

Dalton didn't really know what to say, for he didn't understand it himself. He captured another pawn, wondering how to explain it. 'I was invisible to my family. They never liked my behaviour, and they found it best to ignore me. When I was a boy, I wanted attention, even if it meant being punished. I got into many scrapes, and sometimes I dragged Brandon into them with me.' He sobered at the memory. Though he knew his brother's death had resulted from illness, Dalton blamed himself. If one of them had to die, it should have been him.

'After my brother died, I tried to be more like Brandon,' he admitted. 'I tried to be the man my father wanted, but I was never enough. A few years later, I stopped trying to please them, and I just lived my life the way I wanted to.' It was all he could do, for he had come to accept that he would always be the outsider in his own family.

'I'm sorry,' she whispered. She took one of his pawns with her own, and her eyes held sympathy. 'Even if they don't see the man you are, I do.'

Her words warmed him, but he couldn't release the guilt. 'It's my fault he died, Regina. I was the reason he got sick.'

She shook her head. 'People get sick all the time, Dalton.'

'We went to visit Gabriel, and he had come down with scarlet fever. A few days later, Brandon and I were ill. I recovered; he didn't.'

She was staring at him, her face filled with sorrow. 'It's still not your fault.'

He stood from the chess board, unable to believe it. 'They would have been happier if Brandon had lived.' There was no denying that fact.

Then she startled him by reaching for his hand. Slowly, she drew it to her cheek, never taking her eyes from him. Her skin was cool and pale, but she held his hand to her face. 'Will you help me, Dalton?'

Her unexpected touch soothed him in ways words could not. 'With what?'

She met his gaze and admitted, 'I want to enjoy life more. To live and not be afraid. Will you teach me?'

Chapter Nine

Regina awakened at dawn and chose a blue riding habit from Lady Brevershire's belongings. She had decided to take another step towards ridding herself of the ever-present fear. It was time to go out riding alone and face that invisible monster.

Her maid, Nell, had arrived from London late yesterday evening, and the young girl helped her to dress. The riding habit was loose-fitting, but Regina added a belt to secure it. The thought of an early morning ride was invigorating. Today, she would begin her transformation. No longer would she be a wallflower, but instead, she intended to become a rebel.

'Would you like me to pin up your hair, my lady?' Nell asked.

Regina started to agree and then stared at herself in the looking glass. Was there any need to look like a lady? Who would care if she pinned up her hair or not? No one at all.

For the past few years, she had bound back her hair, as if it gave her a sense of control. She didn't want the vivid red colour to attract attention from men, and she'd done what she could to hide it. But now, she decided to weave it into a looser braid.

'No, I'll take care of it.'

Nell offered to help, but Regina did it herself and donned her hat. For a moment, she glanced at the adjoining door that led to Dalton's room.

A true rebel would go and awaken him. Perhaps invite him to join her. But it would be unwise to awaken a sleeping man. He might pull her into the bed with him. Her skin warmed at the thought of being beside him, his body close to hers. A ripple of interest flooded through her, and she could hardly believe she was imagining it. When had she begun to desire Dalton?

Perhaps it was because he had never forced her. Even their false marriage had been an invitation to escape, not an abduction. Even the few kisses they had shared had filled her with yearning.

Her mind was reeling at the knowledge that she was starting to consider the idea of truly marrying him. And that meant sharing his bed.

She closed her eyes, pushing the thought away. No, it was far too soon for that.

'Do you want me to come riding with you, Lady Regina?' Nell asked.

She did, but this wasn't about clinging to the past. It was about overcoming the shadows that haunted her—and this was her first small step.

'No, I'd rather go alone.' She needed time to think about what she wanted to do next. The idea of riding alone seemed both terrifying and wonderful.

'Are you certain? Not even a footman?'

'I'm only going to ride around the grounds. I doubt if anyone would attack me, so long as I remain at

Cairnross.' Upon one of the smaller tables, she spied a dirk within its sheath. 'But I will take this with me, in case anything happens.' Perhaps it was meant to be decorative, but as a precaution, Regina slipped it beneath her belt. If anyone was foolish enough to attack her, she could defend herself.

She tiptoed outside her bedroom door and down the stairs before she walked outside. When she reached the stables, she ordered the groom to saddle a horse for her.

'Will ye be wanting an escort, my lady?' he asked.

'No, thank you. My husband will join me in a little while,' she lied. The groom appeared uncertain, but once he'd helped Regina mount her mare, she urged the animal into a trot.

The morning sun had just risen above the horizon when Regina rode past the cottages and towards the open field. The grass was so green, she marvelled at the intense colour. She nudged the mare into a canter, revelling in the vast freedom. Here, no one could give her orders about what to do or how to behave. She could be as unladylike as she wanted. No one would care.

Regina followed the edge of a copse of trees. In the distance, a loch gleamed in the morning light, threading its way among the birches. The sun was warm on her face, and she smiled as the wind blew her hair back. For a few moments, she breathed in the crisp early summer air, feeling bold, for there was no one here to threaten her.

In many ways, she wished she could have come to Scotland sooner. Instead of being the fearful, shy wallflower, she could embrace the true parts of herself. She decided that she liked being defiant and breaking the rules.

* * *

She explored the estate for nearly an hour before she heard hooves approaching. It was Dalton, and she guessed that Nell or one of the servants had alerted him. Regina waited for a moment, and then realised a true rebel wouldn't remain in place, waiting. If he wanted to join her, he would have to catch her first.

She urged the mare faster, into a hard gallop. The green grasses turned into a blur as she rode across the fields, alongside the loch. She didn't know where she was going or what she intended to do when Dalton caught up to her. For now, it was enough to seize her freedom, and it filled her with joy.

Regina relished the feeling of the wind tearing her braid free. When she glanced behind, he was gaining on her. She saw a low hedge coming close, and she leaned into the animal, preparing to jump. The mare obeyed, and for a moment, Regina felt as if she were flying. The horse was breathing hard with exertion, and she slowed the mare's pace, guiding her towards the trees.

Dalton's stallion took the hedge, sailing across it. Regina drew her horse into a trot, and finally to a walk. She noticed that he was wearing a kilt and a length of tartan, along with a bonnet and a white shirt. His expression held a dark tension, and after he got off his horse, he strode forward as if he were a Scottish warrior in full pursuit. Would he pick her up and carry her off? The thought filled her with a sudden flare of interest.

Regina dismounted and tethered her mare to a nearby tree, stretching from the ride. It had been wonderful to feel so bold and wild. Her hair had come loose from the braid, and she untied the ribbon, letting it fall free.

'Why didn't you wake me?' Dalton demanded, drawing close to her. 'You shouldn't have gone riding alone.' Worry creased his face, and it struck her to realise that he cared about her.

'I wanted a few moments to myself,' she responded. 'And I knew your clan members would never attack their lady. It seemed safe enough.'

'You should have taken an escort. It's never safe for a lady to be alone.'

She knew that well enough. But this was about having the courage to overcome her fears. For five years, she had cowered in the shadows, obeying her father blindly, and forgetting what it was like to make her own decisions. It was now time to break free of those chains and find her courage once more.

'I'm glad you followed me,' she admitted. The words were a bit reckless, and she walked towards the edge of the loch to stare out at the tranquil waters.

But Dalton wasn't going to let this go. 'What if a stranger had accosted you?' he asked softly. 'What would you have done?'

She tapped the dirk at her waist. 'I would have skewered him like a pig.'

He drew closer. Before she could say a word, he had caught her around the waist and tossed the weapon away. 'Now what would you do?' His voice was fierce and demanding. For a moment, she lost her breath, for he appeared as if he intended to kiss her. The strength of his embrace made her aware of his muscled arms and the raw masculinity of this man.

Though she knew he was trying to prove his point,

she was entirely distracted by wanting to feel his mouth on hers. Her body was pressed so close to his, she could feel his desire. But he didn't press her for more. If she wanted his kiss, she would have to claim it herself.

Her heart pounded, and she stood on tiptoe. 'I would do this,' she murmured. With that, she touched her lips to his and kissed him.

The kiss seemed to set her body on fire. She was aching as he feasted upon her, his mouth hot and demanding. Past and present collided as she tried not to let the old fears haunt her. But the longer he kissed her, the more unsteady she felt. She was starting to lose control of herself, and she needed to pull away.

But when she twisted herself free, the sudden movement made her lose her balance. Her footing slipped, and she clung to Dalton. He tried to hold them, but it was too late. With an enormous splash, he fell into the loch—and he took her down with him. The icy water made her yelp, and she struggled to get out. Her riding habit was soaked, as was her hair and hat.

'It's freezing!' she said, grasping at her heavy skirts to try and get out of the shallow water. 'I'm so sorry.'

'Aye, it's verra cold.' He caught her in his arms. 'You could have picked a better day to swim.'

She was trembling so hard, she could barely speak. 'Not today.' Her teeth chattered, and she struggled to wade out of the water. Dalton helped her out, but she felt foolish for making them both fall in. He tried to help her wring the water from her soaked riding habit, but there was nothing to be done about it.

'I suppose that's one way to defend yourself from a man,' he teased. 'That is, if you were wanting to get away. Though you do look rather fetching with your hair soaked.'

'I'm really sorry,' she repeated.

'Sorry you threw me in the loch or sorry for kissing me?' His voice had gone low, and the resonant tone reminded her of a caress.

'I'm not sorry I kissed you,' she answered.

His face transformed, revealing a desire that mirrored hers. 'Neither am I. I wouldn't be sorry if it happened again.' He reached out to take her hand in his. Though his palm was cold, she felt the invisible ties binding them together. He led her back to the horse, and she stopped a moment.

'I think I should walk back to the house. It's unfair to make the poor animal carry me when I'm so wet.'

'You don't have to go so far,' he responded. 'I know a place nearby where we can get dry.' She glanced around but could see nothing. Dalton nodded towards the trees. 'Come with me.'

They continued walking alongside the loch for half a mile, and at last she saw a tiny thatched house in the distance. The wind was freezing against her wet clothes, and she was grateful for any shelter at all. Even so, she asked, 'Are you certain about this? I don't want to intrude upon anyone.'

'The house is mine,' he said. 'I built it when I was younger.'

'You built it?' She had no idea he knew how to construct a dwelling. He was an earl's son, not a commoner. 'I don't understand.'

'I spent a lot of time on my own after Brandon died,' he admitted. 'I wanted a place where I could retreat. Some of the crofters helped me to build it. It's not much, but I can make a fire for us. You can dry your clothes before we go back.'

She imagined a lonely young man, spending hours apart from his family. The cabin stood in a beautiful place, and the loch appeared green in the afternoon sunlight as the water played against the stones. It was peaceful here, but her heart ached for the boy no one had noticed.

Dalton opened the door and held it out for her to enter. The interior was dark, except for one window which was covered by an oil cloth. It smelled musty, as if no one had been here in years. There were hardly any furnishings at all, except for a bed and a single chair. When Regina approached the hearth, she saw a mantel above it. There were polished stones, a few seashells, and a silver necklace that had once belonged to her. She had lost it years ago, never knowing what had happened to it. It was a simple silver chain with an amethyst pendant, hardly worth anything. But why did Dalton have it? 'Where did you get this?'

'I found it the day you came to see me—the day my brother was buried. You lost it, and I kept it for you. I had always intended to give it back, but I forgot to bring it from Scotland.'

He reached for the necklace now, and unfastened it, hanging it around her neck. The silver chain warmed against her skin, and the pendant nestled above her breasts. His hands lingered a moment upon her shoulders, but he said nothing. Then he turned away to build a fire. He stacked peat bricks in the hearth, tucking tinder around it. Regina watched him strike the tinder, and when the flames caught, she moved closer to warm herself.

Dalton studied her a moment. 'I'm going to remove some of my wet clothes to dry them,' he said. 'I won't harm you.' He unbuckled his belt and set it on the floor. Then he removed the length of tartan and turned his back on her. His kilt was next to go, and she realised that his shirt was long enough to hang down to his thighs. Then he returned to the hearth. She didn't know what to think right now, and her mouth had gone dry. Despite the warmth of the fire, her skin rose up with goose bumps.

'Your turn,' he said. 'If you'll allow me.'

He won't make demands, she reminded herself.

Even so, she was afraid to let down her guard. For so long, she had guarded herself, keeping a tight control over every aspect of her life. But now, Dalton was offering her the choice.

Silently, she unfastened the belt and set it on the table. Then she turned her back and murmured, 'Will you help me with this gown?'

Regina felt his hands upon the laces, and it took him a moment to untie them. Slowly, he helped her lift the gown away. Now she stood before him, wearing only her undergarments. She felt exposed, completely vulnerable to him. His green eyes fixed upon her, and he asked, 'What else would you like me to remove?'

The old Regina would have said nothing. She would have returned to the house, shutting herself in her room and drying her clothes by the fire alone. Not any more.

Her hands were shaking, but Regina turned her back to him once more. 'Will you help me loosen my corset?'

Again, she felt his hands upon her. Slowly, he untied the laces. He took his time, removing one lace, then another. It was almost seductive, the way he loosened her stays. And yet, she was terrified to expose herself to him. But she lifted her arms, allowing him to remove the corset until she stood only in her chemise and petticoats.

The fine linen was soaked against her skin, and she saw the dark look of desire in his eyes. She knew that the wet clothing hid nothing from his gaze, and she covered herself with one arm.

'Don't be afraid of me, Regina,' he said huskily. 'You are in complete command.'

She didn't know whether to believe that. At the moment, her husband looked as if he wanted to remove every last inch of fabric covering her body. Clad only in his shirt, he turned to the fire with his hands outstretched.

'Do you want to be more daring,' he asked, 'or should I leave you alone?'

Regina remained silent, which was the answer he'd expected. And he understood that. But he had glimpsed her naked body beneath the thin wet fabric, and the hunger it had aroused was beyond anything he'd ever felt before. He wanted to pleasure this woman, to watch her come apart in his arms. He wanted her to arch her back, digging her fingers into the coverlet while her release made her tremble.

But he already knew it would not be today.

He suspected Regina had been raped or attacked in some way. Her father had helped her cover it up, and that was why they were being blackmailed. If the wealthiest heiress in London had been ruined, no one would want her any more.

But after the scandal he and Regina had caused with their false marriage, it hardly mattered now. Even if the past was revealed, he could protect her with his family name—that is, if he could convince her to wed him legally.

Dalton walked to a small trunk on the other side of the room and withdrew a wool blanket. He brought it to Regina and laid it across her shoulders. 'Here,' he offered. 'This should help you.'

She drew the blanket around her. 'Dalton, I haven't been very kind to you. You've done so much for me. But I *am* grateful. I want you to know that.'

He was startled when she touched her hand to his chest. For a moment, her palm rested upon his heartbeat, and he savoured the simple touch.

'I suppose I should have asked you to help me climb a tree,' she said ruefully. 'At least we wouldn't have been soaked.' She thought a moment and then added, 'Or perhaps I shouldn't have stopped kissing you.'

Her words washed over him with a silent promise. The edges of the blanket did nothing to hide the delicate lines of her body, the dip of her slender waist, and the full breasts revealed by the wet chemise. He wanted to tear away the fabric and kiss every inch of her skin, tormenting her as she tormented him now.

'As I said before, you are in command.' Dalton faced her, and he wanted her to know that he would remain patient, even if it killed him. She reminded him of a wild animal, too frightened to come close. Seeing her fear sobered him, and Dalton took a step away, hoping she would be soothed by it. 'I would never ask for more than you can give.'

Her tension did seem to ease, and she pulled the

edges of the blanket closed. For a short time, neither said anything. He knew she was trying to decide what to do now.

'I enjoyed meeting your grandfather yesterday,' she said, changing the subject. 'He is a dear man.'

His grandfather had been the one family member he'd been close to, after all these years. 'Thank you for indulging him in his fantasies,' he said to Regina. 'He has lost most of his recent memories. I've asked his housekeeper to let him be, and we have found that he is happier. I come to see him when I can.'

'Sometimes dreams are more pleasant than the truth,' she answered. 'I liked his dream.'

'He liked you, as well,' Dalton said. 'But he'll have no memory of it in the morning.'

'He might not,' she agreed, 'but he will remember the kindness. Feelings last longer than words.'

He recognised the truth of that. His feelings for her had lasted for years. But both of them had grown up and changed. He had put her on a pedestal, an ideal woman he'd adored. And yet, there were so many secrets she held. He wanted to know her better, but she was unwilling to talk about what had happened before.

If they were ever to have a true marriage, he needed to break down the barrier between them and gain her trust. And perhaps that meant indulging her desire to be rebellious.

'What other daring things were you wanting to do?' he asked. 'Climb a tree? Learn to swim? Or was there something else even more daring?'

'I think I've had enough swimming for today,' she remarked, lifting her sodden petticoat.

Her clothing was so wet, it clung to her skin. At

this rate, they would be here for hours—which didn't bother him at all. Still, he would rather be with a half-naked woman when he was warm and not wearing wet clothing.

'It will take some time for our clothes to dry,' he remarked. He eyed her for a moment, and then decided to dry off more thoroughly. If she wanted to engage in daring behaviour, so be it.

He turned towards the fire and stripped off the remainder of his clothing, save his drawers.

'Dalton what are you doing?' she asked. He could hear the uncertainty in her tone.

'Getting dry,' he answered. 'It won't take so very long now. You ought to consider doing the same.'

'You would like that, wouldn't you?'

He laughed wickedly. 'You *do* have a blanket. There's no reason you couldn't lay your corset and chemise out to dry before the fire.'

'Or we could walk back to the house and put on dry clothes,' she reminded him. 'It would be much faster.'

'What would the servants say when they see us in such a state?'

'They wouldn't care,' she answered. 'After all, they believe we are married.'

'But we're not, are we?' His voice grew lower, more seductive. 'It's terrible scandal, what we're doing now.'

'You're the one being scandalous,' she accused.

'Am I? I thought you were the one who wanted to be bolder, not so afraid.' He stared at her, and her gaze drifted over his bare chest, lingering below his waist. His body grew erect at her stare, and he imagined peeling back the fabric, kissing her cold flesh until her nipples rose up in arousal. 'Are you afraid of me?'

'No,' she whispered.

'Liar.' He moved in closer, reaching for the edges of her blanket. 'I can see you trembling.' Her blue eyes held an intensity as she met his gaze. Her red hair was dark from the water, tangled against her shoulders. 'What are you afraid of?'

'I'm afraid of the way I feel when I look at you,' she murmured. 'And how I feel when you kiss me.' Her words were a spark, setting him on fire. He wanted to pull her into his arms, to kiss her until she could no longer bear it.

'I want to take away your fear of being touched,' he answered. 'Will you allow it?'

'I don't think you can.'

He half-expected her to pull away, but she didn't. Instead, he took her hand and brought it to his chest. Her hand was still shaking, but she rested her fingertips upon his heart. His pulse was racing, but he didn't move.

'You may touch me if you want,' he said quietly. Her eyes widened slightly, but she gently stroked his chest. Then she moved her hand to his shoulder, tracing the muscles. Her touch was taking him apart, and he loved every moment of it.

If he didn't stop her, he was going to lose control of himself. Then he captured her palm and brought it to his mouth. 'It's your choice, Regina. Come to my room tonight, and I will only show you pleasure.'

Chapter Ten

It was late when Dalton heard his bedchamber door opening softly. He sat up in bed and saw Regina entering, a brass candle holder in her hand. She wore a white dressing gown, and her auburn hair spilled over her shoulders. In the dim light of the candle, her face appeared pale.

Though he had invited her here, she still seemed nervous. 'Are you all right, Regina?' he enquired. 'Do you need anything?'

For a long moment, she did not answer. Her nerves were palpable, but he did not press her for more. Instead, she blew out the candle and set it upon a nearby table. He felt her slight weight as she sat upon the mattress.

'I came to talk to you,' she murmured. 'And I wanted no one to overhear what I have to say.' She pulled the coverlet over her as if it were a shield. In the darkness, he could hear the swift tempo of her breathing.

Dalton turned to his side, resting his head upon his hand. The soft rose scent of her body revealed the soap she had used in her bath. He longed to pull her into his arms, to press his mouth against her nape and feel her backside nestled against him. But that would only terrify her, for he was naked beneath the sheets.

'I am listening,' he said. She had come to him of her own free will, and he intended to offer whatever she needed.

'I need to tell you what happened to me,' she whispered. 'Why I am afraid to be touched.' Her voice held fear, and he remained still, knowing what this cost her. Though he suspected what she was about to say, he would be careful not to frighten her more.

His hand curled over hers, offering silent reassurance. She took his palm and squeezed it, though she kept her face turned from him.

'I never intended to tell you,' she began. 'But I feel that I should. I know you are wondering why my father was being blackmailed, and I am trusting you to keep this secret.'

He stroked the edge of her palm with his thumb. 'I will never speak of it to anyone. You have my word.'

She took a deep breath, as if gathering her courage. 'Almost five years ago, when I made my debut, there was a baron who was kind to me. Lord Mallencourt was his name.' Her words held a slight tremor, and she gripped his hand tighter.

Dalton didn't recognise the name, but he could feel the tension emanating from Regina. She paused a moment and then continued. 'He flirted with me and made me feel as if he adored me above all others. I was only eighteen, and I believed every word he said.'

He knew the sort of man she was describing—an arrogant rake who believed he was entitled to a woman's affections. Regina let go of his hand suddenly, curling away from him. 'One night, my mother and I were at a ball. My father was returning home that night from his travels, so he was not with us. I danced with Lord Mallencourt, and afterwards, he asked me for my hand in marriage. I was impulsive and agreed to wed him. He wanted to speak to Papa right away, even though it was late.'

'This was before your father intended a betrothal between you and Locharr?' Dalton clarified. He wasn't certain when the laird and Regina's father had made their arrangement.

'It was, yes. Our fathers were friends, but they had not yet finalised a match between us.' She took a breath to steady herself. 'I believed I was in love with Lord Mallencourt, and I was overjoyed by the prospect of marriage. He was an impulsive man, and he wanted to ask Papa for my hand that very night. I agreed and told Mother that I had a headache and was leaving. Lord Mallencourt drove me home in his carriage, and he stole kisses along the way. I was wanton in my behaviour, and I kissed him back.'

She gripped his hand harder, drawing his arm around her as if to shield herself. Dalton pressed a kiss against her shoulder. 'You don't have to say any more, if you are afraid.'

She was silent for a long pause. Then she said, 'I don't want to say it. But you need to understand why I am so afraid.'

His mood tightened, for he wasn't about to give up on her. But more, he held the need for vengeance on behalf of her honour. He wanted to hold her, to comfort her. But he knew if he dared to touch her now, it would only cause her to shrink away.

Regina's voice broke in a sob, and she admitted, 'He took me home, but Papa had not yet arrived. Lord Mallencourt insisted on waiting, though it was entirely too late at night for him to be there. Our footman, Frederick, was not pleased and warned me about a scandal—especially when Lord Mallencourt waited in the parlour alone with me.'

'Why did your footman not stay with you?' Dalton asked.

'Because I ordered him to go. I was stupid and naive, wanting to be alone with the man I thought I loved.' Her voice grew shaky, as if she were afraid to say more. And though he ought to reassure her that she did not have to tell the tale, he wanted to hear the rest.

'After Frederick left, the baron kissed me. But it was not like his other kisses—these were rough, and I didn't like them. He swore that he was eager to wed me, and that I should lie with him so my father could not deny his suit. When I protested and tried to push him away, he shoved a handkerchief in my mouth so I could not scream. He locked me inside with him.' She began crying, and this time, Dalton touched her shoulder. He offered his support while she wept, and inwardly, he wished to God that he could kill the man.

'He pressed me against the wall and tore my gown,' she continued. 'I tried to scream, but the handkerchief muffled the sound when I tried. And when he reached beneath my gown and pushed his fingers inside me, I knew he wasn't going to stop when I asked him to. I fought him hard.'

She wept, her shoulders shaking as she cried in his arms. 'I have never been so frightened in my life. But then Papa came and broke down the door. Frederick had gone for help, even though I'd sent him away.' Her voice broke off amid her tears.

'Your father stopped Mallencourt, didn't he?'

She nodded her head. 'I am still a virgin, Dalton. He did not rape me, though he tried.' Her voice held a tremor, and she added, 'But I think someone saw something that night. The blackmail began only a week later. I didn't know until recently, but Papa received help from Lachlan's father. I think my marriage was part of his arrangement to pay Locharr back.'

Now he was beginning to understand. 'Did Lachlan know of this?'

'No. I never told him or anyone else. Not even Mother knows of the attack.'

He was quiet for a time, and then adjusted the sheets around himself. 'Regina, may I hold you?'

She was still crying, but she turned to face him. He brought her into his embrace, tucking her face against his chest, though he was careful not to let their lower bodies touch. 'It's all right,' he said softly. 'It wasn't your fault.'

'But it was,' she insisted. 'If I hadn't brought him back to the house…if I hadn't let him inside or sent the footman away—'

'It's not your fault,' he repeated. She had been through hell, and he didn't want her to blame herself. He stroked her hair back, touching his forehead to hers.

She was silent, breathing slowly. But there was more he needed to know. 'What happened to Mallencourt?' he asked. 'He deserves a bullet in his heart for what he did to you.'

After another long pause, she said, 'Papa made certain he would never hurt me or anyone else again.'

'Good.' But he could feel her tension heightening, despite her confession.

'Dalton…there's more. I don't want to hide this from you,' she continued. 'But no one has seen Mallencourt since that night,' she continued. 'Not even his family.'

And with that, he was starting to realise what she meant. 'Is he dead?'

'Yes,' she whispered.

Dalton couldn't fault the earl, if he had killed Mallencourt. He would have done the same. Any man who tried to attack a woman deserved what he got. But it explained the reason for the blackmail. It might have been their footman, Frederick—or more likely a relative of Mallencourt, seeking revenge. He didn't know, but he hoped the Bow Street Runner would send answers soon.

'Dalton, do you—do you understand why I never wanted to marry? And why I'm not able to be a true wife to you yet?' she whispered. 'The memories are too harsh.'

He turned her to face him, cupping her cheek gently. 'I understand why you were afraid. And I am glad your father stopped him.' More than that, it gave him hope that one day he might gain her full trust.

'Thank you for telling me of this, Regina,' he said against her cheek. He kissed her gently and was reassured when she kissed him back.

'I am still ashamed of what happened,' she admitted with a sigh.

'Don't be. The fault lay with Mallencourt, not you.' He touched his hand to her cheek, wiping the tears away.

'Is it all right if I sleep beside you tonight?' she whispered.

God, yes. It would torment him in an unholy way, but it was the first step towards a real marriage. 'Of course. But you should know that I am wearing nothing, Regina.'

It was one matter for her to sleep in a separate room. It was quite another to feel her warmth against him. He could easily imagine lifting her nightdress to her waist, caressing her bare hip and touching her intimately. But it was far too soon for that. Instead, he placed a pillow between them so she would not feel threatened.

'I know you won't hurt me,' she said.

'Never,' he swore.

She let out a sigh and snuggled with her backside against the pillow between them. His body was already aroused at her proximity, but he grew rock hard when she pulled his arms around her. Against his forearms, he could feel the soft curve of her breasts, and his desire only deepened. He pulled the coverlet over her, keeping his hands relaxed.

She remained facing away from him, though his feet tangled with hers. Her skin was cold, and he warmed her with his thighs against her legs. At first, she remained ramrod stiff, her fingers clutching the coverlet. But when he didn't move, he gradually felt her beginning to relax. Her shoulders lowered, and eventually, her breathing grew more even until she fell asleep.

Dalton remained awake, as if keeping vigil over his wife. She had put such faith in him, he felt the intrinsic need to protect her. The confession she had spoken had utterly drained her, but he was grateful that she had finally trusted him with the truth.

He kept his arms around her, but despite having her so close, a voice inside warned that this was not over yet. The Bow Street Runner might uncover more than Dalton wanted him to—and above all, he had to keep Regina safe.

Regina awakened just before dawn, tangled up in her husband's embrace. The pillow was now on the floor, and his leg rested over her hip. She grew aware of his hard length against her spine. It should have terrified her, but she realised that he was still sleeping, and it was a natural reaction to her body.

Guilt weighed down on her. He believed she had told him everything about the night of her attack— that the blackmail was because she had been attacked by a man in her father's house. She closed her eyes, wishing that was all.

You need to tell him, her conscience warned.

But right now, it felt good to be in his arms, to feel beloved. If she told him the rest of it, everything would change.

Her cheeks burned with the lies of omission. Did he truly need to know? His Bow Street Runner could still continue the investigation and learn the identity of her father's blackmailer. Was that not enough?

She wasn't certain about anything any more.

God above, she prayed that no one ever learned the truth. Although most people believed that Mallencourt had been drunk that night and had fallen into the Thames and drowned, she didn't know what had stopped any further investigations. Possibly her father had bribed the police. She had never asked, for she didn't want to know. But the fear consumed her, that somehow, someone had witnessed Mallencourt's arrival at her house and subsequent death.

She wanted to believe that it was over, that she was away from the danger. And yet, she couldn't be sure.

Dalton had saved her from public humiliation at her own wedding, and he was so much more than she had known. She wanted to be a true wife to him, but she didn't know if she could bury her past.

The warmth of his body comforted her, despite the evidence of his arousal. And the more she thought about his touch, a soft deepening of awareness slid over her skin. She wanted to feel his caress, to forget about the past.

It was a bold wickedness, for they were not truly married. She had put him off the wedding, not wanting to entangle him in the mess of her life. But now, she was beginning to believe she had been wrong about Dalton.

He left no doubt that he wanted her. But his endless patience made her wonder if she ought to reconsider. She no longer wanted to live in fear, and didn't that mean facing her worst fear of all?

In the darkness, she could feel the warmth of his body against hers. Dalton's hand was at her waist, and she wondered what it would feel like to have his palm upon her bare breast.

It was a risk, for Mallencourt had squeezed her breast roughly as he had shoved her against the wall. There had only been force when he had touched her, and she wondered what it would be like to have Dalton's hands upon her skin. Perhaps it was a way to eradicate the old memory and replace it with a better one. The very thought sent a sudden thrill within her.

She reached for the first button on her nightdress, flicking it free. Then another. As she exposed herself, her heartbeat quickened. This was a test to see if she could bear his touch.

Slowly, she brought Dalton's hand to her bare breast. The warmth and weight of his hand felt good, even as she wondered what she was doing. For a time, his hand merely rested upon her skin, and she was grateful for it.

Then he moved his fingertips against her and murmured, 'Will you let me touch you, Regina?'

She closed her eyes, feeling the blush upon her cheeks. 'Yes,' she whispered. She had wanted to awaken him, but now, she didn't know if this had gone too far. His thumb gently stroked her nipple, and it rose up from his attention. Deep between her legs, she felt a rush of sensation, as if he were caressing her there.

Slowly, with exquisite patience, he drew his fingers over her breast, encouraging the swollen bud. She gasped at the sensation, a restless feeling rising within her.

'May I kiss you?' he asked.

She turned her face to his, but instead of him capturing her lips, he lowered his mouth to her bare breast. The heat and gentle suction against her sensitive nipple made her grip his hair, arching in shock. A cry of her own arousal escaped her lips as he kissed her breast.

It was nothing like the night of her attack. Dalton worshipped her body, reverently swirling his tongue around her nipple. She grew wet between her legs, not understanding how he could make her feel so good. The incredible feelings rose and ebbed like a tide, and she needed more. Fumbling with the buttons, she tried to reveal more of herself, but he captured her wrists and pressed them back gently.

'Allow me.' His voice was husky, and he released her hands, waiting for permission.

'All right.' She closed her eyes, surrendering to his will. But he was gentle as he eased her nightdress from her shoulders, lowering it to her waist.

'You are in command of me, Regina,' he murmured. 'If you don't like any of this, tell me, and I will stop.'

She believed him. But she wanted him to know that she was willing to take the first steps towards reclaiming a normal life as his bride. 'I'll try not to be afraid,' she promised. 'Just…continue to go slowly.'

'You have my word,' he swore. Then he touched her other breast, fondling it as he had the first. She savoured the sensation, and he began to circle her nipple in a rhythm. He lowered his mouth to the second breast, while tracing the wet skin of her first.

Her breathing shuddered, and she wanted more from him—but she couldn't understand what it was. He was driving her to the edge of a precipice, but she wasn't ready to make love to him yet. Instead, he was evoking such a strong arousal, she didn't know what to do.

'Give me your hand,' he ordered, and she did.

Slowly, he reached down and lifted the hem of her nightdress. His hand trailed against her calves, past her knees, to her thighs. And against her will, she began to tremble.

'Relax,' he bade her. 'This will feel good.'

She tensed as he took her hand, holding it. Again, he kissed her nipple, suckling gently until the intense feelings made her breathing shift into soft moans.

Then he took her hand and brought it to the place between her legs where she was wet. His hand remained atop hers, and he drew his mouth to her ear. He suckled at the lobe, and a jolt made her shiver.

'Touch yourself here while I kiss you,' he ordered. 'I want to drive away every memory of him. I don't want you imagining his hands there any more.'

Her shock turned to embarrassment, for she had not ever considered this. But the pressure of his hand against her intimate juncture was so tempting, she hesitated.

'I don't know how,' she apologised.

With that, he held her hand again, guiding it in slow circles. Her fingertips brushed against a nodule of flesh that brought a spear of pleasure deep inside. 'Like this,' he said. 'I'm going to touch your breasts, but I want you to touch yourself wherever you want. If it feels good to you, do it more.'

He eased her thighs apart and guided her hand to the wetness between her legs. Then he lay on his side so she could no longer feel the ridge of his erection. Instead, he kissed one breast while he fingered the second. He laved at her nipple in a slow, deep rhythm, and she decided to mimic it.

Never before had she touched herself. Mallencourt's groping had made her feel dirty, and she hadn't wanted to. But with Dalton, she understood that this was about reclaiming her own power. She experimented with one fingertip, circling the hooded nodule. It felt even better when she moved it back and forth, and an almost savage wave of arousal flooded over her. She inhaled sharply, biting back a moan.

'That's it,' Dalton encouraged her. He switched to kiss the opposite breast, and his thumb rubbed her first nipple. She felt the wetness coating her fingers, and she felt the core of her body reaching and straining for more.

'I don't know—I can't—' Words failed her, for she didn't understand what was happening.

'Don't speak,' he said. 'Just keep touching yourself. Know that I want you to experience only pleasure. Keep going, Regina. I need to see you come apart for me.'

She had no idea what he meant by that, but he put his hand atop hers. 'It's all right.'

He guided her fingertips to her opening, and she gasped at the sensation as she continued to explore herself. She wasn't certain what to do, but Dalton encouraged her. 'Put your finger inside yourself. Then move it in and out.'

She slid her middle finger into her opening, and the unexpected pleasure brought tears to her eyes. He rested the heel of his palm against her hooded flesh, and the gentle pressure felt so good, she could hardly bear it. With every stroke, she felt herself rising. Reclaiming herself.

Her breathing came in gasps, and she quickened her pace. Dalton answered it by teasing her sensitive nodule with his thumb while he stroked her nipple with his tongue.

'Put another finger inside,' he ordered.

She did, and her body ached at the sweet torment of the thick pressure. The sensations came together, and when Dalton caressed her, she sobbed as a tremor took her. She was afraid of what was happening, and she stopped moving her fingers, keeping them buried inside.

It didn't matter. The feeling of his tongue and the

sweet sensation of his fingers forced her over the edge. An almost violent wave of pleasure claimed her, a shimmering release that spread from between her legs down to her toes and up through her breasts. She arched her back, and Dalton rewarded her by suckling harder. She couldn't stop herself from shaking, and he captured her mouth then, kissing her hard as she came apart in his arms.

It was shattering to feel such pleasure, and she rode the crest of the wave until her body convulsed. She could not help but cling to him, not even caring that she could feel his hard body against hers.

He would never hurt her. And tears spilled from her eyes when she realised that it might truly be possible to enjoy a real marriage with this man.

Travis Sidney stared at the note unfolded before him. He had been working on behalf of Lord Camford for weeks now, tracking down the identity of Lady Regina's blackmailer. But now, new evidence had surfaced. He let out a sigh and pushed the paper aside.

'This complicates matters,' he told the magistrate. 'It seems that a great deal was covered up in the death of Mallencourt.'

'The law must prevail above all,' the magistrate replied. 'It is not for us to decide when to follow it.'

Travis knew that, and yet, he had to consider the anonymous blackmailer who had written to him. She claimed she had been there on the night Mallencourt had died. Her testimony upended everything he had been hired to do.

This was no longer a case of blackmail, but instead, a case of manslaughter. Namely, that of Baron Mallencourt, five years ago. Lord Mallencourt's family had mistakenly believed that he had drowned in the Thames after a night of drinking.

But now, this blackmailer claimed that Mallencourt's body had been deposited in the Thomas after he was already dead.

Travis didn't know what he should do now. Yet, the magistrate was right. Above all else, justice should be served. 'I'll leave now,' he told the magistrate. 'Camford needs to know about this.'

But he knew the viscount wouldn't like it at all. Not with the new threat it posed.

'My lord, Gabriel MacKinnon is here to see you. And he has…someone with him.' The butler appeared uneasy by the announcement, but Dalton rose from his desk and followed MacLachor. As they entered the hallway, he saw his wife returning from the garden with a basket filled with roses. Regina smiled warmly at him, and the sight of her brought an aching joy within him. Last night had given him hope that there could be so much more between them.

'Just a moment,' he told the butler. He crossed the hallway and stole a kiss from his wife. Her cheeks blushed, but she did not look displeased.

'I thought the house could use some flowers.'

'I agree.' He imagined laying her atop a bed of rose petals, the scent mingling with her skin.

MacLachor cleared his throat. 'My lord, this is a matter of some urgency. If you'll just follow me.'

'What is it?' Regina asked.

'Gabriel is here,' Dalton answered. 'With a guest, I'm told. You may come with me, if you wish.'

He saw no harm in it, though MacLachor seemed to disagree and was already shaking his head. 'My lord, I do not think that would be wise.'

Dalton took the basket from her and set it down, taking her hand in his. 'It will be fine.' He led Regina towards the parlour, ignoring MacLachor's discomfort.

But when he opened the door and saw Lord Havershire bound like a prisoner, he understood the butler's reasoning.

Regina gasped and went to the earl. 'Father, what has happened?'

The earl's clothing was ragged, and Dalton recognised it as the attire Havershire had worn to the wedding. His face was dirty, and blood stained the front of his shirt. He turned his face away from his daughter and coughed heavily into his sleeve.

Gabriel met Dalton's gaze. 'Havershire tried to kill Frances Goodson,' he informed them, 'and nearly succeeded.'

'Dear God.' Regina dropped to her knees before her father. 'Papa, why would you do this?'

The earl didn't answer, but MacKinnon said, 'He thought if Frances were dead, then the laird would marry you.'

An act of desperation, Dalton realised. One bordering on madness.

'Papa,' she pleaded. 'I was never going to marry the laird.' But the older man did not react to her words. His face was stony, as if he were lost in thought. Regina turned stricken. 'Why would you do this?'

But the earl remained silent. Dalton suspected that the man was unable to explain anything. And in truth, Havershire was lucky to be alive. If any man tried to kill Regina, Dalton wouldn't hesitate to protect her. The laird had shown mercy by letting Havershire live, and no doubt, it was for Regina's sake.

Dalton exchanged a look with his friend, not knowing what would happen now. Gabriel let out a dark sigh. 'Frances is fighting for her life, and Lachlan bade me to take the earl to London. He promised not to press charges, as long as he never sees Havershire again.'

'That can be arranged,' Dalton answered. 'But leave him here, with us. Do not take him to London.' In the earl's state of unrest, he could not be trusted.

Gabriel hesitated, and then nodded. 'I will let Lachlan believe he's in London. But he will be your responsibility now.'

'So be it. But he must be confined so that he cannot harm others.' Dalton sent a pointed look towards Regina. He didn't want her to believe the earl could come and go as he pleased. Especially when he had threatened Lachlan's wife.

Regina gave him a nod of assent as she rose to her feet. 'My father is very ill,' she said to the butler. 'He will need his own room and the care of a physician. He is suffering from consumption.'

'I will find a room for him,' MacLachor promised. He glanced at Dalton, who nodded permission for him to leave.

'We need to talk in private,' Dalton told his wife. 'Your father can remain here in the meantime.'

'But the ropes,' she protested. 'He need not be bound.'

He understood her frustration. 'As soon as his room is prepared, we will take off the ropes,' Dalton said. 'And I will see to it that he has a meal. For now, we need to make some decisions.' He offered his arm, but Regina hesitated before she took it.

He led her back to his study and closed the door. His wife appeared pale and shaken by what she had seen. 'I don't understand. I know Papa was angry with me for marrying you, but why would he believe he could stop the laird from marrying Miss Goodson? Why would he be that desperate?'

'I don't know.'

'It seems that he lost sight of everything. All sense of right and wrong.' Regina's voice was numb, and she sank into a chair. 'Perhaps the blackmailer did something. Perhaps this involved money.'

Dalton came to stand behind her, and he rested his hands upon her shoulders. 'You needn't worry about wealth, Regina. I will repay your father's debts, if it is necessary.'

But his words did little to allay her worries. Although she had confided the reasons for the blackmail, there were many details she had omitted. For instance—her father's role in Mallencourt's death.

The scandal of near rape was bad enough, but the baron's disappearance had a more sinister cast. Dalton went to stand before her, needing to see her eyes. 'Regina, there is something I must know. Did someone witness your father killing Lord Mallencourt?'

'No,' she whispered. But her face had gone white, and he suspected that the earl had hired someone else to handle the matter, if he had not struck the killing blow.

'You know that I will help him, for your sake.' Dalton knelt down and cupped her face. 'But I need to know everything.'

A tear spilled over her cheek. 'I'm so sorry I brought you into all this.' She pulled him close and hugged him tightly. 'You deserved better.'

'Don't,' he warned. 'I wanted to wed you. And I still want to marry you here, one day when you're ready.' He leaned in to kiss her and tasted the salt from her tears. 'We can begin anew.'

She ventured a smile. 'I would like that.'

Regina sat beside her father, gently bathing his raw wrists. His stare was vacant, as if he had given up hope on life. She didn't know the right words to say to him, for she couldn't understand what had driven him to such despair. All she could do was wash the dried blood away, hoping he would speak to her.

For a long time, his hands were limp, and he gave no reaction to her ministrations. Then she finally broke the silence. 'It will be all right, Papa. I—I am happy here with Lord Camford.'

Again, there was nothing. But she took a strip of linen and wrapped it around his left wrist. 'You would like him, I think. He has given me everything I need.' She tied off the bandage and took a second strip.

It seemed strange, talking about Dalton in this way. But it was true that he had given her a sense of hope, as well as a home. He had done everything to take care of her. And last night, he had given her a glimpse of what it was to be touched with love instead of force. She had warmed to it, and the memory made her body crave more.

She now wanted a true wedding with Dalton, and she believed it might be possible to one day lie with him and have children. He had given her such hopes, she longed to share them with her father. It might bring him back to reality.

'We are going to be married again legally. This time, it will be here, according to the Scottish traditions. I have begun making the plans, and I will write to Mother to ask her to come.'

She intended to meet with Mrs Hughes today and plan the menu for the wedding feast. Then she would ask the housekeeper to have her wedding gown cleaned so Regina could wear it a second time.

As she bandaged her father's right wrist, he started coughing again. To distract him, Regina spoke about the roses she planned to cut from the garden. She kept up a stream of conversation, but he was like a statue, with no response to her words.

At last, she could bear it no longer. She crossed her arms and regarded him. 'Whatever possessed you to do such a thing? Why would you hurt Miss Goodson?'

'I was very drunk,' her father admitted. 'I was angry and foolish. I—I don't know why I did it. But… I do pray that she will be all right.'

'I never wanted to marry Locharr,' she said. 'It was an arrangement between you and Tavin MacKinloch, nothing more.'

Her father's face reddened, and he spoke at last. 'It was a good match for you, Regina. Camford was not the man I chose.'

A flare of anger caught her. 'No, but he was the man who chose me. He tried to stop me from being humiliated when Locharr ran off to marry his governess.'

Ned stared at her. 'And whose fault was that?'

His words dug into her consciousness, and she could

not believe he would be that callous. 'You're not blaming *me* for this, are you?'

He shrugged. 'They do call you the Lady of Ice. Perhaps if you had been kinder, not so cold, he might have married you instead.'

She took a step back, feeling as if he'd slapped her. In a tremulous voice, she added, 'You, of all people, know why I am cold to men. How can you make this my fault?'

'It was years ago, Regina. You have to face your fear and move on.'

Which was exactly what she was trying to do. But she was done with being his pawn, obeying him without question. 'Do not ever try to interfere with our lives again,' she said. 'Lachlan made his choice, and so have I.'

'You are not married to the viscount. The ceremony was a farce.'

'No one knows that but us,' she pointed out. 'And it can easily be remedied.' She couldn't believe that he was arguing with her after all this. 'Dalton is a good man.' In a low voice, she added, 'He has offered to forgo a dowry, and he will repay your debt to Locharr.' In a cool voice she added, 'That *is* why I was supposed to wed him, is it not? You didn't have enough money to pay the blackmailer years ago, and you borrowed from the laird.'

When he made no denial, her spirits sank. 'Do I have any dowry at all? Or was that a lie, too?'

'A small one. Only five thousand pounds.' Her father sighed. 'I made some poor investments, years ago. You're right, that I didn't have enough money to pay the blackmail, much less your dowry. Tavin offered to help, and he agreed that I would pay him back as part of your dowry.' He shrugged. 'The debt is still there, though I don't want to give fifteen thousand pounds to MacKinloch and that governess. It was meant for you and the laird.'

'If you borrowed money, then it must be repaid to their clan. You don't have a choice, Papa.'

Ned's face grew pained. 'I feel as if I'm giving money to the woman who stole the life you should have had.'

She understood his feelings, but he was honour-bound to repay his debts. The laird's people had suffered over the years, and her dowry would have provided for their needs. 'You don't have to pay the money,' she said. 'Dalton has offered to repay the debt on our behalf.'

'I don't want you beholden to him, Regina.'

Her frustration only deepened. He had no right to criticise her choices, even if he only meant to protect her. 'You mean *you* don't want to be beholden.' She glared at him and added, 'Dalton is a viscount and the heir to an earldom. There is nothing wrong with my choice to wed him.'

'Does he know what happened?' Her father regarded her with a pointed look.

'Some of it,' she hedged. 'Not everything.'

Ned sighed, and his shoulders lowered. A moment later, he reached for his handkerchief and coughed again. 'I don't want anyone else involved. It's not too late, Regina. If you want to walk away from this marriage, it can still be done.'

But that wasn't what she wanted at all. With Dalton, she had found a patient man who did not force her into anything she wasn't ready for. Last night, he had shown her that the intimacy between a husband and a wife could be wondrous.

'I will not leave him,' she said. 'Not after everything he has done for me.'

'And what will you do if the blackmailer does not stop? What if...the worst is revealed?' he demanded.

'I will be in Scotland, under Lord Camford's protection.'

Her father's coughing grew worse, and he struggled to regain control. 'I know you believe that, Regina. But I fear you cannot hide your secrets for ever.'

She met his gaze. 'Even so, I will try.'

Chapter Eleven

Dalton found Regina at the far end of the garden. She had reached to grasp a tree limb and was struggling to pull herself up. Her petticoats tangled with her legs, and she couldn't quite gain a foothold.

He strode across the gravel pathway and asked, 'Do you need help?'

'I never expected tree-climbing to be this difficult,' she admitted. 'I really should have borrowed a pair of trousers from the stable lad.'

Dalton thought about having a pair made for her. It was not ladylike, aye, but he very much wanted to see the rounded curve of her backside in the trousers. And then he could remove them later.

He came closer to the tree and gathered her into his arms. 'What are you doing?' she asked. In answer to her question, he lifted her high until she could grasp the thick branch and pull herself over. Regina was laughing as she struggled, but she managed to take a seat. 'Thank you for your help.'

Dalton climbed up after her, and he chose the branch

next to hers. 'As trees go, the one you chose wasn't
so bad.'

'I don't think it's in any danger of breaking.' She
tried to adjust her skirts and held on to the tree trunk.

Dalton climbed nearer and stood on a branch below
hers. He rested both hands on either side of the tree,
trapping her in his embrace. Regina touched his hair,
and he murmured in a low voice, 'Did you enjoy last
night?'

'Yes.' Her arms wound around his neck, and he captured her lips, kissing her hard. She returned the kiss,
and he wanted to coax her into more.

'Thank you for not sending my father away,' she
whispered. 'He's made so many mistakes, but I don't
want him to go to prison.'

Dalton touched a strand of her hair and slid it behind one ear. 'I will protect you, and your family, Regina.' He stole another kiss and added, 'But I need to
talk to you about the Bow Street Runner.'

He didn't blame Lord Havershire, if he had indeed
arranged for Mallencourt's death. But he now understood why the blackmailer was such a grave problem.
'I received a letter from the Runner this morning. He's
travelling here to speak with us.'

Her face paled, and she shook her head. 'I don't
want to speak to him. If he's caught the blackmailer,
that's good, but why would he come here?'

'He may need you to testify in court against the
blackmailer. I imagine that's all it is.'

But Regina was already climbing down from the
tree. 'I don't want to see him, Dalton.' She appeared
unsettled, and he guessed it was because she was afraid
of what the Runner had learned.

'Then perhaps he could speak with your father. We have to put an end to the blackmail.' He wanted Regina to know that he would do anything to make her feel safe again. Only after she laid her fears to rest, could she look towards a future with him.

'No!' She let go of the branch and dropped the short distance to the ground. 'I'm not about to subject Papa to an interrogation. Not after what's happened with Miss Goodson. And he's very ill right now.' Her voice was tremulous, and Dalton climbed down to walk with her.

'It will be all right,' he said. The man had claimed that it was necessary to speak with Regina, and Dalton guessed it was because she could answer questions about the blackmail notes. But she was more fearful of him speaking to her father—likely to protect him.

'Keep him away from me,' she insisted. 'Don't let him come to Scotland.'

It was too late to send the man away, for he would arrive in a day or two. 'He is already on his way,' he admitted.

With that, she hurried away from him, making him wish he'd never told her. But although the Runner was coming here, he had promised Regina that he would put an end to the blackmail.

And he intended to see it through.

Regina put a leather lead on her dog, Arthur, and hurried down the pathway leading from the estate. Her emotions gathered up in a tight ball, and she was holding back tears. She knew Dalton believed he was helping her, but she was terrified that the Bow Street

Runner had learned the truth about Lord Mallencourt's death.

She couldn't imagine any other reason why he would come to Scotland. If the Runner had merely learned the identity of the blackmailer, he would have sent a letter about the arrest. There was no need for him to come here, unless he had learned something more.

Arthur stopped to sniff the ground, and Regina's fragile hold on the tears broke free. She let herself cry as she continued walking. But soon enough, she saw Dalton's grandfather standing beside a stone wall. She wiped her tears away and approached him, wondering if he was lost.

'Good afternoon, Lord Cairnross,' she said. 'Have you come to pay a call upon Dalton?'

The old man appeared confused for a moment. 'Dalton,' he repeated. 'Nay, I've come to see Brandon.'

Regina's heart sank, for she realised the earl was still caught up in the past. There was no sense in telling him that Brandon was dead. Instead, she drew closer and asked, 'Would you like to walk with me?'

He brightened at that and offered his arm. 'I should always be glad to escort a bonny lass,' he answered. 'Especially on a day as fine as this one.'

'Why have you come to see Brandon?' she asked.

'He will be needing my instruction on how to manage the estate,' the earl answered. 'Such a hard-working, responsible lad he is.' His smile deepened, and he asked, 'Has Brandon begun to court you?'

She shook her head. 'No, but Dalton has.'

The earl laughed heartily. 'Dalton is still very young. You'll have to wait a few years for him to grow up. But even when he does, Dalton is a wild one. His parents have had their fill of him.'

She wasn't entirely surprised, but she saw an opportunity to learn more about her almost-husband. 'Why? What has he done?'

Lord Cairnross's mood shifted, and his smile faded. Regina waited for him to speak, and when he did not, she asked again, 'My lord, what happened with Dalton?'

The older man patted her hand and led her back into the garden. 'He's a lost soul, that one is. Mark my words, he'll ne'er forgive himself. I can't say if his father will, either.'

It seemed that his thoughts had shifted back to the present, for he was speaking of Brandon's death. Was that the reason why Dalton had felt abandoned by his family? Did they truly believe that he had caused his brother's death? He had blamed himself before, but she hadn't wanted to dwell on it. His pain had evoked memories of the lonely adolescent boy on the day his brother had been buried. She didn't like seeing Dalton in pain.

'It wasn't his fault,' Regina murmured. 'And there is more to Dalton than people see.'

The earl sobered. 'But you see it, don't you lass?' His expression shifted into sadness.

She nodded and took his hand in hers. 'I know you and your family grieve the loss of Brandon. But Dalton has done everything he can to take care of Cairnross and his father's estates. He is a good man, and no one should blame him for a tragedy that happened in the past.'

The earl squeezed her palm. There was a fleeting

moment of understanding before he turned and walked back towards his house. Regina followed him at a slow pace until she saw that he had made it back safely. But his remarks made her wonder about Dalton's family. His mother and brother were dead, and she had never even met his father.

Her heart ached for Dalton, and she continued walking along the path. While she knew that he wanted to help her overcome her past, she didn't want to entangle him in danger.

The arrival of the Bow Street Runner would inevitably reveal secrets she didn't want her husband to know. She stopped to look back at the house, wondering if she should even go through with a true marriage. She had told her father she intended to do so, but now, she wondered if that was wise. At least now, Dalton still had his freedom. If the worst happened, and the truth was revealed, she could know that he was safe and unharmed.

She passed by the tree she had climbed earlier, and the sight of it only conjured memories of his embrace. She had loved his kiss, loved the way he needed her touch.

She loved him.

Regina closed her eyes, and she could hardly bear the storm of emotion pouring into her heart.

You cannot marry him, her head warned. *When he learns the truth, he will despise your family. Give him the chance to walk away.*

But selfishly, she wanted a few nights with him. She wanted to overcome her fears and give Dalton her innocence, as penance for what she had to do next—leave him.

Likely, it would hurt, and there was a chance the old memories would suffocate her...but she was willing to take the risk for Dalton's sake.

She took a deep breath, gathering her courage. Tonight, then. She would go to him and push away the darker memories of her past. In doing so, she would reclaim the life she'd wanted, spending these last few days showing him how much she loved him.

And when the Bow Street Runner arrived, she would take her father and go.

It was late at night when his door opened. Regina stood at the entrance, her hair down around her shoulders. 'May I come in?' she asked.

The sight of her warmed him. 'You never have to ask,' he answered. 'You may come and sleep beside me every night if you wish.' Though he didn't believe that was why she was here, he wanted her to know that she was always welcome.

She blushed and closed the door behind her. But instead of coming to the bed, she sat down in a chair beside the fire. It was dying down, and he took a poker to revive the flames.

'I'm sorry for the way I reacted earlier,' she said. 'It's just that...these days with you have been so good, I didn't want to think about the past. I didn't want the Bow Street Runner to ruin everything.'

'I won't let that happen,' he promised. But even so, her face held doubts, as if she believed he might change his mind. Despite her confession about Mallencourt's death, he sensed a reserve, as if she had not told him everything. Likely it was meant to protect her father—but now was not the time to speak of it.

'Thank you for taking my father in,' she continued. 'And if I didn't say it before, I am also thankful that you married me in London. You turned an awful day into something wonderful.'

Dalton came to sit across from her in the opposite chair. Though he didn't truly consider it a choice, she'd needed his help. 'Of course.' He set the poker aside and regarded her. She appeared nervous, and he wondered if she wanted to talk or whether she wanted comfort.

She answered his unspoken question when she stood from her chair and approached him. Then she knelt down and put her arms around his waist. Her offering deepened his desire until he was fighting the urge to claim her. 'Dalton,' she whispered. 'I don't want to think about the past any more. I only want to enjoy this time with you.'

God, yes. Her words were like a flame touched to oil. But he knew he had to be so careful, to coax her gently so she would not be afraid.

'Come here,' he murmured, lifting her to sit on his lap. Her skin allured him with the faint scent of flowers. His body was aching with raw lust, but he fought it back. She needed tenderness, not conquest. She leaned in to kiss him, and he took her mouth, returning the affection and sliding his tongue over the seam of her lips.

It was all he could do not to carry her off to bed. His heart was roaring in his chest, and as her tongue met his, he grew rock hard. The more she kissed him, the more he started losing control. He needed a moment to gain command of himself, and he pulled back.

'May I undress you?' he asked softly.

She nodded, her eyes wide in the firelight. He helped her to stand and then slid her wrapper from her shoulders. Her nightdress was of the finest linen, and he could see the curve of her breasts beneath it. He led her to the bed and bade her to sit down. Then he knelt before her, as if to worship.

'Do you want me to remove your gown, or would you like to take it off?' He wanted her to have the choice, to feel as if she held power over him.

'I want you to do it,' she breathed.

Dalton reached for the buttons, unfastening them one by one. He savoured the moment, revealing her bare flesh slowly. Then he reached for the hem of her gown and eased it higher. She stood from the bed, and as he lifted it, his palms caressed her thighs and hips. She closed her eyes at the contact, but it did not seem that she was afraid. His hands lingered upon her waist, and then when he removed the nightdress, he revealed her naked body. Her skin was golden in the firelight, and he caught his breath. Her breasts were slightly larger than his hands, and her waist dipped in before it curved back to her hips.

'You are beautiful, Regina. I could stand and look at you for the rest of my life.' He took her hands, drinking in the sight of her. Then he brought her hands to his shirt buttons and waited.

She seemed shy, but slowly, she unfastened the three buttons before lifting his shirt over his head. Her gaze fixed upon his chest, and he brought her hands to his heart. 'You can touch me if you want to.'

Tentatively, her fingers moved over his chest, and she traced the outline of his pectoral muscle. 'Your skin is so warm.'

He inhaled at her touch and guided her hands to his trousers. 'Undress me, Regina.'

She appeared hesitant again, but he waited for her to unfasten the buttons. Her fingers brushed against his hard length, and he bit back a groan.

Regina stopped instantly. 'Did I hurt you?'

'No. It's just that I want you so badly. I need your touch.'

She waited a moment and then removed his trousers, followed by his small clothes. Now that he was naked, he sensed her fears rising. 'It's all right, Regina. If you need me to stop at any time, I will.'

She nodded but brought her hands back to his chest. It seemed that she was uncertain about what to do, so he reassured her. 'Touch me any way you want to.'

'I don't know what you like,' she admitted.

'I like your hands upon me in any way that pleases you.'

While she touched his chest, he ran his fingertip along the curve of her breast, circling slowly until he reached the puckered nipple. 'You seem a little cold.' He teased the tip, and she jolted.

'They do call me the Lady of Ice,' she murmured.

'Then I'll have to set you on fire.' He took her nipple into his mouth, swirling his tongue until she gripped his shoulders and arched back. His hands moved down to cup her bottom, and he lifted her up, wrapping her legs around his waist. He carried her over to the bed and laid her down. Then he moved on his side, drawing her leg over his hip.

'Do you still want this?'

Regina could scarcely breathe. But she wanted this night with Dalton, to drive away her demons and to give him something of herself.

'Yes,' she whispered. Her voice was trembling, and her fears seemed to double.

But instead, he drew her hand to his manhood. In turn, he rested his fingertips against her intimate curls. 'Then touch me. And I will do the same to you.'

'I thought—' Her words broke off when his thumb began to caress her. He seemed to know her secret places, and he knew just how to invoke pleasure.

'You thought what?' Again, he circled slowly, and a spiral of white-hot need gathered between her legs. She was rising to him, pressing back as he stroked.

'I thought you would be inside me now.'

He laughed softly, and his voice was dark, filled with promise. 'Later, darling. For now, I want to warm you until your body craves mine.'

He slid two fingers inside her, and she was shocked at how easily her body accepted him. He kissed her breast, suckling gently as he moved his hand in rhythm. She hardly recognised the noise that came from her mouth when he found the sweet spot inside her. Her body welcomed his touch, and she touched his velvet shaft as he stroked her. They moved together, and as he invaded and withdrew, she moved her hand upon his hard length. She was startled when a bead of fluid emerged from the tip of him, and she caressed it with her thumb.

Dalton growled and caught her hand. 'If you keep doing that, our night together will be entirely too short.' Then he pulled her hips to the edge of the bed and knelt down.

'I want to taste you, Regina,' he said, kissing her inner thigh. She nearly bolted upright when he parted her curls and licked her intimately. Dear God, his tongue. He explored her sensitive flesh, dipping softly against her wetness. Her hands dug into the coverlet, and she keened a sobbing cry when he began to stroke her nodule with his tongue. It was gentle, and yet, the pressure made her clench her inner muscles, wanting so much more.

'Dalton, I can't,' she breathed. 'Please… I need you.'

But he ignored her, working her with his mouth and suckling against her until she seized up and arched her back. The shattering pleasure rained over her, leaving her helpless except to enjoy the fierce release that erupted. She was so wet, needing his body inside hers. But he seemed unwilling to claim her, as if he didn't want to hurt her.

Regina sat up and took his head in her hands. 'Lie down on the bed,' she commanded. 'It's my turn.'

He stood, his erection raging as he lay back. She leaned down and discovered the pleasure of touching him. He was at her mercy as she caressed him, and when she put her mouth upon him, he surged forward.

'Regina, slow down.'

But she suckled against him, loving the power of making him feel the same way he'd made her feel. She ran her tongue along his hard length, and his entire body went rigid.

'Stop,' he pleaded, and she did, wondering if she had hurt him. Dalton was breathing hard, but he drew her to straddle him. He took her hips in his hands and guided himself to her entrance.

But he didn't force himself inside. No, he closed his eyes, waiting. And she understood that he was giving himself to her. He would never force her, never make her feel powerless.

Instead, he was surrendering to her pleasure. And she revelled in the knowledge that she was in command.

It was awkward at first, but she took the head of him inside. She was still a virgin, and the fit was tight. The strain upon his face was like a man caught up in torment. And as she started to move, he hissed.

'I love you, Regina,' he said. 'I always have.'

She wanted to answer the words, but her brain warned her not to. Not if she had to leave him. It would be cruel to say it and then go. Instead, she held back her love for him and brought his hands back to her breasts. 'Will you touch me again?'

He did, and he rolled one nipple between his thumb and forefinger. She felt her body giving in, welcoming him as she used her body weight to sink lower. There was a slight pinching sensation, and then he was fully sheathed inside her.

Again, she expected him to begin thrusting. Instead, he sat up and took her breast in his mouth. She was overcome by the echo within her womb and could not help but move against him.

'That's it, darling. Just like that.'

She rose up and then sank against him, unaccustomed to the sensation of having him deep inside. But she discovered that as she moved, some of her earlier pleasure returned. She changed the angle of her thrust and found that it heightened her sensation when she squeezed against him.

Dalton was responding to her, meeting her thrusts with his own. But instead of feeling as if he had taken the lead, it felt as if he were trying to give her what she wanted.

She tried to go faster, and when she bumped against him, her body began to tremble. Each penetration brought her closer to the brink, but she was afraid to reach for it.

'Dalton,' she said, bringing his mouth to hers. She kissed him lightly and then pleaded, 'Will you make love to me now?'

He rolled her to her back but kept her on the end of the bed. As he bent over her, he lifted her hips higher, and then began a timeless rhythm.

She gloried in the feeling of him gliding in and out, and she murmured, 'Yes. Like this.'

He was gentle, and yet, she desired more. She wanted to feel the height of sensation again, and she tried to quicken his pace.

'Not yet,' he whispered, slowing down. 'Savour it. Feel me touching you. Trust me, Regina, and let go.'

He continued the relentless give and take, with such slight pressure, that she started to quake with the stroking. Over and over, he entered and withdrew, but again, it was with such tenderness, she wanted to grasp his hips and demand more.

But her body recognised the pleasure he was giving, and she suddenly felt a part of her awakening, climbing higher. The ball of sensation tightened inside, caressed so gently, until it unravelled within her. Every fibre of her being came apart, rippling with the wave of pleasure so strong, she squeezed his shaft inside and cried out her release. He continued the pleasure as she arched hard, shaking until he emptied himself within.

She wrapped her legs around him, feeling her own emotions growing raw. He had given her everything, taking away the past until there was only love between them.

She wanted to weep at the thought of leaving. God help her, she didn't know if she had the strength.

He was collapsed on top of her, but his hands traced a soft caress upon her hip. 'Are you all right?' he asked.

'Yes,' she lied. But not because of the physical release between them. It was the knowledge that he would soon be dragged into the sordid truth about Mallencourt's death. She had wanted to avoid it—had hoped that no one would ever find out. But now that the Bow Street Runner was travelling here, he would confront her and her father about what had happened that night. And the only way to avoid it was to leave and hope that no one could find them.

'You seem troubled,' he said, withdrawing from her body. 'Do you regret this?'

She shook her head and forced a smile. 'It was wonderful, Dalton.' To emphasise her words, she reached up to kiss him.

But as he drew her body to his, wrapping the coverlet around them, she could not help but feel as if their time was running out.

Something was very wrong with his wife. Although she now spent the nights in his bed, Dalton sensed her distraction. It was as if she were trying to separate herself. During the daytime, she hardly spoke to him any more, while at night, she welcomed him into her arms. He had invited her to go out riding yesterday, but she had declined, saying that she was worried about her father. He didn't know how to bridge the distance between them, nor did he understand why she had suddenly changed.

She was in the parlour with her father, drinking tea, when he asked, 'Regina, may I speak with you for a moment?'

'Of course. Papa, will you excuse me?'

The earl nodded. In the past few days, his appearance had grown haggard, and he seemed to have weakened. Though Dalton had asked if Regina wanted him to summon a physician, she had declined.

He offered his arm, and she took it. There was tension in her demeanour, and as soon as they were alone, she asked, 'What is it? Has someone arrived?'

'No, not yet.' He started to lead her outside, but she stopped walking.

'Oh. Was there something else you needed from me?'

'I wanted to spend time with you,' he said. He put his hand upon the small of her back. 'Let us speak outside, away from everyone else.'

She didn't argue with him, and he took her hand in his. They walked past the estate grounds, well beyond the garden, until they reached the shores of the loch. The morning sunlight gleamed upon the silvery water, with only the slight movement of a fish breaking the surface. 'You've been avoiding me, Regina.'

At that, she flushed. 'How can you say that after last night?'

Although he didn't want to fight with her, he needed to understand why she had withdrawn. 'You barely speak to me during the day. Any time I've asked you to go riding or to walk the dog, you find a reason not to go. Have I done something to offend you?'

Remorse slid over her face, and she shook her head. 'Not at all. I'm just…distracted right now.'

'Is something wrong?' The words escaped before he could stop them. 'Do you no longer wish to be my wife?'

Her eyes filled up with tears, and she stared out at the loch. Her silence was damning, and it was as if she'd thrust an invisible dagger into his gut. He didn't know what to say, not when she made no denial. For a long moment, he waited for her to speak, and when she did not, he asked, 'And what if there is a child?'

'There isn't,' she said softly. 'My courses started this morning.'

But somehow the knowledge only seemed to widen the distance between them. He didn't understand what had changed, beyond their intimacy.

'Tell me what has changed since we became lovers,' he said. 'You owe me that much.'

A tear slid down her cheek. But still, she didn't answer. He wanted to confront her, to demand the answers. But he did not want to risk frightening her.

'Because you deserve better than this,' she said. 'I thought I could run away from my past, but now I see it isn't possible. And I won't do anything that could bring ruin to your life.'

He reached for her hand, but she pulled away. 'You're afraid,' he accused. 'Why? Is it because of your father?'

She turned her back. 'Dalton, please let it be.'

'I'm not afraid of anything he has done. Whatever it was, it's over and done with. We will keep him confined to Cairnross. I can help your mother hire a land steward to look after Havershire. It will be all right.'

'No. You don't understand,' she said, swiping at her tears. 'If the Bow Street Runner has learned what happened the night I was attacked—if he knows that Mallencourt died at our house—it will all be over. There's nothing we can do.'

He stared at her, at the raw fear in her eyes, and her refusal to consider seeking help from him. She had no faith in him to defend her family.

'I need to leave, Dalton. I need to take my father and disappear.'

He was already shaking his head. 'No. You're not going anywhere.'

She was starting to stride away from him, but he caught her by the waist and pulled her into his arms. 'I've waited years for you, Regina. And I'll be damned if I'll let you go.'

He captured her mouth, kissing her hard. But it was more than staking a claim upon her—it was the need to know whether she truly didn't want him. He framed her face with his hands, trying to make her see how he loved her. 'Trust me,' he said against her lips. 'I will guard you both.'

She did kiss him back, but he tasted the salt of her tears. She wound her arms around his neck, weeping silently as he kissed her. He softened his mouth against hers, and at last held her close.

'Don't go, Regina. Let me fight for you.'

But after he pulled back, he could see the doubt in her eyes. She kept his hand in hers and said, 'Let's go back home, Dalton.'

It wasn't a yes—but it was the best he could get from her.

As they neared the house, he saw a coach stopped

in front of the stairs. Regina stiffened at the sight of it, and he tightened his grip on her hand.

'It's him, isn't it?' she murmured.

'We don't know that yet.' But he could tell from her posture that she didn't believe it. They went inside, and MacLachor confirmed, 'The Bow Street Runner has arrived, my lord. I bade him to wait in the parlour.'

Regina had gone utterly white, and he thanked the butler. To his wife, he said, 'It will be all right. He may have news for us.'

'I should have left yesterday,' she murmured beneath her breath. 'Now it's too late.'

He squeezed her hand in reassurance, and when they entered the room, she remained at his side. The Bow Street Runner stood and greeted them. 'Lord Camford, thank you for agreeing to see me.'

Dalton gave a nod and then said, 'Lady Camford, may I present Mr Travis Sidney.'

Regina lowered her head in acknowledgement, but Mr Sidney's expression turned solemn. 'I regret that my presence may cause some distress. That was not my intention.'

'I am certain that whatever you've learned, we can resolve it,' Dalton answered. 'Please, sit.' He glanced at the Earl of Havershire, who was staring at the opposite side of the room. He held a handkerchief in one hand, and his expression appeared weary.

'You asked me to find out who was blackmailing the earl and his family,' the man began. 'It took a few weeks, but I did find out that it was a woman. One who was rather desperate for funds.' He cleared his throat and met Regina's gaze with regret. 'She was there at your residence, waiting for you that night before you arrived home from the ball.'

His wife paled and touched her hand to her mouth. 'Was it my maid? Nell's grandfather was there that night. Did she come to visit him? I thought they were loyal to us, but perhaps I was mistaken.'

Mr Sidney shook his head slowly. 'No, my lady. It was not Nell.' He turned to Dalton and said, 'May I speak privately with you, my lord?'

'My wife may stay and hear all of it,' he countered. 'This does involve her.'

The man shook his head. 'I have risked a great deal by coming here unofficially. This is not my jurisdiction, but out of courtesy, I felt it best to tell you what I've learned. And I fear, I must insist that we speak alone. That includes Havershire.'

Dalton felt Regina's icy fingers, and she seemed unsteady on her feet. 'It will be all right,' he told her. 'We'll talk of it later.' He pressed a kiss to her forehead, and she risked a look back before she took her father's arm.

Before they left, Havershire paused at the doorway. 'I will keep her safe, Camford. No matter what happens.' With that, he escorted her out.

Dalton didn't know what to think of that cryptic remark, but he intended to ask later. The Bow Street Runner waited until he was certain they were alone. A few moments later, he lowered his voice. 'There are some complications you should be aware of, my lord. The blackmailer provided some anonymous details that could prove troublesome, should they come to light.'

He sobered, knowing what the man was about to say. 'It's about Mallencourt, isn't it?'

Mr Sidney nodded. 'The night he…died, the coroner ruled his death an accident. But the blackmailer has threatened to go to the press with details about how his death was a murder instead.'

'It was not murder,' Dalton argued. He wanted to reveal more but decided to hold back the truth.

'That may be. But even a breath of this scandal would ruin both your families.' Mr Sidney cleared his throat. 'I am certain your father would not want this.'

Dalton had no doubt of it. If the earl learned that he was now entangled in a cover up of manslaughter, his father would never speak to him again.

'You asked me to identify the blackmailer.' Mr Sidney reached for a pen and ink on a nearby table and scratched a name upon the paper. 'This is she. But there is danger in this. If she is arrested for her blackmail, she has enough family connections to cause irreparable damage to your name.'

Dalton stared at the name in disbelief. This would indeed cause Regina pain. He crumpled up the paper and walked over to toss it in the hearth. It caught fire and blazed, turning the name into ash. 'What do you advise?'

'Keep your wife here, in Scotland. She is out of London jurisdiction here and can be kept safe. Let the blackmailer reveal the knowledge, if she will, and there is a chance that no one will believe her. Since she is destitute with no father to speak for her, she could be viewed as manipulative or scheming to gain money.'

Dalton thought about it for a time and said, 'So we are calling her out?'

The Bow Street Runner paused. 'I have known men

like Mallencourt. I wouldn't let a dog near him, much less a lady. I am willing to let the past remain there.'

'So be it.' It wasn't the greatest solution, but it was best for all families involved. 'I will speak with my wife and let her know that she cannot return to London.'

Mr Sidney stood from his chair and extended his hand. 'And should anyone ask you, I did not travel to Scotland, nor did we have this conversation.'

Chapter Twelve

Regina was pacing in Dalton's bedchamber, waiting for the news, when finally, the door opened. 'What did you learn?'

He went to sit on the edge of the bed. 'The investigator believes it's best if you remain in Scotland. It will be safer for you to avoid scandal. The woman has threatened to tell everyone about Mallencourt, if she is arrested for blackmail. She has enough influence to cause problems for both our families. But Sidney thinks that no one will believe her, since it happened so long ago, and she is rather desperate for funds.' He paused a moment and said, 'I think he's right. If you stay in Scotland, and we say nothing, it's for the best.'

She couldn't imagine how a servant or a commoner could have so much power. No one in the press would believe such slander. 'Who was it, Dalton?'

His mouth tightened, but he admitted, 'It was Lord Blyton's daughter, Lady Anne.'

Anne? It felt as if she'd taken a blow to her stomach. At first, denial rose to her lips. Anne was her friend. They had laughed together, attended outings along the

Serpentine, and she could not imagine such a thing. 'How is this possible? Why would she—?' Her words broke off as she considered it. Anne's father had died years ago. Her mother had many daughters, and the earl had left them penniless. No doubt Anne was trying to survive—but the betrayal cut her deeply.

'Never mind,' she murmured. 'I know why.' She clutched her hands together. 'I never knew she was there that night.'

'Mr Sidney doesn't think she actually saw anything,' Dalton said. 'But she was aware that Mallencourt was there and that he was dead the following day.'

Inwardly, Regina felt as if she had swallowed stones. Had anything been real? Or was their friendship only a means of Anne getting closer? She had spent many days with her, sometimes inviting her to stay over the night. They had spent long hours talking, and she supposed Anne had come over that night and was waiting for her. She had not attended the ball, for since her father's death, the family had received few invitations.

'Will the blackmail stop, do you think?'

Dalton shrugged. 'Possibly. Now that we know who it was.' He reached for her hand and squeezed it. 'Are you all right?'

She didn't know. It felt as if her entire friendship had been a lie, and it hurt to know that the bright, spirited young woman had been stealing thousands of pounds a year from her father. Had Papa known this? Had he paid the money to avoid scandal? Or was it charity? Somehow, she didn't believe it was the latter, for Ned had borrowed money from Tavin MacKinloch over the years to pay it. Her father had remained silent about their finances, never alluding to his financial troubles. It seemed that he had only revealed his debts to Arabella after he had restored his wealth— but he had not breathed a word about the blackmail.

'I don't know what to think of all this,' she admitted, 'but I agree that it would be best to keep it quiet.' She thought about writing to her former friend to offer financial help, if she would cease the blackmail and remain quiet. But then, there was no guarantee that Anne would agree. It felt as if she didn't even know her friend any more.

'What do you want to do if she reveals everything?' he ventured. 'What then?'

The truth weighed heavily upon her, and she knew she had to tell him the truth. He could not help her if he didn't know what had happened. 'Dalton, there is more about that night. There are things I didn't tell you.'

His face tensed, and silence descended between them. She could feel his worry, his censure. For so long, she had hidden behind shadows, hoping that no one would ever know, save her father. But she could not keep this from him any longer. She simply didn't know how to begin.

Dalton finally broke the stillness, saying, 'Then tell me what happened. All of it, this time.'

Regina saw no other choice. She steeled herself and then faced Dalton. 'The night when I was attacked, I let you believe that Papa broke the door down to save me. That…wasn't entirely what happened.'

Her hands began to shake, and her courage faltered. He would truly think the worst of her after this. The blood pulsed within her veins, quickening her fears. 'Our footman, Frederick, had gone to find another key after Mallencourt locked us inside. He didn't hear me scream, because the baron had shoved a handkerchief in my mouth.'

Just speaking of that night brought back terrible memories. She remembered her dry mouth, the blend of fear and rage rising inside her as she had tried to fight back. A part of her had remained alert during the attempted rape, and she had pretended to lose her balance.

'I—suspected that Lord Mallencourt would rape me before anyone could help, and I had to find a way to stop him. He forced me up against the wall, and I was not strong enough to push him away. So, I let my weight fall towards the hearth.'

Dalton was listening to her, his gaze intent and focused. She didn't know what he thought of her, but she continued. 'When he tried to pull me back, I seized a fireplace poker and struck him in the head. He lost his balance and fell backwards.' Bile rose up in her throat, and she struggled to keep back the nausea. 'H-he cracked his skull against the stone hearth.'

Even now, she was haunted by the blood spreading out upon the white marble. At the time, she'd believed he was merely unconscious. But after Mallencourt didn't move again, she realised what she had done. He was dead, and she was at fault for it. The paralysing guilt had haunted her ever since, and it was a burden she could never surrender.

'My father did break down the door. But when he came inside, Mallencourt was already dead. I killed him.'

Her tears did fall now, but Dalton was staring at her as if she were a stranger. There was a blend of horror and disbelief in his expression…which was exactly why she had not spoken of it before.

She waited for him to speak, but he simply stared at her as if she were a stranger. Finally, she lifted her gaze to his. There was a storm brewing in his eyes.

'Why didn't you tell me the truth?' he asked quietly. His voice held a chill, and after what he'd just learned about her, no doubt he was furious.

'I didn't want to see you looking at me the way you are now,' she answered softly. 'I didn't want you to despise me for what I did.'

She waited for him to deny it, but his face hardened with anger. 'I am your husband in every way that matters, Regina. There was no reason to hide all this. Not from me.'

'If you had known that I killed Mallencourt, you never would have wanted to marry me.' She was quite certain of that. 'I cannot change what I did. But I can keep my past from hurting you.'

'Is that why you didn't want to marry me in Scotland?' he guessed. 'Because you didn't think I was strong enough to protect you?'

'What man wants to wed a murderer?' she countered. 'I didn't want you tangled up in any of this. It wasn't fair to you.'

'But it was all right to share my bed, to risk a child?' he shot back. 'Why would you use me in that way?'

His words struck her cold, for that was exactly what she had done. She had never thought of it that way, but she *had* used him to overcome her fears. He had taught her that the union between a man and a woman could be beautiful…but she had never intended it to be permanent between them.

Her heart ached, and tears rose to her eyes. 'Dalton, I'm sorry. I shouldn't have done that.'

He was pacing, his restlessness evident. Then he paused a moment and studied her. 'You were planning to run away, weren't you? That's why you've been so distant.'

She nodded. 'When you told me the Bow Street Runner was coming here, I suspected he had learned the truth. I didn't see a choice but to leave.'

The bleakness in his eyes nearly shredded her heart. 'Did you never once believe that I would want to protect you?' He shook his head in disgust. 'You gave up on our marriage before it even had a chance.'

'I thought I was protecting *you*,' she answered dully. 'If you weren't truly my husband, then your family name would not be dragged into scandal.' Though it was in his nature, wanting to guard her, there were consequences for her actions. While some might agree that it was an accidental death from self-defence, others might call her a murderer. She didn't want Dalton to be whispered about in drawing rooms for the rest of his life. He deserved better.

'It's far too late for that, Regina. Everyone saw us married in London. Even if they realise it was not a true marriage, they will speak poorly of us.' He stopped and regarded her. 'And if I am not legally your husband, if any charges are brought against you, then I can do nothing.'

She shook her head. 'I never wanted you to be caught up in this, Dalton.' It wasn't fair or right. Inwardly, she was trembling with fear.

'Because you have no faith in me?'

'No. It's because I deserve whatever happens to

me.' A shudder crossed over her as she thought of the hangman's noose. 'I was young, I was reckless, and I caused a man to die.' The guilt filled her up inside, drowning her with the knowledge that she could never undo those sins.

'It wasn't your fault!' he insisted. 'You are not to blame for it.'

'They will say it was my fault,' she said quietly. 'After all, I allowed him to pay a call upon me so late at night. A true lady would never do such a thing. They will say that I encouraged him, that I made him promises. And then they will say that I killed him.'

'It was an accident,' he said hoarsely. 'You know this.'

She did, but she was also realistic about how society would see her. They would be delighted at the idea of her wrongdoing.

'My father and our footman helped to dispose of his body. What we did was wrong.' At the time, they had all feared the worst. Her father had been determined to keep anyone from learning the truth, and Frederick had agreed to help.

'What Mallencourt did was wrong, also.' His words weighed upon her, though she didn't truly believe they were comparable. The baron had attacked her, and she had taken his life.

'I've always known I might have to face the consequences for what I did,' she admitted. 'It's why I wanted to disappear in Scotland.'

He stared at her for a time. 'Are you really giving up on us, Regina? Or are you simply afraid?'

A hard lump caught in her throat, her heart aching. 'I'm sorry, Dalton. I'm so sorry for what I've done. If you want me to take my father and leave, I will understand.' She didn't want him to share this burden—not when there was no good outcome.

'And what if I want to help you?' he asked quietly.

She closed her eyes. 'I think it would be better if you just let me go.'

Dalton couldn't believe what she was saying. He moved in close, taking her waist in his hands. 'So, none of this was real? You came to Scotland to escape your past, and you won't allow me to protect you. I've said that I love you, but that means nothing.'

Her eyes were filled with tears, but she took his hands and stepped back. 'I never wanted to involve you in this.'

It burned him that she had no faith, no trust in him. But worse came the realisation that she didn't love him in return. He had done everything he could for her, and it wasn't enough. A darkness unfurled inside with frustration at himself.

He was responsible for bringing her into danger. By hiring the Bow Street Runner, Mr Sidney had re-opened the investigation and learned the truth about Mallencourt's death. If Dalton had not interfered, she might not be in this situation.

'I'm trying to do the right thing, Dalton,' she whispered. 'I'm setting you free to live the life you deserve.'

But he didn't want to be free. For just once in his life, he wanted to be enough.

He released her from his grasp, feeling as if their makeshift marriage had shattered. Instead, she would walk away, abandoning everything they had built together.

The door closed behind her, and he sank into a chair. Would she truly rather run away than allow him to help her? Did he mean that little to her? His mind was numb, his insides churning.

She wanted him to let her face this disaster alone. But he refused to remain passive. Whether or not they were married by law, he had agreed to take care of her for better or for worse. She needed him, even if she didn't want his help.

She was his wife in body and spirit, if not legally. Dalton didn't care that she had pushed him away. He intended to do everything in his power to help her— no matter what it took. Even if she didn't love him, he would stand by her side and defend her.

He decided to speak to Lord Havershire, to find out what could be done. And he also intended to confront Lady Anne, to discover why she had turned against her friend. While neither the earl, nor Regina, could visit London, there was nothing to prevent him from doing so.

Dalton left the room and saw one of the housemaids tidying up the parlour. 'Have you seen Lord Havershire?'

The girl's face turned confused. 'He left, my lord.'

'What do you mean, he left?' Dalton's mood tightened, for the earl ought to be here. Had he turned coward and run? He crossed to the window and saw Mr Sidney's coach departing but no one else.

'He went with the man who came calling,' the maid answered. 'He didna pack any clothes, but he just… went away.'

'Did you hear him say anything? Did he speak to anyone?'

'He only said that he had to leave, to help his daughter.' Then a moment later, she added, 'He did go to see Lady Camford before he left. And he seemed sad after he said goodbye.'

Havershire was clearly planning something, but what? A coldness caught Dalton as he mulled it over. If Havershire returned to London, everything could unravel. The earl was already unstable after he'd tried to kill Miss Goodson. God help him if the man was going after Lady Anne.

Or there was another possibility. Dalton knew what he would do, if he were in the man's place. The earl was dying of consumption, and everyone knew it. If Havershire went willingly to the authorities and confessed to murder, Regina would never face charges. But more than that, the earl could risk losing everything.

Dalton bit back a foul curse. Why had Mr Sidney agreed to take the earl with him? After everything they had discussed, why take the risk?

'Tell MacLachor to pack my belongings for London. I'm leaving immediately.' Havershire would need someone to intervene and pull him back to reality.

Dalton's mind was spinning with all that needed to be done, but as he focused his thoughts, he recognised that he ought to seek help from his father. As a peer, Lord Brevershire held a great deal of influence.

He won't want to help you, his brain warned. When had his father ever noticed him or even treated him like a son? John blamed him for Brandon's death. He had always been disappointed or indifferent to Dalton's efforts to please him.

But if it was necessary to humble himself before the earl, to save Regina and her family, he would do it without question.

Regina had never felt so alone in all her life. Over the past week, she could hardly bear it, worrying about Dalton and her father. Papa hadn't said much about why he was leaving, but he'd confessed that he missed Arabella and wanted to see her.

She suspected he was planning more than that, from what he'd promised Dalton. Her fears had only doubled as she questioned what her father would do. But how could she argue with him, if he wanted to see Mother again?

She was so grateful that Dalton had gone after him. If anyone could keep Ned out of trouble, it was him. Even so, she could not relinquish her apprehensions. At night, she had slept in Dalton's bed, wishing he were still there. Although she didn't regret revealing the truth to him, it had changed their relationship. And she didn't know if it could be rebuilt after she had kept secrets from him for so long.

Regina tried not to think of the emptiness stretching out between them. Dalton had tried to give her a good life, a good marriage. For a time, she had hoped she could abandon the past and reach for the future she wanted. It had almost seemed possible, until now.

You're feeling sorry for yourself, her inner voice chided. *Stop moping about like a wallflower.*

The worst had happened, and he now knew everything. She could either bemoan her fate, or she could take steps to improve her circumstances. It was time to cast off the chains of the past and stand up for what she wanted.

Or *who* she wanted. And in this case, it was most definitely Dalton St George.

She realised now, that it had been a mistake to offer him his freedom. What kind of a coward was she, suggesting that she take her father and go? At the time, she'd been caught up in her fog of misery, feeling as if she had entangled Dalton in a trap.

His words haunted her now.

I've said that I love you, but that means nothing.

That wasn't true at all. He meant everything to her. And it was her fear and panic clouding her judgement, making it impossible to find the right words. She'd been terrified that Mr Sidney had come to arrest her for murder.

But he'd only come to warn her. She'd been given a second chance at life, as long as she remained in Scotland. Perhaps it was time to stop being a victim and start taking command of herself and her life. Then she could find a way to rebuild her marriage.

Regina decided to pay a call on his grandfather to learn more about him. The older man had become dear to her, and what better way to brighten her day than to climb aboard a sailing vessel bound to imaginary India? She smiled at the thought.

MacLachor was kind enough to bring Arthur and the leather lead so she could take him on a walk with her. The puppy was thrilled to be out in the sunshine, and she had to hold him back to keep him from running.

'Will you be wanting me to accompany you to meet the Earl of Cairnross, my lady?' the footman asked.

'No, thank you. I will simply walk to his house and perhaps I might coax Lord Cairnross to walk back with me. I should be home within a few hours.'

'As you will, then.'

Regina breathed in the fresh air, letting it lift away her melancholy. The air was growing cooler, and she was glad she had worn a pelisse with her gown. The dog was barking, straining at the lead, and she tried to keep her grip firm but gentle.

She slowed her pace while the puppy sniffed at the ground, and a sudden sadness washed over her with the realisation that she truly couldn't return to London any more.

But her mother would never live anywhere else… and Ned was sick. When her father eventually died, Regina couldn't imagine Arabella coming to live here. It made her wonder if she would ever see them again.

In the distance, she saw Lord Cairnross standing outside his house. His pallor was grey, and there was a solemnity to his demeanour. The housekeeper was speaking to him, but he waved her off. Regina wondered if this was not a good day, after all.

'Good morning, Lord Cairnross,' she said when she reached his side. 'How are you feeling today?'

His stare was vacant, but he did perk up when Arthur jumped up, resting his paws on the earl's knees.

'I'll stay with him,' she told Mrs Howard.

The housekeeper nodded. 'I'll put on tea and biscuits, then.'

Regina waited to see if the earl would speak, and when he did not, she enquired, 'Would you like to go for a walk with Arthur and me?'

Again, he said nothing. The only sign that he heard

anything was when he reached down to pet the dog's head. Something had pulled him deep into memory, and Regina decided to confide in him.

'Dalton has gone to London, to bring back my father. He left after we received some troubling news.' She felt a slight chill and said, 'If you still have your ship, I wouldn't mind it if you sailed me to an island somewhere. As long as you bring Dalton along.'

It still pained her to remember the way he had looked at her when he'd learned that she had killed Mallencourt. As if she were some horrifying creature. A dark pain caught her with the fear that he wouldn't want her any more.

Don't think in that way, she warned herself. *Find a way to win him back.*

'My sailing days are over, I fear, lassie,' Lord Cairnross said.

'Why do you say that?' She studied his face carefully, and there did seem to be lucidity in his eyes.

'I am weary. I miss my wife. I'm an old man, not good for much of anything any more. And some days, what is left of my mind goes wandering.'

'I met you on one of those days, and I liked you very much,' Regina said. 'Come and walk with me. Tell me about Dalton when he was younger. How did he and Brandon get on?' She touched his arm gently, and at last, he offered it. With the lead in one hand and her other hand resting on the crook of his arm, they began a slow walk.

'Brandon was the perfect son; Dalton was the very devil. I liked them both, but my daughter much preferred her angel. Her heart broke when Brandon died, and it turned her husband against Dalton, too.

'The truth was, Ailsa was much more like Dalton than she wanted to admit. She was every bit as wild as he was. Sometimes she behaved like a lady, and she certainly knew all the etiquette and deportment—enough to marry an English earl. But she and Dalton were too alike. Both headstrong and stubborn.'

'After Brandon died, what happened to Dalton?'

'He tried to fill his brother's shoes. Tried to be the good son. But his parents grieved so hard, they couldn't bear to see him. He had to teach himself what he needed to know. And I was here, so I wasn't able to help him. I didn't know how bad it was until he told me, years later.'

She kept her arm in his, noticing how his physical strength seemed to improve as they spoke. His mood was lifting, and she was glad to help him.

'I am in need of your help, Lord Cairnross. Unfortunately, my husband and I had a…a disagreement, and I want to know how to win him back. I hurt his pride, and I don't know how to gain his forgiveness.'

The earl seemed to think it over. 'Dalton is a proud one, aye. But he admires strength of will. Tell him you're sorry and spend the night in his bed, and all will be well, lass.'

Her cheeks burned at his frank admission, but she supposed there was something to be said for actions speaking louder than words. 'If he comes home, I will do that indeed.'

'If he comes home,' the earl scoffed. 'Ha. Go and fetch him yourself, lass.'

Regina smiled and bid him farewell. Her spirits were already lifted after visiting with Lord Cairnross, and as she walked with the dog, she spied a coach drawing near to the house. Was it Dalton and her father?

She hurried closer, clutching at her skirts as she approached. But instead of stopping near the doors, the coach continued towards her.

Arthur began barking and straining at the lead, but she held him back, suddenly suspicious.

When the coach drew to a stop, the driver called out, 'Lady Regina?'

'Lady Camford,' she corrected, even though it wasn't true.

At that, the door to the coach swung open, and a stocky man stepped out. 'Your husband bid me to come and bring you to him.'

Regina took a step backwards. *No, he did not,* were the words that came to her lips. Instead, she replied, 'Why?'

At her question, the man appeared irritated. 'If a husband bids his wife to come, she should not be asking why.'

'If a strange man bids me to get into a coach, I have every reason to be asking why.' She took several steps back. Arthur barked furiously at the man, and she dropped the lead, turning to run.

'Lord Cairnross!' she called out, though he was already inside. 'Help me!'

Strong arms seized her waist, and she fought with all her strength, elbowing the man as she twisted and turned. It was like her nightmare all over again. Regina screamed, but the two men subdued her, shoving a handkerchief in her mouth and throwing her into the coach. The other man got inside with her and closed the door. Within moments, she felt the horses start trotting, and she fell forward, barely catching her balance. She reached for the door handle, but her assailant grabbed her wrist and twisted it until she cried out in pain.

No one could hear from the gag in her mouth. God help her, not again. Not this.

As the coach pulled away, Elliott MacLachor, Earl of Cairnross, held out his spyglass and stared at it. 'Bloody pirates. They've stolen the princess.' He strode inside the house and said to his housekeeper, 'Mrs Howard. A coach came and took Lady Camford away. Will you help me rescue her?'

Mrs Howard gripped her broomstick, her mouth open. 'My lord, is this one of your imaginings?'

Elliott opened the door and pointed outside. 'See for yourself. I willna be letting savages take our princess. Fetch my pistols.'

She hurried outside and saw the puppy barking, its leather lead trailing behind as he raced to follow the coach. 'Oh, dear God. What's happened?'

'They took her,' Elliott repeated. 'We have to stop them.'

A dawning realisation broke over the woman, and she shouted for one of the younger lads. 'Hamish! Quickly, tell MacLachor that Her Ladyship has been taken.' She wrung her hands in panic. 'What can we do? His Lordship is gone and so is her father. There's no one left.'

'No one but us,' Elliott said. 'We will have to help her.'

The housekeeper stared at him, shock in her eyes. 'I canna go with you, my lord. I'm too old.'

Elliott took her hands. 'So am I. But she needs us, Mrs Howard.'

Her frail palms were trembling, but she gave a nod. She took a deep breath and steeled herself. 'I'll get the pistols. You get a coach and horses.'

Before he knew what to make of that, she added, 'Don't be letting them out of your sight, my lord. We'll follow them and bring her home. I can promise you that.'

Over the past few days, despite Dalton's attempts to intercept the coach with Mr Sidney and Lord Havershire, he had been unable to catch up to them. It seemed that the men had not taken the main roads, and by the time he'd realised this, it was too late.

But he knew where they were going. And so, he'd decided to travel as fast as he could, switching horses often, in order to reach London first. He needed to understand what had happened and how severe the threat was against Regina's family.

If there was little danger, he would do what he could to help. But he worried that he might have no legal rights. Since she had refused to call him her husband, he was bound by her father's wishes. It infuriated him, being so helpless. But he had sworn to himself that he would do everything in his power to save her from harm. Even if that meant lowering his pride.

He ordered his coachman to drive him to his father's house. Though he doubted if the earl would help him, he had to try. Lord Brevershire had connections in Parliament, and he hoped the earl could use his influence to help him.

Dalton walked inside the house and gave his coat and hat to the footman. 'Where is my father?' he asked.

'His Lordship is in his study,' the footman answered.

Dalton thanked him and strode through the hallway. He walked inside and saw his father bent over a ledger, writing calmly.

'Father,' he greeted the man solemnly.

The earl did not look up from his papers, but merely answered, 'Dalton.'

He waited to see if his father would say anything further, but there was nothing.

Careful, he warned himself. *You need his help.*

'Do you have time to talk?' he asked, still waiting in the doorway.

'Not now,' Brevershire answered, still recording columns of numbers. 'Perhaps later this evening.'

'It's important,' Dalton continued. 'I am in need of your guidance.'

His father paused to set down his pen. He removed his spectacles and sighed. 'I heard about your impulsive wedding. You must be aware of how the scandal impacted our family name. I could not go anywhere without someone speaking of it.'

'I didn't want Regina to be humiliated and abandoned on her wedding day,' Dalton said. 'I have no regrets.'

'All of London was talking of it,' the earl said. 'I could go nowhere without someone laughing at our family. Do you understand the embarrassment you brought upon us? Did you even think of the consequences?'

'I thought of her,' he admitted. 'And I suspect that

if Mother had been in a similar situation, you'd have done the same.'

'Did you ever wed her legally?' his father prompted.

He didn't answer his father's question. If he replied no, his father would do nothing to help him. Then again, he wasn't certain his father would help him now. 'Regina is my responsibility. She is in some…trouble at the moment, and I came to beg for your help.'

'Beg?' His father's face turned incredulous. 'When have you ever begged for anything? Making rash decisions has always been your way, Dalton. Like that wedding.'

'I know I've made mistakes in the past. But I want to believe that you and I can work together.'

The earl appeared doubtful, but Dalton refused to back down. He took a deep breath and steeled himself. 'Regina was attacked several years ago, and the man who hurt her is now dead. Her father was receiving blackmail demands.'

Brevershire stood from his desk, his expression grim. 'One scandal after another.'

'She is an innocent,' Dalton argued. 'I am asking for her sake. You know a great deal of people in London. With your influence, I might be able to protect her.'

His father stared at him, and there was no denying that he didn't want to be involved. But Dalton refused to back down.

'I know I am not the son and heir you wanted,' he said. 'But I cannot stand by and do nothing. Regina is everything to me. I love her, and I will do everything in my power to help her.'

The earl regarded him with a long look. 'You want

me to use my influence to convince others that her family is blameless?'

'If it's possible, yes.'

His father's expression turned grim. 'It may not be. We cannot control what others think.'

'I have a plan…though it is rather unusual. But if you help me save her, I will do whatever you wish of me. I will become like Brandon, if that is what you want.'

His father sighed and shook his head. 'You could never be Brandon.'

The words stung, but Dalton nodded. 'Then what is it you want? What can I do?'

His father reached out and touched his shoulder. The weight of his hand was startling, for he could not remember the last time the earl had touched him. 'I never wanted you to be Brandon.'

'You never told me what you *did* want,' Dalton said.

His father stared off at the bookcase. 'Grief is a difficult thing. There were times when I thought I was over his death, but then you would do something that reminded me of Brandon. It nearly brought me to my knees.' John's grip tightened on his shoulder. 'Every time I saw you, I thought of him. You were more alike than you knew.'

An ache caught in Dalton's gut at his words. 'I thought you never wanted anything to do with me. Because I was the reason he grew sick. If I hadn't taken him to see Gabriel—'

'It wasn't your fault,' John interrupted. He turned to face him squarely. 'But losing a son isn't something you ever get over.'

'You still had a son left,' Dalton said, his voice heavy. 'And I knew I wasn't the one you wanted.'

John looked as if he'd been struck in the face. 'You believed that?'

Dalton shrugged. 'What else was I to think?'

His father met his gaze for a long moment, searching for the words. 'I only wanted you to curb your impulses and think before you acted. Being an earl means you have to put the needs of others before your own.'

'I have,' Dalton answered, his voice raw with emotion. 'I am putting *her* above all else.'

For a long moment, John stared at him, as if taking his measure—as if he were seeing his son for the first time in years. At last, he answered, 'Good. Then perhaps there's hope for a new beginning. For all of us.'

Chapter Thirteen

In the dim light of the coach, Regina decided that she would no longer be a victim. The man had bound her hands in front of her, and she did not know who had hired him. He was little more than a thief-taker. But she would have her answers.

She pressed her face against the side of the coach until part of the handkerchief was caught against her cheek. Slowly, she pulled, until she managed to free it from her mouth. Her tongue was dry, but she managed to cough.

'Clever thing, aren't you?' he said.

'Not clever enough to avoid captivity,' she remarked, coughing again. He barked a laugh at that and handed her a flask of something. She wasn't certain what it was, but she took it with her bound hands and ventured a sip.

The whisky burned a path down her throat, but she managed to drink another swallow to clear her throat.

'We're stopping for the night soon,' he told her. 'If you're a good girl, you can sleep in a room with me.'

Where she could be attacked? It wasn't at all a good

idea. 'Why stop at all?' she asked. 'I assume you were paid to bring me to someone. Won't you get more if you bring me there faster?'

He laughed again. 'We have to change horses and get food. But if you want to keep travelling I've no objection.'

'I would much rather continue travelling.' She straightened and stared outside the window. 'But I'd also like to know who hired you. And what your name is.'

He let out a snort and took a sip from the flask. Then his gaze drifted over her body. 'I suppose you would. Hobson's my name.'

She waited, but he did not reveal who had paid him to capture her. It was doubtful that this could be Lady Anne's family. They had nothing at all. And if it were the authorities, then Mr Sidney would have taken her then.

No, it was someone else. A dark thought occurred to her, and she wondered if she dared voice it. The coach was slowing down, and she needed to know. 'Did Mallencourt's family pay you well?'

A sly smile spread over his face. 'Clever, as I said.'

Dear God. If the Mallencourts had discovered that their son's death was not an accident, it was possible that they could bring charges against her and her father. It would be difficult, but not impossible. If they had the money to hire a thief-taker, then what else would they dare?

'Be a good girl and stay quiet while I get food and change the horses.' He reached out and stroked her cheek before he tied her ropes to the interior of the coach.

Disgust roiled in her stomach, but she didn't flinch at all. The more she cowered or surrendered, the more he would dare.

'And if you're friendly, I'll keep you comfortable when they remand you into custody,' he offered. 'No chains to bruise this soft skin.' He slid her hair back from her neck, resting his hand there.

Revulsion rose up, and she suppressed her shudder. All the horrifying memories of Mallencourt returned, along with the wrenching fear. But she forced herself to ignore him, giving him nothing for the liberties he'd taken.

He left the coach, and she waited in the dim light while someone changed the horses. She tried to reach for the door handle, but it was jammed shut. With her feet, she tried to kick it, but she heard the distinct rattle of chains.

Regina cursed at that. She had based her plans on escaping right here and now. Instead, it seemed that she would have to rethink it. If they brought her into custody, there was one definite problem for the Mallencourts. Dalton had said it earlier—if the coroner had already ruled the death an accident five years ago, it would take a great deal to overturn it.

If she clung to that, insisting her innocence, she might be able to avoid a trial.

Outside, the rattling noise continued, until at last, Hobson pulled the door open. He got inside, and she could smell the heavenly aroma of fresh bread. She had never wanted to eat so much in all her life.

Within moments, the coach was back on the road, and she watched as Hobson took out a piece of the bread. 'I suppose you want this, don't you?'

Don't answer, she warned herself. *The price is too high.*

He took a bite, chewing with his mouth open. 'I'll give you a piece. But you'll have to pay me.'

She knew the sort of payment he wanted, and again, she behaved as if he wasn't there. He reached out to pinch her roughly. 'Do you think you're something special, *milady?* You're naught but a whore anyhow. Living as mistress to that viscount. You might as well give me what I want.' He leaned in as if to kiss her, and Regina spat in his face.

Pain exploded across her cheek when he struck her with his fist. She was stunned into silence, and Hobson added, 'You won't escape, if that's what you're thinking. Remember who is your master, milady, and you'll find that I can be generous to those who please me.'

She lifted her chin and glared back at him. 'You should think of what happened to the last man who touched me against my will.' A trickle of blood ran down from her nose, but she refused to back down. Her words were an open threat, but she hardly cared.

'Use your wits, Hobson. What do you think will happen to you if you violate the daughter of an earl? I *will* tell him what you did, and my father will use his position and power to ensure that you suffer. Whereas if you bring me home, who do you think will pay more? The Mallencourts, who have nothing, or an earl? Even my husband will offer more than enough for my safe return.'

He was starting to falter, but he argued, 'You'd just

have me arrested as a thief-taker. I'd be in prison for this.'

'It's not too late,' she insisted. 'You made a mistake, but one that can be corrected.'

She would not be a victim again, too terrified to fight back. This time, she would use her arguments, her words as weapons. He was still trying to think, but she could see that her words were starting to change his mind.

Hobson continued to eat in front of her, and her stomach growled with raging hunger. She gladly accepted the pangs, as long as he kept his hands to himself. It would be another long night of travelling. She dared not close her eyes, though.

'Think upon it,' she told the man. 'There is still time to change your mind.' Her courage kept her voice calm, but inwardly, she remained troubled. To keep herself from panicking, she forced herself to think of Dalton.

Dear God, she missed him. She had loved waking up in the morning with his arms around her. He'd made her feel beloved, and turning away from him had been the hardest thing she'd ever done. It was a physical ache to be apart from him.

But love was about choosing what was right, not her own selfish needs. She'd had to give him the choice, the chance to walk away from this scandal. Letting him go was the right thing to do, even if it tore her heart out. Even now, she didn't know what he would say or do when he saw her again. She didn't know if he'd gone to help her father out of obligation, or whether he still loved her.

Hobson continued drinking from the flask, and in time, his head drifted back, and he began to snore. Regina renewed her efforts to free herself from the ropes, though she wasn't entirely certain what she could do, even if her hands were unbound.

Even so, she refused to give up.

Three days later

The last thing Dalton expected to see was a pirate and a housekeeper charging into his father's house. His grandfather's hair was tucked beneath a cap, and he had a cutlass strapped to his side. A blend of exhaustion and excitement lined the old man's face.

His father, Lord Brevershire, was staring at his father-in-law. 'Cairnross, is that you? What the devil are you wearing?'

The older man came forward and brandished his cutlass. To Dalton, he said, 'Laddie, we must go and rescue the princess. She was taken by ruffians, and we tracked them to the southern islands.'

'Who took her?' Dalton's instincts flared up, and he immediately understood that Regina was in danger.

'A thief-taker,' Mrs Howard said. 'Bold as you please. He rode up in a coach and snatched her out from under us. But Lord Cairnross and I followed her. We ne'er let her out of our sight, not once, did we?'

'Not once,' he repeated. 'And we must go now to fetch her back. Now that we have reinforcements.' The look in his eyes made it clear that he considered Dalton to be the reinforcements.

And Grandfather was right about that. He would do everything to help Regina, but he needed more information. 'Where did he take her?'

'Near the Tower,' he whispered. 'I'll have to show you where they are.'

'The driver knows?' Dalton verified, and his grandfather nodded. He told a footman to fetch his coat and hat.

'Just how much have you had to drink tonight, Cairnross?' Brevershire asked. 'You seem rather deep in your cups.' He folded his copy of *The Times* and set it aside.

At that, the old earl glared at him. 'How dare you, sir. Do not accuse me of being a drunkard when your granddaughter has been kidnapped.'

'By ruffians,' Brevershire repeated drily. His tone said that he didn't believe a word of Cairnross's tale.

'Aye, of course. Who else?'

But Dalton believed it. He was already putting on his coat and hat. 'Let's go now, Grandfather.'

'At least your son has some sense,' Cairnross pronounced. 'Aye, laddie, we'll go now and save her.' He sheathed his cutlass and turned to go. To Mrs Howard, he commanded, 'Stay here and gather a feast for us, so that when we return, we may feed the lass.'

Mrs Howard bobbed a curtsy, and bid them, 'Be safe, and bring our lassie home.'

Lord Cairnross gave a strong salute. 'So I shall.'

All during the coach ride, Dalton tried to sort out the fact from fancy. He'd learned that Regina was taken by a hired man and that his grandfather and Mrs Howard had tracked her all the way to London.

'Did they stop at inns along the way?' he questioned.

'Nay, laddie. They changed horses and bought food,

but they didna stay overnight.' His grandfather added, 'I was only going to bring one driver, but Mrs Howard said we should bring two, so they could take turns sleeping. She was right, as usual.'

'Why did they take her?' he wondered aloud.

The question seemed to sober his grandfather. 'I don't ken, laddie. But we will save her, aye?'

He nodded. His thoughts wandered back to the day he had gone after her father. Lord Havershire was now safely at home in the care of a physician and his wife. Dalton had spoken to the household, strictly reminding them to keep the earl quiet and rested. He still didn't know why Havershire had left, but he knew he had to address the issue of Mallencourt's death.

To his surprise, he saw that the driver had brought them to the Mallencourt residence. A dark uneasiness caught in his gut.

They knew. And if he didn't do something, they might take their own vengeance out on Regina.

Dalton didn't know how he would approach this situation, but he thought a moment and made his plans. Then he told his grandfather of his intention. 'Can you help me with this? We'll split up and see if we can find her.'

There was a flicker of unrest in the old earl's eyes, but he inclined his head. ''Tis dangerous, but aye, I can indeed, laddie.' He rested his hand upon his cutlass. 'You can depend on me. I've had a great deal of experience in battle.'

Whatever thoughts were going through the older man's head, Dalton could not say. But they had only one chance to save Regina, and he would do whatever he could.

Dalton left his grandfather behind in the coach and approached the front door. He sounded the knocker, though it was well past the hour for guests. He continued rapping on the knocker until at last, a footman arrived.

'Lord Mallencourt isn't receiving callers. Come back in the morning.' Before he could close the door, Dalton pushed his way through.

'I will leave, as soon as I have my wife,' he said smoothly.

At that, a look of alarm flashed over the footman's face. 'My lord, I don't think—'

'Let him in, Hugh,' a voice spoke. 'Lord Camford and I have much to discuss regarding his wife's behaviour.'

Dalton studied the younger man, Mallencourt's brother, and likely the new heir. 'We do have much to discuss. Kidnapping is not an offence I will allow to pass lightly.'

'Nor will I allow her to get away with murder.' Mallencourt's face held a cool solemnity. His dark brown hair framed a face with stony grey eyes. 'She will be brought to trial.'

'I demand that you give Lady Camford back, before I bring the law to support my case,' Dalton insisted. 'As my wife, she is my responsibility.' He hoped rather fervently that no one knew the truth about their marriage.

'I have arranged a meeting with the local magistrate,' Mallencourt said. 'We will discuss the details of my brother's death and determine whether new charges should be brought forth.'

'His death was ruled an accident,' Dalton said. 'What do you hope to accomplish with this?' He was stalling, trying to draw out the man into conversation. His grandfather needed time to search for Regina.

'I want justice,' Mallencourt answered. 'The world deserves to know how my brother died.'

'The world knows how he died. You cannot overturn anything.'

'We shall see,' Mallencourt answered. 'In the meantime, you will be leaving.'

'Not without my wife.' He started to move forwards, but this time, two footmen flanked him on either side.

'She is not here on the premises,' Mallencourt said. 'But I will bring her to the magistrate's in a few days and send word. You may see her then.'

Dalton didn't know if the man was telling the truth or not, but he had given his grandfather all the time he could. He considered the idea of forcing his way in, but it might cause stronger consequences in the long run. At least he knew who had taken her and why.

He turned his back on Mallencourt, turning over the problem in his mind. He was vaguely aware of the servants closing the door on him, and he wrenched the door of the coach open.

There he found his grandfather happily sitting across from Regina. A breath of relief rushed through him. He didn't know how Cairnross had found her, but the distraction had worked.

Dalton could hardly blink before she was in his arms, half-crying. He closed the coach door, and the driver took them away.

'Well done,' he said to his grandfather. 'Did you have any difficulty finding her?'

'I used your distraction to my advantage,' Cairnross answered. 'Went through the servants' quarters and rescued the princess. There was only one locked door, so I knew that was where she was imprisoned.' He beamed and added, 'They were daft enough to leave the key in the lock.'

'Did anyone see you?'

Regina shook her head, still gripping him tightly. 'They were too worried about you to even think about me. When Lord Cairnross showed up at my door, he unlocked it and took me outside the servants' entrance.'

'Thank God,' he breathed. To his grandfather he added, 'Well done, sailor.' His grandfather saluted him, leaning back in the coach with pride.

Regina kept her hand in Dalton's, so thankful that he was here with her now. She could hardly tear her gaze from his, and when they arrived at his father's residence, he led her up the stairs to his bedchamber.

'Are you all right?' he asked, when they were alone. 'Did anyone hurt you?' He reached out and touched the bruise on her cheek.

She shook her head. 'It's nothing serious. Just a few bruises.'

'This looks like someone hit you.' His thumb caressed the spot, but she caught his hand.

'I don't want to think of that now. I'm home safe, with you. That's all that matters.' She brought his arms to her waist and rested her arms around his neck. Right now, she refused to consider what lay ahead or what scandal could impede their happiness. Instead, she needed to be in his arms, to let him know how much he meant to her.

'Let me defend you, Regina,' he murmured against her hair. 'With whatever lies ahead.'

She lifted her face to his and kissed him. 'I was wrong to leave you. And whatever happens, we will stay together,' she promised.

He undressed her slowly, and she did the same to him, savouring each touch. It felt like an eternity since he'd held her, and she welcomed the hard lines of his body against hers.

'I am sorry for pushing you away,' she said. 'I thought at the time, that I was protecting you from the scandal. I never meant to doubt your ability to defend me.'

His hands moved over her bare breasts, and she gave a soft cry as her body grew aroused to his touch. 'The danger's not over yet. Mallencourt wants to overturn the coroner's cause of death.'

She had suspected as much, but hearing it brought the terror only closer. 'Do you think he can?'

Dalton trailed his mouth down her throat, his hands sliding lower. 'He can try. But I won't let him hurt you, Regina.' His mouth closed over her breast as he parted her legs. She gripped his hair, raising up her knees as she grew wet with need. 'And when this is over, I want you to marry me.'

He entered her in one swift stroke. Her body welcomed him inside, and her heart was so filled with love and fear for the future, she could hardly bear it. 'I will,' she promised.

He clasped her hands in his, and his green eyes held the intensity of a lifetime. Slowly, he made love to her, and with every stroke, she felt their bodies becoming one. 'I don't want to die, Dalton. Please…don't let them bring charges against me.'

'I won't let anything happen,' he swore. 'I will hire

attorneys for you, if needed...but it is my hope that
nothing is overturned, and we will put an end to it.'

To underscore his words, he seized her hips and
thrust deeply inside. She squeezed him within and
wrapped her legs around his waist. He quickened his
pace, and she felt her breathing mimic his thrusts. As
he penetrated her, she felt herself rising higher, straining as he pushed her to the edge.

'I love you, Regina,' he said. Over and over, he took
her, and he demanded, 'Let yourself go. I want to watch
you reach the edge.'

He ground against her, and the contact was a sear-
ing touch that fisted inside her and then shattered into
a thousand pieces. She clenched his length as she shuddered, and he rode her release, echoing her pleasure
when he took his own. She heard his groan against
her lips as he emptied himself and collapsed atop her.

'I love you,' she whispered. 'And I have faith in
you.'

He held her close, but neither knew what the future
would bring. They lay together in the darkness, and
she asked, 'Was there any word from Anne?'

He shook his head. 'She refused to accept my call
a few days ago. Which was not surprising.'

'What will you do about her?' She traced her hand
over his hard shoulder, marvelling at his lines of
strength.

'Sidney thinks I should leave it alone. I disagree.'
He caught her hand and brought it to his heart. Beneath
her fingers, she could feel the beating, and she pressed
a kiss to his bare skin.

'I am going to meet with an attorney before we go
to the magistrate. He will represent you and ensure

that we follow the law. I believe that, in the end, we can prevail.'

She didn't voice her fears, for there were two enemies against her—Mallencourt and Lady Anne. Though she wanted to keep faith that there was a chance of acquittal, a part of her feared the worst. She had heard of women who had been hanged for murder. A cold chill flooded through her at the thought. She didn't want to die—especially when she had been a victim of Mallencourt's violence.

A tremble caught her, and she clutched at the thin coverlet. If Anne had been the blackmailer, why would she turn against her? Regina had mistakenly believed that they were friends. Though she had known of her friend's poverty, never had she imagined that their friendship was false.

What had Anne witnessed? Had she truly been there that night, waiting for her? Or was that a lie, too? She didn't know. Though she tried to sleep, it would not come. All she could think about was the meeting with the magistrate and whether she would survive the outcome.

'What of my father?' she asked Dalton. 'Have you seen him?'

He shook his head. 'He has kept to himself. Thus far, he has remained with your mother at home.'

She was glad to hear that he had arrived there safely. And although he had bid her farewell, she could not relinquish her worry. Perhaps his illness had worsened, and he wanted to spend the remainder of his days at home with Mother. But she didn't want to think of him suffering.

Another thought occurred to her, and she asked,

'Will Papa have to speak to the magistrate on my behalf, as well?'

'I think it's best if the attorney handles his testimony,' Dalton countered. 'We cannot afford a moment of madness.' She knew he was referring to her father's act of violence against Miss Goodson.

His arms closed around her, and she knew she was putting her life in his hands. Everything came down to this meeting with the magistrate—and she feared the worst.

Over the past few days, Lord Brevershire had been more demanding than Dalton had ever known. Both of them had stayed up late each night, going over their plans. And yet, he could not have been more grateful for his father's help. Dalton had offered to live in Scotland, retiring to a quiet life with Regina, if they managed to save her.

Instead, John had demanded that he take on more responsibilities, including caring for all the estates and handling their investments. He had no choice but to take on the full weight of the earldom, though the title was not yet his.

Dalton wanted to believe that he and his father would succeed, but the truth was, he had no idea. They had set their plans in motion, writing countless letters until his fingers were stained with ink and sore. Right now, he felt as if he were in the midst of a war, fighting for his wife's survival. But he would spend every coin he had if it meant protecting her.

He had hired the best attorney in London for her, and they had spent all morning discussing her case. Mr Hortense Whitley had listened, taken copious notes, and he had also sent word to the magistrate, moving the meeting to later in the afternoon.

'You have a good chance of winning,' he said to Dalton, 'but do not let your wife or her father speak to the magistrate. They could incriminate themselves without even knowing it.'

'Regina will do as we ask,' Dalton said. Earlier that morning, they had agreed that she would remain in hiding to keep her safe. 'It's her father who could be questionable. I asked him to join us this morning, so you can advise him.'

'We have a few advantages,' Mr Whitley said. 'Namely, the cost of a trial would be high, and Mallencourt's family would have to pay for it. It has also been several years since the ruling, so time is on our side. Last, the blackmail would only incriminate Lady Anne—or it could possibly be used against the Mallencourts. It all depends on whether that comes out in the meeting.'

'What is the purpose of resurrecting this case?' Dalton asked. 'What do they hope to gain?'

The attorney shrugged. 'Power and influence, I suspect. If they believe they have an advantage over your family, it would be a means of intimidation…'

And likely that was the true reason. The threat of scandal had forced Havershire to pay thousands of pounds to protect his daughter's good name. The Mallencourts might have the same goal, of extortion.

It was rather like an elaborate game of chess. The winner would have to make sacrifices and accept losses for the overall good. And Dalton had already made his first move.

The door opened, and Lord Havershire walked inside. Dalton stood and greeted the man, asking, 'Won't you sit down and join us?'

The earl did so, and he folded his hands in his lap. The attorney was about to go over their plans, when Havershire suddenly broke into a racking cough. He covered his mouth with a handkerchief and took a moment to clear his throat. Then he said, 'Forgive me. I fear, my health is not what it used to be.'

'Of course,' the attorney said. 'If you would care for some tea…'

'In a moment.' The earl waved him off. 'Before you begin speaking of your plans, there is something we should discuss.'

'Go on.' The attorney dipped his pen in the inkwell and regarded him.

Lord Havershire's gaze moved from Dalton to the attorney. 'This situation is about human greed, is it not? The vultures wish to strip us of everything, in order to benefit themselves. Even if we indulge them, it will never be enough.'

He coughed again, his shoulders shaking from the exertion. 'I know this, because I borrowed money to pay the blackmailer for nearly five years. To me, it was a worthwhile endeavour because it protected our family name. Tavin MacKinloch loaned me the money when some of my investments failed. I managed to rebuild our wealth last year, and now that I have the funds to repay his family, and restore Regina's dowry, I owe a great debt to the laird.'

'I have already repaid your debt,' Dalton informed him. 'For Regina's sake.' He had quietly taken care of it, giving Lachlan the money that his family was owed.

The earl sobered. 'Then I will return the funds to

you, for I take care of my own debts. But now, we must do everything in our power to protect my daughter. I am prepared to make the sacrifice.' His gaze moved from one man to the next. 'If that means shouldering the blame for Mallencourt's death, I will do so.'

The attorney rose from his chair. 'No, sir. Absolutely not. You risk losing your title, your estates—no. You must not confess to a murder you did not commit.'

'There was no murder at all,' Dalton interjected. 'Mallencourt's death was accidental.'

'Indeed,' the attorney said, 'but we must tread carefully. Had you not attempted to cover up his death, there would be no question of it being an accident. As it is, that could be construed as a crime.'

'I saw no other choice,' Havershire admitted. 'I couldn't bring such a scandal upon our family. Regina's future would have been ruined.' He sank down into a chair. 'I am dying. I don't care what they do to me, so long as we save her.'

Dalton thought a moment about their circumstances. 'I don't think it will be necessary. We will meet with the magistrate and come to an agreement.' In this instance, he believed that the Mallencourts would never back down—not unless it was to their benefit to do so. He was counting on it.

'My lord, do not say anything,' the attorney advised. 'No good will come of it.'

Dalton could see that Havershire was struggling at the idea of letting others fight for his daughter. 'I will not let her be imprisoned or face death. Never.'

'Nor will I,' Dalton reminded him. He met the earl's agitated expression with his own steady resolve. 'I swear it to you.'

Chapter Fourteen

Regina spent the first half-hour alone in a small office. Her father, Dalton, and the attorney had asked her to remain apart from the others, so she had sat in the tiny space with little more than a chair and a single desk.

The sound of voices and footsteps approached, and the door swung open. She was startled to see her former friend, Lady Anne, standing there. Anne's face was red, as if she had been crying. She clutched her hands together and stood close to the doorway.

'Regina? Can we talk for a moment?'

She wanted to respond with: *I have nothing to say to you.* Instead, she stared back at her friend and remained silent.

Anne took a breath and said, 'I wanted to tell you how very sorry I am. But you must understand how destitute we are. There is no one to take care of my family. I did what I had to do to survive.'

'You betrayed me,' Regina answered. 'A true friend would have asked for help instead of demanding blackmail.'

'Your father would have done nothing for my family,' Anne said slowly. 'But he would do everything for you. I was careful not to ask for money he couldn't afford. Without his help, my family would never have survived the past five years.'

'You're wrong,' Regina countered. 'He couldn't afford it, and he had to borrow the money. My betrothal to Lachlan MacKinloch was part of his repayment.' Her mouth tightened at the thought of her former friend's demands. 'And now, because of what you've done, I could face imprisonment. Or worse.'

Horror washed over Anne's face. 'No! I promise you, that will not happen. I won't allow it.'

'You can make no promises to me.' Regina turned her back on the young woman. Inwardly, she was seething with anger. She had mistakenly believed that Anne was her friend. She had trusted in her, sharing parts of her life that she had not shared with anyone else. And now, to learn that her best friend was responsible for her father's debts and the blackmail was too much. 'You need to go.'

'I just…wanted you to know that I still consider you my friend. There was nothing else I could think of to help my family.'

'You could have lowered your pride and asked,' Regina said. 'Instead, you betrayed our friendship.' Without another word, she turned away. She heard the sound of Anne weeping, and tears gathered in her own eyes for the loss. It could have been so different between them.

Regina rested her forehead against her hands. Time seemed to stretch out endlessly before she heard the footsteps approaching again. This time, when the door opened, she lifted her face to see who it was. When Dalton stood there, she felt her emotions breaking apart.

'Regina?' he asked. 'Are you all right?'

'No,' she whispered, her voice breaking. She stood up from the chair, feeling so fragile and yet filled with hope. 'I'm not.'

The sight of this man eased her in a way she had never expected. He opened his arms, and she ran to him, heedless of what she had said to him the last time. 'I love you,' he said against her hair, holding her tight. She gripped him as if he were a bastion of strength against the storm of fear coursing within her.

'I love you, too,' she cried. 'Dalton, what will happen to me? I'm so afraid.' Her skin felt icy, and prickles of gooseflesh rose up, despite the heat of his embrace. His mouth came to hers in a warm reassurance, his kiss healing her.

'I'm going to help you,' he promised. 'I swear it.'

She kissed him back, winding her arms around his neck. The comfort did not diminish her fear, but it made it more bearable. For a time, she simply let him hold her, and she was grateful for his embrace.

When he pulled back to look at her, she asked, 'What have they decided?'

'Nothing as yet. I have asked my father to intervene on your behalf,' he said. 'He knows many people in London, and I believe he can use his influence to help.' After a slight pause, he added, 'They want to question you now.'

'I thought I was to say nothing.' She wiped at her tears, and he cupped her face, kissing her again.

'Your attorney will ask the questions,' he said. 'Just

answer him honestly. And know that I will fight for you with every breath I have.'

He held her again while she wept, and she realised that this was what marriage was meant to be. Standing by a loved one, no matter what happened. And for the first time, she realised that she was lost without him.

She braved a smile. 'I want to believe that somehow we will get through this.' Even as she spoke the words, she tried to push away the doubts. Her heart ached at the thought of enduring a lifetime of prison.

There was a slight shadow on Dalton's face, but he did not share his reasons. She suspected that he didn't want to consider the alternative.

His expression sobered, and he reached up to take her face between his hands. 'Are you ready?'

Not really, she wanted to answer but didn't. It was too easy to let her thoughts wander down the path of anxiety.

You're going to survive this, she told herself.

She could only hope it would be true.

After the initial introductions were spoken, the magistrate gestured for all of them to sit. Mallencourt's younger brother was there, along with Lady Anne, Lady Regina, and Lord Havershire. Dalton had hoped that his father would come, but it seemed that John had stayed away.

The clerk stood and said, 'We are gathered together to speak of some new evidence that Reginald Clark, Lord Mallencourt, has discovered in regard to his brother's death. The purpose of this meeting is to determine whether an arrest should be made and whether a trial should be pursued for wrongdoing.'

At that, Hortense Whitely stood. 'Your Worship, I have been appointed as the attorney representing the rights of both the Earl of Havershire and his daughter, Lady Regina.'

'Is that truly necessary, given the absence of a trial?' the magistrate enquired.

'It is. And it is my sincere hope that we may put this matter to rest and avoid a trial altogether.'

The baron appeared irritated but motioned for the clerk to present his concerns. Dalton grimaced when he heard the clerk say, 'It is believed that Lady Regina Crewe, daughter of the Earl of Havershire, did feloniously lure the late Baron Mallencourt to her home. That with malice aforethought, she did bring Lord Mallencourt into the drawing room alone, where she feigned seductive behaviour to the baron before striking him over the head with the intent of murder. And that she instructed her servant to dispose of the body near the River Thames.'

The clerk continued describing the details, but Dalton's gut was churning. Murder, not manslaughter. The picture Mallencourt had evoked was of a heartless Lady of Ice, one who would tempt men, only to lead them to their demise.

Regina's face had gone pale, and Mr Whitley stood. 'Your Worship, I have the coroner's report from five years ago, when Lord Mallencourt's body was found.' He held it out and said, 'If there had been any wrongdoing, it would have been noted at that time.'

The magistrate read over the coroner's notes, his face impassive. His gaze shifted to the new Lord Mallencourt, and he asked, 'If there were doubts about your brother's death, why did you not mention them five years earlier?'

Lord Mallencourt cleared his throat. 'We did not know what happened and trusted the coroner's report. But a few weeks ago, a witness came forward and contacted my family. Lady Anne claims she was there on the night my older brother died.'

Regina's face was deathly white, but she remained silent. From the raw fear on her face, Dalton could see she was struggling to hold back tears. He wanted to comfort her, but he could not speak.

The magistrate eyed the young woman sitting nearby. 'Is this true?'

The young woman stood, her face masking all emotions. 'It is. For a short while, I was there before they arrived.'

'And of whom do you speak when you say "they"?' the magistrate asked.

'Lady Regina and Lord Mallencourt,' she answered. Her face appeared stricken, but she did face Regina at last. There was a silent communication between the two of them, but Dalton could not say what the young woman was thinking.

'And they were returning from a ball?' the magistrate continued.

'They were, yes.'

'Were you present at the same gathering?' he asked.

'No, sir. I was not invited.' Her face flushed, and she looked down at her hands.

'Why, then, did you go to Lady Regina's residence if you knew she was not at home?'

Lady Anne's face reddened. 'Because I did not wish to be at my home. I often stayed with Lady Regina overnight, and I wanted to talk to her after she returned.'

'But you knew it was too late to be paying a social call,' he continued.

'It was,' she agreed, 'but I have come to call on many occasions. I let myself in and went to Regina's rooms to wait for her. No one saw me.'

'And you believe you witnessed something related to Lord Mallencourt's death that night?' the magistrate questioned.

Lady Anne hesitated. 'I was not in the same room with them, so I cannot say for certain.'

The attorney stood and said, 'Your Worship, this is speculation. If she was not in the same room, she cannot even say whether Lord Mallencourt was there. He might have simply driven Lady Regina home and departed.'

'And did he?' the magistrate asked Lady Anne.

Her face crumpled, and she shook her head. 'I—I don't know. All I know is that…the baron was there that night, and the next day he was dead.'

'She knows exactly what happened,' Mallencourt interrupted. 'Because she has been blackmailing the earl for years. When the earl refused to pay, she came to me.'

Lord Havershire started in his chair, but the attorney sent him a warning look while Dalton held his breath. If the earl admitted the truth, it could cost them everything.

'Lord Havershire,' the magistrate said. 'Were you under the threat of blackmail these five years past?'

The earl regarded each of the people in the room—

Lord Mallencourt, Lady Anne, the magistrate, and finally Dalton and Regina.

'I was, yes,' he confessed.

Regina's stomach sank, twisting into nausea. Her father's admission essentially told the magistrate that they had something to hide, something worth the threat of blackmail. And her fears only magnified.

There could be a trial at the House of Lords—not just for her, but for her father, as well, for covering up Mallencourt's death.

The attorney sighed and shook his head. 'Your Worship, I see no reason why we should entertain this conversation any longer. The coroner's report clearly shows—'

'I have more questions,' the magistrate said. He directed his attention to Lady Anne. 'I could easily have you arrested on charges of blackmail. Or, if you tell the truth about what you saw and heard that night, I could dismiss the charges.'

Anne blanched at the confrontation. Her gaze passed from Lord Havershire back to Regina.

Don't do this, Regina warned. But she knew that her life and her father's hung in the balance.

'I'm sorry,' she whispered, tears breaking forth. Then she turned back to the magistrate. 'I…heard voices that night. I went to the stairs, because I thought Regina had returned from the ball. I heard Lord Mallencourt talking with her, so I didn't go down. But I saw them go into the parlour together. And later, I heard him attacking her.'

'You did nothing to help,' Regina interrupted, her own tears streaming down her face. It was too late to hide the evidence any longer, but she seized the opportunity to confront her former friend. 'That blackguard tried to rape me, while you stood by on the stairs and allowed it to happen.'

Anne stared back at her. 'And what could I have done? I didn't know what was happening, and I just… froze.'

Regina didn't look at the magistrate or Mallencourt—only Anne. 'If someone had tried to hurt you, I would have done anything to stop it. I would have tried to open the door or screamed. I wouldn't have stood by, and I certainly wouldn't have tried to extort money out of it.'

'Is that what happened?' the magistrate asked. 'Did the baron try to…defile you?'

Regina closed her eyes and nodded.

'And I broke the door down to help her,' the earl added. At the sound of her father's voice, Regina turned to him. 'Like any father, I would do everything necessary to save my daughter from ruin.'

'Even murder?' Mallencourt prompted.

Regina was shaking her head in horror. 'Papa, no.'

But from the resignation on her father's face, she knew he was intending to confess. He coughed again, a hacking sound that revealed the weakness he was suffering. For long moments, he struggled to breathe, and the magistrate exchanged a look with the attorney.

'I think we have our answers,' Mallencourt said softly. 'My brother did not die by drowning in the Thames after a drunken night.'

The silence that spread throughout the room was damning. Regina felt physically ill, wondering if she should confess the truth. It was the right thing to do, and she could not let her father suffer for her own sins.

But Dalton seemed to sense what she was about to do, and his hand clamped down on hers in a warning.

Chapter Fifteen

'**P**erhaps the greater question is why you would dredge up the past,' Dalton countered, staring hard at Mallencourt. 'Your older brother attacked a lady. His death was ruled an accident by the coroner, but even if his death were manslaughter, I doubt if any jury would convict an earl defending his daughter.'

'You don't know that,' the baron started to say.

'What do you hope to gain?' Dalton pressed further. 'I know the state of your finances, and you cannot afford to pay for another trial. Nor will it bring your brother back.' He softened his tone. 'Which is a good thing, I think. I've heard that you've done a great deal to rebuild your family's name. You're a far better baron than he ever was.'

Mallencourt sobered at that. When Dalton met his eyes, he added, 'I know what it is to live in the shadow of an older brother. And what it is to lose him.'

In that moment, a look of understanding passed between them. He could see the baron faltering, and it gave him reason to hope.

The door opened quietly, and he was startled to see

his father entering the room. The magistrate glanced up, and Lord Brevershire greeted him. 'Forgive me for my tardiness, Harold. I was delayed and could not be here until now.'

Dalton met his father's gaze with a silent question, but the earl did not reveal anything at all.

The magistrate appeared unsettled by the intrusion. 'Did you need to be here, Brevershire?'

'In a matter that affects my son? Of course, I should be here.' John went to Dalton's side, and his expression held silent support. Emotion gathered up inside him, and when his father rested his hand upon his shoulder, Dalton felt his hope rising higher. He met his father's gaze, and in the older man's expression, he saw the strength of an alliance. He was grateful that the earl had seen fit to help him.

'Lord Mallencourt, I think it would be in your best interests to drop these charges,' Brevershire began. 'Your brother had a dreadful reputation in society, and it would be terrible, if everyone learned what he did to Lady Camford.'

Before Mallencourt could answer, the earl went on. 'I also thought you should know that my son and I have made many investments over the past few months, and last week, we purchased the Larkin Factory and the properties at Melford. I believe they represent most of your family's assets.'

Dalton hid his smile, thankful that the purchase had indeed been successful. He hadn't known for certain until just now.

Lord Mallencourt's expression turned shocked. 'You've done what?'

'Oh, it was my son's idea,' Brevershire remarked.

'I understand that your family has been undergoing some financial difficulties. We have now purchased the property and your businesses. I think we may be able to help you rebuild. I look forward to a profitable arrangement between us.'

The magistrate's expression still revealed his confusion. The earl smiled warmly. 'I don't think this discussion needs to go any further. I do believe that all will be well, and there is no need to pursue any unpleasantness. Am I right?' He sent a pointed look towards Lord Mallencourt.

The unspoken message was, *Let the matter go.* For they had effectively purchased every source of income the Mallencourts had. One breath of scandal, and it would all end.

Lord Brevershire then turned to Lady Anne. 'And as for you, I am certain that a lovely young woman like yourself would not want to be embroiled under the accusation of blackmail. It would certainly undermine your hopes of finding a husband. I suspect that you and your sisters could benefit from some assistance—that is, if you mend your ways and if all charges are dropped.'

Anne shook her head. 'It was a misunderstanding, indeed.'

Lord Mallencourt echoed the sentiment, his expression wary. 'I agree that all charges should be dropped.'

Lord Brevershire smiled broadly. 'Excellent. Now that we are all in agreement, let us put an end to all of this. Harold, would you and your wife like to join me for a supper party this evening?'

The magistrate sighed and shrugged. 'I should be glad to.'

Dalton breathed a sigh of relief when the magistrate dismissed them all, effectively rendering no case of wrongful death. Mallencourt's face had gone pale, but it did seem that the baron wanted to avoid scandal and protect his family's assets.

Dalton took Regina's hand in his, and she embraced him hard. 'Everything will be all right.'

She pulled back to look into his eyes, her smile filled with love. 'Yes, it will. And soon, we will return to Scotland.'

Against her ear, he murmured, 'We have a wedding to plan.'

Laughing softly, she squeezed his hands. 'So, we do.'

Two weeks later

The sky was a brilliant blue, and the weather was starting to grow warm. Regina walked through the gardens, which were filled with roses. Colourful ribbons streamed in the wind, and she saw her bridegroom waiting beside the minister. A fiddler played a merry tune, leading the way down the path. Her heart swelled with happiness, and she held back her tears. Her father and mother were there, along with Dalton's grandfather and father. The entire village had come to celebrate, and Mrs Howard was beaming from her seat.

This was the wedding she had dreamed of, as a young girl, before her life had fallen apart. Not a ceremony of wealth and pomp, but instead one with her closest family and friends. She wore the same blue wedding gown as before, but she let her hair hang down loosely about her shoulders. Around her throat,

275 _Michelle Willingham_ 275

she wore the amethyst necklace Dalton had given back to her.

Her mother was smiling at her, and even her father's face had softened. Ever since he had learned of Dalton's means of gaining control over Mallencourt, the earl had heartily approved of the marriage. It had been a strong risk—and yet, there would never be any threat against her again. Of that, she was certain. She had spoken to Dalton's father in private, reassuring him that she loved his son and would do anything to make him happy. Lord Brevershire had softened, and for that, she was grateful.

Her dog, Arthur, sat beside her husband, patiently waiting. They spoke their vows, and Regina promised to love Dalton with all her heart. When he kissed her, she laughed when he swept her off her feet and carried her away to the _cèilidh_. Arthur scampered alongside them, following them to the celebration.

There was music, and she danced with his grandfather and her new father-in-law, who was surprisingly spry. Her own father was too weak to dance, but she saw the broad smile on his face and the joy at seeing her happiness.

Dalton brought her to sit beside him at the high table, and he fed her choice pieces of roasted chicken and soft bread. 'At least now our marriage is legal,' he said.

'It always felt legal to me,' Regina said. 'Even without the licence, I spoke my vows before the first minister and witnesses. You were always my husband, in my heart.'

'You were the wife I've been waiting for, all my

life.' He caressed her cheek, and she held his hand to her face.

'You taught me not to be afraid,' she said softly. 'And how to love.'

He took her hand in his. 'I find that I'm wanting to leave our wedding feast, Regina. At least, for a little while.'

She met his gaze and nearly caught her breath at the desire blazing in his eyes. 'Yes,' she whispered. 'I will come with you.'

Dalton stood and took her hand in his, leading her towards the stables. He ordered the groom to prepare a horse for them to share.

'Where are we going?' she asked.

'To the house I built,' he answered. 'I want to be alone with you.'

She smiled at the memory, and he lifted her atop the mare, swinging up behind her. Then he rode towards the loch and the house he'd built. Although the breeze was cool against her cheeks, his body warmed hers.

The thatched house was as tiny as she remembered, and her body flushed with heat when he dismounted and lifted her into his arms.

'I love you, Dalton,' she said as he carried her across the threshold.

'And I love you.' He lowered her to stand before he turned to close the door and bolt it shut. 'I'll build a fire so you'll be warm when I make love to you.'

She loved the idea of a fire, but she knew that her husband would warm her even faster. While he bent to kindle the flames, she unbuttoned the first few buttons of her gown and then removed her shoes and stockings. Once the blaze had caught, he stood and went to help her undress.

With every inch of skin he bared, he pressed his mouth to her flesh. She was aching for his touch, rising to his call. He unlaced her stays while she helped him remove his shirt. And within moments, they were both naked in the firelight.

She drank in the sight of his hard, strong body. 'My Highlander,' she murmured. 'Come and love me.'

He took her back to the bed, laying her back. With his knuckles, he grazed the cockled tips of her nipples, sending a flood of warmth between her legs. He kissed her gently, his mouth capturing hers. She sighed as his tongue slid inside, mimicking the lovemaking to come.

Regina touched his chest, feeling the pulse of his heartbeat before her hands moved lower. Over the hardened stomach, down to the velvet shaft of his arousal. She cupped him, stroking her hand over his length.

Dalton hissed with pleasure, and he rewarded her by covering her nipple with his warm mouth. He suckled gently, and she felt the wet surge of her own needs. He moved his hand between her legs, finding the nodule of her pleasure. And with his thumb, he gently stroked it, knowing how to draw out the sensation.

Her breathing grew rhythmic, and she fisted his length, loving the way his face strained with need. When she touched the tip of his erection, he groaned and dragged her hips to the edge of the bed.

'Look at me, Regina,' he commanded. He parted her legs, lifting her hips. Then in one swift stroke, he took her. The fierce invasion evoked an unexpected spear of desire. She lifted her hips, watching as he entered and withdrew. The vision of his body joining with hers seemed to arouse her even more, and she heard herself breathing more rapidly.

'Can you feel me, deep inside?' he murmured.

'Yes,' she moaned, urging him faster. 'Don't stop.'

And God help her, her words unleashed a frenzy of madness. His shaft was like iron, and she melted against him, revelling as he thrust inside. No longer was he gentle, but he claimed her as if he could never get enough.

The wildness of his need pushed her off the edge, and she broke apart, her body seizing up with the spasms of pleasure. She squeezed him hard, and he continued to drive deeply inside, until her body quaked again, stroking his length. He lost control, uttering words of how much he loved her, how much he needed her.

And with one final stroke, he flooded her with his release, his body shuddering as he collapsed upon her. She welcomed the weight, knowing that the years ahead would bring only happiness and joy. Perhaps even children.

'Do you know, I never dreamed I could have this,' he murmured against her skin. 'I wanted you, but I thought I would never be enough.'

'You are everything to me,' she answered. 'Always.' She touched his hair, still loving the feel of his body buried inside hers.

He kissed her again and drew his hand over her face. 'I will spend the rest of my life trying to be worthy of you, Regina.'

'No,' she answered gently. 'You already are the man of my dreams. And I will spend the rest of my days loving you.'

Epilogue

D alton walked through the cemetery with Regina, her hand clasped in his. She carried a small posy of roses, which she laid upon her father's grave. Their daughter, Penelope, broke free of his grasp and went after the flowers.

'No, those are for Grandpapa,' Regina said gently.

Dalton recognised the determined look on the little girl's face, and it looked as if she would voice a protest. Instead, he plucked a single blossom from the posy and tucked it behind her ear. 'Grandpapa wouldn't mind giving you this one, sweetheart.'

Regina braved a smile through her tears. 'I'm so glad he got to see her before he died. I know he loved her.'

'He did,' Dalton agreed. 'And she is loved by so many.' Penelope had wrapped his own father around her little finger, crawling into John's lap whenever she wanted a cuddle. 'My father would wage war for her sake.'

Fortunately, it had never come to that. The Mallen-court family recognised that their livelihood depended upon keeping the peace, and thus far, there had been not a trace of scandal. Even Lady Anne had disappeared, remaining quiet about what had happened.

Dalton picked up their daughter and tossed her up, hearing her delighted laugh. She had transformed his existence, and he could not be happier than to have a wife he adored and a daughter of their own.

'Dog,' Penelope demanded, pointing at Arthur, who was sniffing at the ground.

'Yes, that's your dog, too,' Regina said. She tucked her arm in Dalton's and said, 'I do miss Papa. But I am grateful for the time we had and for his blessing. I will always believe that the best day of my life was the day you switched places with Lachlan and married me.'

He kissed her lips softly with Penelope nestled between them. 'I won't be arguing about that, lass.' His smile turned wicked. 'But I think you may need to be carried off by a Highlander, a time or two.'

'I think you may be right.' She answered his smile. 'How about now?'

* * * * *

*If you enjoyed this book, be sure to read the first
book in the Untamed Highlanders miniseries*

The Highlander and the Governess

*And why not check out Michelle Willingham's
Warriors of the Night miniseries*

Forbidden Night with the Warrior
Forbidden Night with the Highlander
Forbidden Night with the Prince